AMULET BOOKS
NEW YORK

Dr. Critchlore's School for Minions

Polar Distress

BOOK THREE

SHEILA GRAU

ILLUSTRATED BY

JOE SUTPHIN

PUBLISHER'S NOTE: This is a work of fiction. Names, characters, places, and incidents are either the product of the author's imagination or are used fictitiously, and any resemblance to actual persons, living or dead, business establishments, events, or locales is entirely coincidental.

Library of Congress Cataloging-in-Publication Data

Names: Grau, Sheila, author. | Sutphin, Joe (Children's book illustrator), illustrator.
Title: Polar distress / by Sheila Grau ; illustrated by Joe Sutphin.
Description: New York : Amulet Books, 2017. | Series: Dr. Critchlore's School for Minions ; book 3 |
Summary: Runt joins a team from his school in icy Upper Worb, where they battle beasts and compete to find a rare mineral against a team from Dr. Pravus's school that includes Runt's former best friend, Syke.
Identifiers: LCCN 2016037984 | ISBN 9781419722943 (hardback)
Subjects: | CYAC: Monsters—Fiction. | Contests—Fiction. | Polar regions—Fiction. | Boarding schools—Fiction. | Schools—Fiction. | Blessing and cursing—Fiction. | Mystery and detective stories. | BISAC: JUVENILE FICTION / Fantasy & Magic. | JUVENILE FICTION / Fairy Tales & Folklore / Adaptations. | JUVENILE FICTION / Humorous Stories.
Classification: LCC PZ7.1.G73 Pol 2017 | DDC [Fic]—dc23
LC record available at https://lccn.loc.gov/2016037984

Text copyright © 2017 Sheila Grau
Illustrations copyright © 2017 Joe Sutphin
Book design by Julia Marvel

Amulet Books and Amulet Paperbacks are registered trademarks of
Harry N. Abrams, Inc.

Printed and bound in U.S.A.
10 9 8 7 6 5 4 3 2 1

Amulet Books are available at special discounts when purchased in quantity for premiums and promotions as well as fundraising or educational use. Special editions can also be created to specification. For details, contact specialsales@abramsbooks.com or the address below.

ABRAMS The Art of Books
115 West 18th Street, New York, NY 10011
abramsbooks.com

FOR RACHEL, RICKY, ALEX, AND DANIEL

CHAPTER 1

If at first you don't succeed, you're fired.
—EVIL OVERLORDS TO NEW RECRUITS

I was pretty sure the apple was poisoned. In my defense, I was really hungry.

It was afternoon, I'd missed lunch, and now I was stuck in my junior henchman classroom, alone with Professor Murphy, who sat behind his giant desk, ignoring me. On my own desk was a plate with the apple, a small cage holding a mouse, a pocket chemistry set, my test sheet, and a pencil.

We'd been studying food safety, an important job for henchmen, because they have to keep their overlords safe from enemies who want to poison their food.

I knew what I had to do: carefully examine the surface of the apple for needle marks and other blemishes, cut a slice, use the poison-detecting mouse, and perform some chemical tests. I'd done it all. One side of the apple had a puncture mark. And even though Professor Murphy had used a "poison" that was safe to eat (but was detectable as a real poison), when I dropped a slice from the punctured side into the mouse's cage, he wouldn't even sniff it. The chemicals starting foaming like a rabid werewolf as soon as they touched the slice. Finally, according to the test, the server had only just been hired (meaning: not trustworthy).

I wrote all of this down, along with my conclusion: The apple was poisoned. My suggested course of action: Arrest the server and feed *him* the apple.

In my mind, I'd completed the test.

And then my stomach growled.

Professor Murphy worked at his desk, scowling as he graded the essay portion of my exam. I stood up, grabbed my practical exam, and approached him. Without looking up, he pointed to a pile of papers on the corner of his desk. I dropped it on top.

"You need a mentor, I believe," he said, still focused on his papers. He hardly ever looked at me. It was as if he thought if he ignored me, I might go away.

He was right, though. I didn't have a mentor. My first mentor, Coach Foley, had gotten rid of me after I failed the first junior henchman test. My second mentor was Mistress Moira, the school seamstress/chocolatier, but she didn't teach a class of minions, and one of the goals of the Junior Henchman Training Program was to teach us how to lead a group of students. Plus, she'd recently taken leave to find the witch who had cursed me.

"I'm assigning you to Tootles," Professor Murphy said.

"Tootles?" I was confused. Tootles wasn't a teacher—he was the head groundskeeper. "But he doesn't teach a class of minions."

"No. He needs help with his Forest Restoration Project and asked me for a volunteer, so I'm assigning you." He finally looked

up at me, and then pointed to my desk. "Return to your seat until the test period is over," he said, so I did.

Well, this bites. All the other third-year junior henchmen trainees had great minions to lead. Rufus's mentor taught the intermediate mummies. Janet had the imps, Jud had some giants, and Frieda led other ogre-men. Even the new kid, Meztli, had a great group of minions—some first-year monkey-men. Who did I have? Nobody. I wasn't going to be able to march around school with my very own minions following me, doing what I told them to do. And, really, that was the best thing about being in the Junior Henchman Program.

I sulked at my desk, alone. We had to take the quiz individually after school. Each of my classmates had already taken it and passed. It wasn't a hard test.

The ticking wall clock echoed in the silent room, a constant reminder of how slowly time can pass. I had fifteen minutes until the period was over. Fifteen minutes, going by in agonizingly slow *tick . . . tick . . . tick*s.

Professor Murphy slashed and swished his red pen across the page with the relish of a fencer. He was killing my essay with a thousand forceful scratches.

I looked at the apple on my desk. My stomach growled.

The pen scratched.

The clock ticked.

I sliced off a piece of apple from the side that hadn't been punctured. I gave a sliver to the mouse, who sniffed it once and then gobbled it up. I ate the rest of the piece. At the sound of my chewing, Professor Murphy looked up. His scowl was so severe, you'd have thought I'd just thrown the apple at the OUTSTANDING EDUCATOR plaque hanging on the wall behind him.

He picked up my test, marked it with a giant red F you could probably see from the top of Mount Curiosity, and then came over and slammed it down onto my desk.

"But I was done," I said. "I went through the protocol. I marked everything I found on the test." I pointed to the paper.

"Your analysis indicated poison—but you just took a bite of the apple."

"It's not real poison, and I missed lunch. I'm really hungry."

"Discipline is vitally important for a henchman," he said. "You will not embarrass me by graduating from this program, getting *my* seal of approval, and failing in the first task your EO assigns you. Do you know how that would make me look?"

Clearly, Professor Murphy hated me. He'd been trying to kick me out of the training program from the moment I entered his classroom. But Dr. Critchlore had placed me in the class. He'd reinstated me after Professor Murphy kicked me out, and then had reinstated me *again* after I'd gotten three "behavioral" strikes. Professor Murphy didn't think I was junior henchman material, and he was super proud of all the students who graduated with his precious "seal of approval."

When he looked back down, I tried to finish my apple slice as quietly as I could, but he heard me.

"You think you can do whatever you want and Dr. Critchlore will save you every time?" he said. "Who do you think you are?"

That was my problem. I didn't know who I was.

CHAPTER 2

Exploding cigars, falling objects, poison, and old age.
—LEADING CAUSES OF DEATH AMONG EVIL OVERLORDS

For most of my life, I'd thought I was a werewolf. My earliest memories are of snuggling with my wolf family, running and playing with them in the forest, and howling together at night. I remember eating out of a bowl on the floor. But then so did my friend Boris, and he's mostly human.

Recently, I thought I might be a vaskor. The vaskor are terrifying creatures with horns and sharp claws, but they use glamour to appear human. My vaskor friend Sara had called me "family." *Maybe I've been walking around disguised all this time,* I thought, *my impressive monster form hidden beneath a runty human disguise.*

Nope. I was 100 percent human. It was a disappointment.

And then I'd learned I was the missing prince of Andirat. A prince with a ridiculously long name that I couldn't even remember. The prince's family had been killed in a military coup, and the country had been split up by the generals who'd led the uprising. I'd spent my life dreaming of finding my family . . . only to discover that they were dead, my country gone.

There was proof: I'd shown up at Dr. Critchlore's School wearing the Andiratian royal attire and medallion, and at four years old I looked just like the prince in the family portrait. Never mind that I didn't have any princely memories. And I wondered how many princes remember eating from a bowl on the floor.

Still, it was all I had to go on, and I needed that clue because I was cursed to die on my sixteenth birthday. I had thick red bands around both wrists, which had shown up after I'd left Stull. Mistress Moira called the marks "a tethering curse," to make sure I didn't go outside the range of the death curse. So, really, I was twice cursed, and I had no idea why. Learning I was a prince was the first clue I had toward figuring that out.

You can see how all this could get a guy down. But wait—there's more! I'd also lost my best friend, Syke, who left the school after finding out that Dr. Critchlore had killed her mother. Syke's mother was a hamadryad, and Dr. Critchlore had burned down the forest where she'd lived to make room for a boulderball field. We'd always believed that he had saved Syke from a fire when she was a baby. What we didn't know was that he was the one who'd started the fire.

Syke had grown up as Dr. Critchlore's ward, but now she hated him. She hated me too for not telling her when I found out the truth. And also because I'd defended Dr. Critchlore. But I knew there had to be another reason for why he'd done it. The story just didn't add up.

Before leaving, Syke had gotten some revenge by using her Tornado in a Can™ to sabotage Dr. Critchlore's office. She'd done some other stuff too, and now, according to Dean Everest, Syke was "persona non grata" at our school. That meant they didn't want her to come back.

She was currently living at the Great Library, next to a forest filled with hamadryads who had known her mother. She took classes at the Kobold Retraining Center, which was kind of ridiculous, because she wasn't a kobold. I had seen her once in the three months she'd been gone, and her anger hadn't faded one bit. She didn't want to come back.

It had been a depressing winter for me.

After my test, I snuck into the kitchen, plopped myself down at Cook's table in the corner, and hunched over my dinner tray, which was piled high with food. I was starving.

Cook leaned against the table, ladle in hand. She tucked a stray hair back under her hairnet and sighed. "Runt, you've always been the happiest kid I've known," she said as I stuffed my face with dinner rolls. She grabbed the last one out of my hand and pointed to my stew.

"I keep thinking things like, I can't wait for third period so I can hang out with Syke and complain about Professor Murphy. Who hates me, by the way." I picked up a spoon and attacked the stew like I was in an eating competition.

"He doesn't hate you," Cook said.

"Yes, he does," I said with a full mouth. Cook shook her head, so I finished chewing before adding, "He's had it in for me ever since Dr. Critchlore selected me as a junior henchman trainee—and then put me back in the program after Professor Murphy kicked me out. Twice."

"Kids always think teachers have it in for them. Teachers aren't like that."

Since when? I wanted to say, but instead I lifted the bowl to my face to finish off my stew. Then I turned to the pasta, mounded high on its own plate.

"It's been three months. You need to get over losing your friend," Cook said. "Tootles and Riga are crushed, you know. They raised her like a daughter . . . and then she runs away like that."

"She probably thought they knew the truth too," I said, still wanting to defend her. "She was mad at everybody here. You saw her."

"Well, she's gone now. And good riddance, I say. After what she did to Dr. Critchlore's office? And to the boulderball stadium? And to the Wall of Heroes? She could have seriously injured someone. I'm telling you, Runt, if that girl was still here, I'd forbid you from associating with her.

"Now, then," she went on. "Moping isn't going to cheer you up. You need to get yourself out there. You have other friends—Darthin and Frankie. Eloni and Boris."

"Yes, but don't you hear yourself?" I slurped up the last noodle and moved on to the chicken fingers. "They're already best friends with each other. I'm like the useless third eyeball on a three-eyed cat."

"Well, go out and find a replacement best friend. And it wouldn't hurt to try a vegetable once in a while." She went over to the counter and returned with some green beans. "Syke's leaving was a blessing in disguise. When you attach yourself too tightly to one person, you miss out on meeting a lot of interesting people. And monsters too, I suppose."

9

She pointed to the beans.

I sighed. I hated green food. Unless it was frosting.

"And cheer up, for goodness' sake!" She put down the ladle and searched her apron pockets until she found her notebook and a pen. She ripped out a page and put it next to my tray. "Write down all the good things in your life . . . Go on."

I stared at the blank page, then looked up at Cook.

She folded her arms and nodded at the paper.

I wrote: *Cook isn't really going to make me eat these mushy green beans.*

She laughed. "Guess again."

I crossed that out and wrote: *Hoopsmash season has started.*

Cook winced. She thought hoopsmash was too violent. Tackle three-ball was okay, but she did not want me playing hoopsmash, which is sort of an indoor combination of Tackle-the-Pill and Shoot for the Hoops.

Doing well in classes (except for JH). I was acing all my classes: Literature, Math, Monster Biology, and Introduction to Sabotage.

I'm a prince, I wrote, but then I crossed that out. I wasn't sure that was good, or that it even mattered. Could you really be a prince if you didn't have a country?

I live in the most amazing place on the planet.
I've grown two inches since school started.
Janet Desmarais smiled at me this morning.

"That's a good list," Cook said. "Feel better?"

"I guess," I said. I tucked my Good List in my pocket and got up to go. "Thanks, Cook. Do you know when Mistress Moira will be back?"

Mistress Moira had left shortly after my return from the Great Library. Nobody knew where she'd gone. Aside from a letter of instruction on how to get rid of my tether curse, I hadn't heard from her. I was hoping she'd be back before the next full moon, because I had a question about her instructions. There was something on her list that I really didn't want to do.

"Nobody knows," Cook answered. "But I'm sure she'll be back soon."

"Why are you sure?"

"Because it makes me feel better to be sure."

"Okay," I said. "Then I'm sure you're not going to make seafood tetrazzini this week."

She was right. I *did* feel better.

I left through the cafeteria, which was filled with the rest of the student body eating and talking. I passed the skeleton table, the siren table, the ogre-man table, and the cool shape-shifter table. As I approached my usual spot in the corner to say hi to the guys, the alarm bell sounded—three quick blasts.

The screen at the end of the room blinked on, showing our fearless leader, Dr. Critchlore, smiling broadly. "Everyone, the day we've all been waiting for has arrived! Please, sit down and pay attention."

I sat down next to Darthin, wondering what Dr. Critchlore was talking about.

CHAPTER 3

*"It's must-see TV! Literally. You have to watch it—
or face large fines and possibly imprisonment."*
—TAGLINE FOR THE SHOW *EVIL OVERLORD DINNER THEATRE*

Dr. Critchlore cleared his throat. "Students and faculty . . . It brings me great pleasure to share with you the following live episode of *Evil Overlord Dinner Theater*. The EOs love to broadcast how they punish people who displease them, and I've been waiting for tonight's episode for months.

"As you know, my nemesis, Dr. Pravus, has been charged with conduct unbefitting a minion-school headmaster. He has broken the Minion School Directives by sabotaging not only us but other minion schools as well. Now, after months of delays, he's finally going to get his due.

"Enjoy."

The scene switched to the council chamber, where five evil overlords sat behind a long desk on an elevated platform, looking down on a contrite Dr. Pravus. I'd seen him in person a few times, and each time I'd felt a desperate urge to crumple into a ball and beg for mercy. Now he stood humbly with his hands clasped in front of him.

Wexmir Smarvy, the EO of Lower Worb, sat at the center of the judges' panel. He was a bull of a man, with a square jaw, a thick mustache, and slicked-back black hair. He leaned forward to speak into his microphone, but no sound came out. A man rushed over to fix the problem, fiddling with some wires on the desk. He tapped the microphone, which echoed with his thumps, then motioned for Smarvy to continue.

Wexmir Smarvy rose from his seat, towering over the worker. He grabbed the poor guy and threw him over the table and onto the floor. Two workers ran out to drag him away. Smarvy sat down as if nothing had happened.

"Dr. Pravus," he read, "you are accused of sabotaging other minion schools for the purpose of driving up demand for your own minions. This is a serious breach of the Minion School Directives, and if found guilty . . . well, you know the punishment."

"I do."

Dr. Critchlore's voice chimed in over the video feed, "School license revoked, public shaming, and then banishment to Skelterdam. Yes!"

"We have written testimony from five schools detailing the sabotage they've experienced," Smarvy continued, "and also the evidence that you were behind it."

"Of course they blame me," Dr. Pravus said. "I am the superior trainer of minions, so naturally they will use any excuse to bring me down. I expect that. But please don't act like I'm not a victim too."

This was met by a few sideways looks by the EOs.

"*You* have been sabotaged?" Fraze Coldheart asked.

"I have." Dr. Pravus turned and sniffed, his body shaking with sobs. He held up a hand to ask for a moment to compose himself. "Yesterday . . ." His voice squeaked. He cleared his throat and continued. "Yesterday, my giant gorilla enclosure was destroyed when a sinkhole opened up beneath it. Every one of my . . . my . . ." He shook his head, sadness turning to anger. "It was sabotage!"

It felt like the breath had been sucked out of the room, both here in the cafeteria and among the evil overlords. Dr. Pravus's giant gorillas, the most terrifying beasts on the Porvian Continent, were gone?

"And I know who did it," Dr. Pravus said.

I looked at Darthin, who looked at Frankie, who looked at Eloni, who looked at Boris, who looked confused.

"Critchlore?" Eloni asked.

"No, not Critchlore," I said. "Sabotage is one thing. But this— Someone murdered those gorillas."

After the shock had passed, Fraze Coldheart asked, "Who? And why?"

Dr. Pravus frowned at him, which I thought was very bold.

"Pravus sure hates Coldheart," Eloni said, echoing my thoughts. "I wonder why."

"Maybe Fraze Coldheart stole Pravus's dessert," Boris said, with a hard scowl at Eloni. Eloni got up to get another dessert for Boris.

On the screen, Pravus turned to Wexmir Smarvy as if he had asked the question.

"Everyone knows my giant gorillas are the most dangerous beasts on the Porvian Continent," Dr. Pravus said. "Despite that ridiculous rumor about their falling in love too easily. Please. One untrained teenager shouldn't be taken as representative of the group. They are strong and intelligent. Unstoppable!

"And so a rival of mine—I'm not naming names, but a man so desperate to reach my level that he'd do anything to bring me down, Dr. Critch—um . . . *someone* applied a rock-dissolving substance to the ground below, and *pffft*! Now they're gone." He bowed his head. "I blame myself," he said, wiping a tear. "The enclosure was just outside our school grounds. If only I'd made the area more secure."

"Your giant gorillas . . . perished?"

Dr. Pravus nodded his head. "Every last one."

There were murmurs among the EOs. Wexmir Smarvy looked smugly happy. He'd already recruited some giant gorillas, and now he had the only ones left.

"That liar!" Dr. Critchlore's voice exploded out of the television. "He did it himself, to deflect the blame!"

"It's strange timing, don't you think?" Fraze Coldheart said,

15

echoing Dr. Critchlore's suspicions. "The day before you are to appear before us, you suffer the same crime that you are accused of committing."

"It's hard not to think that you staged this yourself," Maya Tupo added.

"It's what I would have done," Cera Bacculus agreed.

"I'm flattered that you believe me so cunning," Dr. Pravus said. "Unfortunately, it is not the case. I've been much too busy with my latest project. You see, I've come into a bit of information about a minion that will make my giant gorillas look like helpless little imps in comparison."

A chorus of boos filled the cafeteria as imps threw food at the screen.

"I'm very close. I have assembled the, er, subjects. I only need to make sure they are properly trained. I assure you, you will not be disappointed. In addition—"

Wexmir Smarvy held his hand up to stop him. The EOs covered their microphones and conferred quietly with one another. Very quickly they were ready to give their verdict.

"Dr. Pravus," Wexmir Smarvy said, "we are of the opinion that you had a hand in the sabotage of the other schools. It's not without a little admiration that we've followed your tactics. But this sabotaging behavior must stop, and we cannot allow rule breaking to go unpunished.

"My suggestion of banishment has been overruled by my colleagues, who point out that you've excelled at training minions for over two decades. We're also intrigued about this new minion of yours. So, in conclusion, if you pay a restitution minion to each school and promise not to sabotage again, we will dismiss this case."

"I promise," Dr. Pravus said, looking as sincere as an imp promising not to prank anybody.

The video feed cut to Dr. Critchlore, who looked livid. His voice roared, "So he gets away with it! Not a lick of punishment! It's outrageous!" He collected his composure and stared right at us. "Students, this is disastrous news, which will have dire consequences for us. Dire! I am hereby invoking the Prime Imperative. Stand by for instructions."

We looked at one another, wondering what this meant.

"Did he say he was in Voking?" Boris asked. "Because I was in Voking once. There's nothing to do there."

Darthin explained that Dr. Critchlore meant he was making a command. But none of us had ever heard of the Prime Imperative.

"Well, 'prime' means of the first importance," Darthin, our human dictionary, said, "and 'imperative,' when used as a noun, means an absolute requirement. Whatever it is, it sounds ominous."

"You've never heard of it happening before?" Frankie asked me. I shook my head.

Rumors swirled through the room, causing more panic and unease than a ghost invasion.

"He's going to ask us to attack the Pravus Academy," a monkey-man guessed.

"That's crazy," said the monkey-man next to him. "We'd be crushed, and Dr. Critchlore would be banished to Skelterdam."

"I bet he's going to get rid of all the humans," an upperclassman

17

said. "Get back to training monsters. That's the first duty of a minion school."

I didn't know if it was the green beans or the rumors, but suddenly I felt very sick.

The next morning everyone showed up to breakfast early, hoping to hear more about the Prime Imperative. My human table was met by more than a few looks of pity. Some monsters pointed to us and then made slashing gestures across their throats, clearly indicating they thought we were goners.

"Maybe we could transfer to Minion Prep?" Darthin said.

My stomach clenched. I'd grown up here. I didn't want to go anywhere else.

At last the giant screen on the wall of the cafeteria blinked on, and our headmaster's face greeted us.

"Good morning," he said. He looked exhausted, like he'd been up all night. "I know you are all wondering about the Prime Imperative."

My breath caught in my throat.

"I have to apologize. I overreacted after seeing my archenemy escape the punishment he so richly deserved." He smiled. "We're fine. Everything's fine. There's no need to worry about anything."

Students murmured and looked at one another, confusion plain on each face. This was quite a switch in attitude.

"Indeed, everything is peachy keen. Things are going so well, in fact, that I've decided we all deserve a little fun. How about we move the annual Minion Games up in the schedule? In fact, let's start them right now!"

The whole room erupted in cheers. Everyone loved the Minion Games. They normally took place near the end of the year—a week of fun and games after the grueling work of the term. It was, without a doubt, the highlight of the school year.

"See? How could things not be *completely fine* if we are giving up our studies to play?" Dr. Critchlore continued. "Competition teams will be assigned . . . this evening! The contest will begin tomorrow! Let the games begin!"

Everyone in the cafeteria whooped with happiness. But then I noticed the look on Dr. Critchlore's face before the screen blinked off. He looked frightened.

CHAPTER 4

Hard work beats monsters if monsters don't work hard.
—PEP TALK FOR HUMANS DURING LAST YEAR'S MINION GAMES

On the way to my first-period class with my new mentor, the head groundskeeper, I thought about the Minion Games and how they weren't going to be as much fun without Syke. The Minion Games are made for monsters, but Syke always found a way for us to help our team. We'd always been teammates. But now she was gone.

It was nearly spring, and the air felt fresh and cool. On my way to Tootles's tree house I noticed new growth popping up from the ground, along with two dirty hands. One of the new zombies liked to sleep buried in the garden.

Tootles and his wife, Riga, had been at the school longer than anybody. He'd been castle groundskeeper to Dr. Critchlore's father, and Riga worked in construction, assembling many of the mock buildings that we used for training and the sets that we used for the fashion show.

They'd also raised Syke when Dr. Critchlore had agreed to take care of her after her parents died. Dr. Critchlore was too busy for most parenting tasks, and Tootles and Riga had always wanted a child of their own.

While Tootles didn't teach a class of minions I could help lead, there *was* an upside to working with him. Now I'd have some time alone with him to ask some questions. I had a feeling he knew more about why Dr. Critchlore had burned down Syke's mother's tree than he'd told me. Didn't he know it was a hamadryad-protected forest? If so, why'd he let Dr. Critchlore destroy it?

If I could find the answers to those questions, maybe Syke would come back.

Tootles wasn't in his tree house, but Riga, dressed for work in her overalls, with safety glasses perched on her graying hair, told me where to find him: out behind the castle, working on the Forest Restoration Project. The FRP was a peace offering Dr. Critchlore had made to the hamadryads when they'd come to check on Syke. Syke had left before work had started.

The new forest was going to be located on the far side of the Aviary, stretching out from the base of Mount Curiosity, with a narrow river running along the far edge. It was a wide patch of land, now speckled with small tree saplings.

I found Tootles planting a group of white-trunked birch trees near the river.

"Hi, Tootles," I said.

He stood up, removing a glove to shake my hand. He wore his white hair in a ponytail, and his skin was weathered and tan. "Runt, how are you?"

"Okay, I guess," I said. "I can almost imagine how the forest is going to look."

"It will be perfect. I'm going to put a little clearing in the center, with a pond. Just like Syke wanted."

"That's nice and all, but she won't come back," I said. "Not while she believes that Dr. Critchlore killed her mother. Plus, she knows some people here are mad at her because of the sabotage."

A few weeks ago, when I'd gone to the Great Library with Professor Zaida to collect some books, Syke had barely talked to me. But Sara, the girl explorer/vaskor who'd saved me from Dr. Pravus, had. She was close friends with Syke now, and she'd told me that Syke knew her acts of sabotage were unforgivable. Syke didn't care, because she wasn't ever coming back.

Tootles looked sad. "She may not come back," he agreed. "I'm going to finish it, though. I owe it to them."

"Them?"

"Syke and her mother, Karya."

"Tootles, I've asked you a million times, but can you please, *please* tell me what happened? You've worked here forever. You must have known it was a hamadryad-protected forest."

"I did." He turned back to his work, trying to cut off this conversation.

"So why did you let him burn it down? I know it wasn't to make a boulderball field. He could have made it right here, in this clearing. It's not that far from the castle."

"Runt, I've told you—I can't talk about it."

Why not? I wanted to scream. But that strategy hadn't worked when I tried it a few weeks ago. It hadn't worked with him or Cook or Riga or Uncle Ludwig or anyone who'd been living here when the fire happened. Nobody would tell me anything.

"Tootles," I said, "you and I know that the story you're telling me doesn't make sense. It makes no sense that Dr. Critchlore burned down the forest. First of all, why burn it down? Why not have the giants pull out the trees? They could have cleared the land in a day without the risk of a fire."

"Runt, these are grown-up things. It's complicated. Now, did Professor Murphy send you here?"

"Yes," I said with a sigh. "He said you needed help with something."

Tootles led me over to where he'd grouped the trees he was going to plant. There were hundreds of planter boxes covering the field. A few were turned upside down, and I assumed that Tootles had already planted those trees. Six boxes were upright and empty.

"Those are the ones that got away," he said.

"Huh?"

"They were going to be a surprise for Syke: enchanted weeping blue atlas cedars. They're strongly rooted as adults, but as saplings, they tend to wander off."

I did not know that.

"How? Why? Where?" I mumbled.

"I thought these were firmly rooted. I don't know how they got out of their boxes. There are six of them. I raised them in my secret greenhouse. I'm pretty sure they won't go far. They're attracted to water: streams and lakes. They're also somewhat . . ."

"Weak? Slow? Easy to catch?" I prompted.

"Uh . . . no."

"Cuddly? Friendly? Helpful?"

"Sadly, no. They are mischievous and sneaky and very strong. You won't be able to subdue them physically."

23

"What do you want me to do, then?"

"Convince them to come back here."

"*Convince* them?" I said. "Like . . . with words?"

"Yes," he said. "As adults, they're quite charming and excellent conversationalists."

"But as saplings?"

"Not so much."

I sighed. "Should I start looking by the river or the lake?"

"Actually . . ." He winced, like he was afraid to go on.

"What?"

"My biggest fear is that they've gone to the swamp. I don't want them to secure their roots there."

"Um . . . you *do* know there's a swamp creature in there."

"Yes, thanks for your concern," Tootles said, putting his gloves back on and returning to his work. "But the trees are hardy. They'll be fine."

"I was talking about me!"

Tootles laughed. "You'll be fine too. I saw you evade a swamp creature in the hedge maze, remember?"

I did. "Okay, fine. I was planning to go to the swamp after school. For . . . something else."

"Perfect. Thank you, Runt."

With luck, I could round up the trees and have a new mentor by the end of the day. A real mentor. With monster minions.

CHAPTER 5

Legend tells us an Undefeatable Minion was created generations ago.
It caused so much horrific damage that the knowledge of
how it came to be was locked away, never to be used again.
—*THE HISTORY OF WAR*, BY DUNGA POX

After that, I headed to my junior henchman class. The six desks were arranged in an arc, facing the front and Professor Murphy's enormous desk.

I took my seat next to Meztli, the exchange student were-jaguar from the southern continent of Orgal. Next to him was Jud, a werewolf, and then came Rufus, the alpha werewolf, and then Janet, the most perfect girl ever. She was smart and funny and nice, and had a smile that made me feel fluttery inside when it was aimed at me. At the far end of the row sat Frieda, the ogre.

Our test scores had been posted on the board. Professor Murphy was the sort of teacher who thought humiliation motivated a minion to work harder. It had the opposite effect on me—it made me feel like quitting.

There I was, on the bottom, with a giant F next to my name. Janet, Freida, and Jud had As, Meztli had a B-minus, and Rufus had a C-minus. Rufus might be Professor Murphy's favorite, but it wasn't due to hard work. He did only enough to pass and no more.

"You got an F?" Meztli whispered to me.

"I ate the apple," I said. "You?"

"I ate the mouse."

Ew. He must have noticed my expression. "I'm a cat." He shrugged. "Nobody said not to."

Professor Murphy began a lecture that summed up our lesson on food safety. The loud clock seemed to slow down again, and the whole room felt smothered by boredom. I watched Meztli swat his pencil to the edge of his desk. He looked at it for a second and then pushed it off.

At last Professor Murphy turned to the subject we were all waiting for—the Minion Games.

"Our next subject was going to be interrogation techniques, but it will have to wait," he said. "As you know, Dr. Pravus has not been banished, as we'd hoped. This, in itself, is not a problem for our school, as Dr. Critchlore is the superior trainer of minions. However, Dr. Pravus now possesses a dangerous piece of information."

Unlike the others, I already knew that Dr. Pravus had broken into the Great Library and stolen *The Top Secret Book of Minions— Translated Edition.* We'd stopped him from taking over the library and erased his memory of its location, but not before he'd passed the dangerous book to his henchman. The *TSBM* was believed to contain the secret instructions for creating an Undefeatable Minion.

"As he mentioned, he's currently training a minion so fierce it will put all others to shame. That minion, we believe, is the legendary Undefeatable Minion."

The five kids next to me gasped. Realizing I wasn't supposed to know this already, I gasped too, a second later, which made everyone look at me like I was an idiot.

"The only way to stop Pravus from taking over the minion business is to make our own Undefeatable Minion," Professor Murphy went on. "Dr. Critchlore has the same information, but it's coded in an ancient language that has been very difficult to decipher. This means that Pravus has a huge lead on us."

"What exactly is an Undefeatable Minion?" Janet asked.

"They were first created accidentally hundreds of years ago, or so legend tells us. A freak convergence of random events gave birth to the most powerful, indestructible beasts ever known. They killed everything and destroyed entire cities. So devastating was their power that the knowledge of their creation was placed in a coded book, which was then hidden away."

"If they couldn't be defeated, what happened to them?" Frieda asked.

"We don't know." Professor Murphy said. "That's why they are thought to be mythical."

"How does something become indestructible?" Jud asked.

"We don't know that, either. To re-create those random events, we think we need four things. The first one is a mineral, which Dr. Frankenhammer believes is the key ingredient for a potion of some kind. If we are to catch up with Dr. Pravus, we need to find that mineral.

"Chances are, if it's that vital, it won't be for sale in the local mineral store. We'll have to go out and find it ourselves, much as we do when we go on field trips to find the death flower that Dr. Frankenhammer uses for his zombie-repellent potion. Dr. Critchlore plans to assemble teams to search for the mineral."

Professor Murphy began pacing. "We're using the Minion Games to evaluate every student here, to determine which minions will best be able to perform certain tasks.

"You junior henchmen trainees are privileged to know this information, and it must remain secret." He turned to me with an extra-hard stare. "To the rest of the student body, this year's Minion Games are no different from any other year. A time for fun. But you junior henchman trainees will know that these games are the most important test the minions will ever face, because the fate of the school lies in the results. We expect you to do your best and, as future leaders, to get the best out of others."

Rufus and Jud fist-bumped. They loved the Minion Games, which they regularly dominated. The Minion Games highlighted monster skills, of which I had . . . none.

"As you know," Professor Murphy went on, "junior henchmen trainees are placed on teams with the minions they're leading through the mentor program. For you third-years, this will be the first test of your skills as a leader. You've had a few months of training. Let's see what you and your minions can do.

"I shouldn't have to tell you that this will factor into your final grade. While regular classes have been postponed, my evaluation will rest solely on your performance in the games. Those of you who are struggling"—he pointed to Rufus's and my names on the board—"now have a chance to improve."

"But, sir?" I said. "I don't have any minions to lead."

"Runt." Professor Murphy sighed. "As I often say, one must learn to lead oneself successfully before leading others."

"So . . . that means?"

"You need to stop relying on others to fix your problems."

I felt my face grow warm, and I slouched lower in my chair.

When Professor Murphy dismissed us, I reached the door at the same time as Frieda, who looked as worried as I felt.

"What's the matter?" I asked her as we left the classroom. "You love the games."

"I do, but my ogre-men first-years don't listen to me," she said.

"Because you're a girl?" I asked.

"No, because they're ogre-men. They don't listen to anybody."

Rufus turned around at this. "You need to be tough with them, Frieda. Scream at them, physically threaten them. You're too nice. You have to rule by intimidation."

Frieda looked puzzled. I don't think anyone had ever told her that she was too nice. She routinely sat on smaller kids, pretending she didn't see them.

"My mummies do what I say," Rufus bragged. "Why? Because if they don't, I'll unwrap them."

"You can't!" I said. That was a terrible threat.

"Make 'em too scared to fail," Rufus said, ignoring me. "*That's* motivation."

We reached the castle foyer and everyone headed outside for free period, but I veered over to the dungeon stairs. Before heading down, I felt a hand on my arm.

"Runt," Janet said. She looked at the front door, which had just closed behind Rufus, then turned back to me. "I just wanted to tell you that I'm leaving school for a couple weeks."

"Oh?" I said, unable to mask my disappointment. "Do you need someone to collect your homework?"

"No, I'm fine," she said. "I just wanted to tell you to be careful."

"Sure, okay," I said.

"No, you don't understand." She grabbed both of my arms, and my insides fluttered with happiness. Janet Desmarais was talking to me. Touching me. Where was that slow clock when you needed it? I didn't want this moment to end.

"You need to be *really* careful," she said. "Rufus is so mad that you're still in the Junior Henchmen Program. I don't know why he hates you so much, but I've heard him joke about how accidents happen all the time, especially to weak little humans. I know he's joking, but he also kind of isn't—you know?"

"Don't worry," I said. "I've gotten good at avoiding him. Have a great trip."

"Thanks," she said. Then she hugged me and whispered in my ear, "Runt, you're not who you think you are."

I gasped. Partly because of the electric thrill I felt from hearing those words, and partly because I'd just spotted Rufus coming back inside to look for Janet. And here I stood, hugging her. I think his canines grew two inches as he snarled at me.

CHAPTER 6

*The Monoliths of Andirat are towering blocks of
stone carved with huge faces.
They are all that stand in the once proud capital of Andirat City.*
—*ANDIRAT, A HISTORY*

I used to spend my free period with Syke. We'd walk around the grounds, pretending to spy on people. Or she'd try to convince me to sneak into secret places and then mock me when I wouldn't, so I'd have to come up with something more fun to do, like a tree-climbing race, which she always won, even when she gave me a ten-minute head start.

Unfortunately for me, that free time was another thing I'd lost. Now I faced my toughest teacher, in secret.

Professor Zaida.

Every free period I met her in Uncle Ludwig's secret library, which was hidden below the regular library, so she could teach me about Andirat, a country that didn't exist anymore, and how to be a prince, which was a ridiculous notion. Me? A prince? Whenever I took an online Minion Career Aptitude Test, I usually got something like "Dungeon Cleaner," "Target Practice Dummy," or "Blame This Guy."

But I was a prince, so I had to learn to act like one. My family, the

Natherlys, had ruled Andirat, a country across the ocean, for two hundred peaceful years, up until eight years ago, when Andirat's five generals revolted and took over. I was the only member of the royal family to escape alive.

Before Andirat, my ancestors had ruled a country right here on the Porvian Continent called Erudyten. It had been a peaceful and wealthy country until it was attacked by its jealous neighbors, forcing the ruling family to flee across the ocean. So that was twice in history my ancestors were defeated in battle and had their countries torn up. Not a good track record, if you ask me.

I sat in front of a giant book about the fall of Erudyten, unable to stop thinking about Janet's hug. Professor Zaida twice told me to get "that stupid smile" off my face and concentrate.

"Your grandfather, Charles Natherly the third, was obsessed with reclaiming his ancestral homeland. Erudyten is now four countries—Riggen, Brix, Carkley, and Voran—which are ruled by four of the most oppressive evil overlords here on the Porvian Continent," she said. "Your grandfather wanted to reunify Erudyten and free those people from their oppression."

"Huh? Oh, right. My grandfather. I called him Papa Chuck," I said. "He read me bedtime stories and taught me how to spit."

She frowned at me. We both knew I didn't remember my grandfather, or any of my relatives. I joked, but really I was sad that I had to learn about my family from a book, that they weren't around for me to get to know them.

"Runt," she admonished. "This is important."

"I'm sorry. It's just . . . Shouldn't we be looking for the witch who cursed me? Why does it matter what my dead grandfather wanted?

He's gone. Erudyten is gone. It was destroyed two hundred years ago."

Professor Zaida was as obsessed with Erudyten as my late grandfather. She was a covert librarian of the Great Library, which had been built to save the books in Erudyten from being destroyed by the invading armies. Through the centuries the librarians have dedicated their lives to protecting those books.

"Mistress Moira is searching for whoever cursed you. There's nothing you and I can do that she can't do better. My job is to prepare you for what comes next. You need to learn about leadership. Now—"

She stopped abruptly as Uncle Ludwig passed by our table, muttering to himself, as usual. His life's goal was to find the Great Library, the secret repository of all the world's knowledge. He knew that an Archivist of the Great Library worked at Dr. Critchlore's, and he was determined to find out who it was so he could find the library.

I was sitting across from an Archivist, and she and I both knew exactly where the Great Library was located.

"Why don't you tell him?" I asked Professor Zaida as Uncle Ludwig disappeared with a handful of research papers. I knew that Professor Zaida was worried he couldn't keep a secret, but she shouldn't have worried about him—*I* was the one who couldn't keep a secret. And I was supposed to be helping him. How was I supposed to keep pretending to look for it?

"I cannot divulge anything about the Great Library." She looked at me sternly. "And neither can you. Fortunately for you, we're almost done moving it, so you have nothing to tell."

"That's good. But I know Pravus's henchman poisoned a bunch of your operatives. You must need more people. Why not him?"

"It's complicated."

"Are you still mad that he never thought you could be an Archivist?"

"I'm used to people underestimating me, Runt," she said, probably referring to the fact that she was a little person. "Now let's get back to work. Your grandfather—and your father too—were disgusted by what the EOs had done to the beautiful homeland of their ancestors. His generals wanted to invade, starting with attacks on Fraze Coldheart in Riggen, the location of Erudyten's former capital city, but your father was working on a diplomatic solution—"

I shook my head. "Why do I need to know this?"

"It's your heritage," she said. "Runt, you are the last in a line of great leaders. You must be ready to lead those who would follow you against the generals who overthrew your family."

"Nobody will follow me," I said, laughing. "I don't know if you've noticed, but I'm kind of a joke around here. Everyone knows I spent my whole life thinking I was a werewolf. They know I'm an idiot."

"No, Runt," she said. "You are a prince."

I sighed. "Tell that to Professor Murphy. Maybe then he'll respect me."

"In other words, you're not interested in earning his respect. You want it given to you for an achievement you had nothing to do with."

"Well, when you put it that way . . . yes."

"Runt, that's no way to earn someone's respect. It's what you *do* that matters, not titles, or whom you know, or what you say about yourself. Prove that you are worthy of his respect."

That was an impossible task, but I was tired of trying to convince grown-ups that he hated me.

"And we discussed this," she said. "We're keeping your identity a secret. For your protection."

"So I shouldn't tell anyone?"

"No!"

Oops.

I'd told Syke, and I was pretty sure that Janet knew too. Once, after she'd gotten my medallion back from the imp who'd stolen it, she told me that if I found out I was a missing prince, she hoped I would remember the people who had been nice to me. At the time I'd thought she was being silly, but now? She must know. But how?

Uncle Ludwig returned from upstairs. He came right over to our table.

"Critchlore asked me for a book on minerals," he said. "They've reached a breakthrough in deciphering *The Top Secret Book of Minions*. He thinks we need something called sudithium. Ever heard of it, Professor Zaida?"

"I don't think so," she answered.

"He also wants a list of meteorite-impact craters," Uncle Ludwig said. "I have my own mysteries to solve—without any help, I might add." He glared at me.

"Sometimes the greatest secrets are hidden in the most obvious places," Professor Zaida said.

Uncle Ludwig gave her a funny look and then went back to

the stacks, mumbling something about quitters. Professor Zaida winked at me. She enjoyed toying with Uncle Ludwig.

I leaned over to her and whispered, "Do you know what sudithium is?"

"No, I really don't," she said. "But we've let Dr. Critchlore use the resources of the Great Library to decipher his book, and we'll help him research that question as well."

"Okay, then, how about getting me a book about the Oti tribe?" I asked. My vaskor friend, Sara, had told me that she was "Oti," but I'd never heard of that tribe, and Uncle Ludwig didn't have any information about them in his library.

"That's not important right now," Professor Zaida said.

I slumped in my chair. I needed to learn more about Sara, and the rest of the vaskor. A few months ago, when I'd visited the Great Library, I may have, sort of, freed her from her spell of obedience to the royal family.

It had seemed like a nice thing to do at the time.

CHAPTER 7

Three secret elements are not included in the periodic table. These elements are thought to be so dangerous that scientists refuse to share their information concerning their existence.
—*SECRETS OF THE MODERN WORLD*, VOLUME 1,625

I asked Darthin about sudithium as we sat down to lunch with Boris and Eloni.

"It's a very rare element, believed to come from outer space, and it's found in places where meteorites have crashed. It's pale greenish silver in color."

"How do you know all that?"

"I overheard Dr. Frankenhammer talking to Dr. Critchlore about it in the lab this morning. Ever since Pravus escaped punishment, Critchlore's been panicking." He leaned in to whisper. "You guys, I think Dr. Pravus is trying to create the legendary Undefeatable Minion. That's what he was implying during *Evil Overlord Dinner Theater*."

"Something's up—that's for sure," Eloni said. "After PE I was helping Coach Foley put the dodge boulders away in the shed. Critchlore showed up. He didn't know I was in the shed, so he started telling Coach Foley that he needs him to help arrange teams to go out on search missions. It sounded like he knows where they want to go—they just need to decide who's going."

This was exactly what Professor Murphy had wanted to keep secret. I wondered how soon it would be before I was blamed for the leak of information.

"Field trips? To where?" Boris asked.

"I've looked into it," Darthin said, because of course he had. "Guys, one of the largest impact craters on the Porvian Continent is in Upper Worb."

"Hey, that's where you're from," Boris said.

"I know. What if he wants me to go?" Darthin looked worried now. "I don't want to go back. You can't imagine how terrible it is there. What if they won't let me leave?"

"What's so terrible about it?" I asked. "I mean, I know there's Irma Trackno and her crazy rules about nightly tributes. But your family is there. Don't you miss them?"   .

"I do. I'd love to bring them some lightbulbs. And toilet paper. They get only one roll a month. But the crater is way north, and I've heard stories . . . The beasts there are huge and vicious. There's a reason why the Supremely Wonderful Irma Trackno has never recruited minions from outside her realm. She doesn't need to."

"Relax," I said. "I'm sure Dr. Critchlore won't send you." I didn't want to be mean, but I'd seen baby rabbits that were braver than Darthin. Critchlore would have to be nuts to send him on a field assignment.

Frankie sat down at the table, dropping his tray and resting his head on his folded arms next to it.

"What's up, Frankie?" Eloni asked.

"Nothing," he said into the table. His body shook with sobs, which was good. When he tried to keep his feelings bottled up, his head tended to pop off.

"Want to talk about it?" I asked.

"He's been working with Dr. Frankenhammer," Darthin explained.

"That's good, right?" I said. Frankie usually wanted to spend more time with his dad.

Darthin shook his head and whispered, "Dr. Frankenhammer is studying him, to see what he did wrong, so he can make a better version. He feels threatened by this talk about an Undefeatable Minion, thinks it's ridiculous that everyone believes a centuries-old book can create a better minion than he can."

"Oh, no," I said. I felt so bad for my friend. His father—er, creator—was a perfectionist. Frankie was amazing in so many ways too. It was cruel to only see his faults and ignore his talents.

"What'd he tell you this time?" Darthin asked.

Frankie lifted his head, sniffed, and said, "I'm too emotional." Then he plopped his head back down.

I was worried about my roommates. I couldn't do anything for Frankie, but maybe I could help ease Darthin's worries by talking to Dr. Critchlore. I was sure Darthin wouldn't be chosen for a field trip, but I knew he wouldn't be convinced unless I told him that those words came from our headmaster himself. I decided to go visit Dr. Critchlore before my next class.

There was a new, younger guy behind the secretary's desk. It looked like Professor Vodum had been fired after he'd tried to trick Dr.

Critchlore into giving him a better job. This new guy was crisp and neat, from his haircut and clothes to the desk in front of him. He was focused on his work, opening and sorting the mail with quick efficiency and a sour look on his face that reminded me of someone.

Dr. Critchlore's office door was open. It looked exactly like it had before Syke's sabotage, but with three smaller portraits of Dr. Critchlore replacing the giant one that used to hang behind the secretary's desk.

"Um, hi," I said to the new guy. "Professor Vodum's not coming back?"

"Mr. Vodum is now a recruiting assistant," the new guy replied. "He's performing his duties off campus. If you are looking for him, I can pass along a message."

He opened his desk and pulled out a pad of paper. The letter-head read, "From the desk of Barry Merrybench."

I felt my jaw drop open in shock. "Are you related to Miss Merrybench, the late former secretary?"

"I'm her nephew," he said. "Did you know her?"

"Yes," I said. I managed to keep myself from adding, "She tried to kill me." Instead, I smiled and said, "Can I see Dr. Critchlore?"

"Don't be ridiculous," he answered. "He's much too important to see students. There's a string of command, you know. If you have a problem, you start with your teacher, then your guidance counselor, then the dean of students. They will bring any unresolved issues to our headmaster."

"But I always—"

"Oh, I know who you are now." He stood up and came around

the desk and stood in front of me, blocking my access to Dr. Critch-lore's office. "Karen told me about you. You're Runt Higgins."

"But Miss Merrybench is dead," I said.

"Is she?" he asked sarcastically.

"Yes. She was eaten by zombies."

"Was she? Did anyone find a body?"

He grabbed my arm and dragged me out of the office while that horror-filled sentence seeped into my brain. Was it possible? No. It couldn't be.

As we reached the door, we bumped into two of the most hid-eous, disgusting, terrifying creatures I'd ever seen. They stood over six feet tall, with moist reddish brown skin, like a slug. Huge round mouths that looked like giant suction cups filled up most of their heads, with thousands of tiny teeth.

I screamed. I knew what these were. Giant leech-men. They sucked the blood out of anything and everything they met.

Barry Merrybench and I stepped back. One of the creatures held out a piece of paper. Barry took it and read aloud: "Dear Dr. Critchlore, Here are two new students I think will do quite well in the 'HOLY BLACK TERROR, WHAT IS THAT THING?!' program. Yours, Head Recruiter Vodum."

"You have *got* to be kidding me," I said.

CHAPTER 8

*"Get That Thing Out of Here!" "What Did I Just Step In?" and
"We're Going to Need a Bigger Net."*
—OTHER SPECIAL PROGRAMS AT DR. CRITCHLORE'S SCHOOL

My last class of the day was Introduction to Sabotage. The teacher based his entire lecture on what Syke had done before leaving. He covered the blackboard with complicated diagrams of the stables, the grandstands, Dr. Critchlore's office, and the Wall of Heroes. He gazed at his work, shook his head, and muttered, "Four attack zones . . . perfectly timed execution . . . clean getaway. How'd she do it?"

Everyone looked at me, but I had no idea.

Once class was over, the moment I'd been dreading arrived. I had to go to the swamp.

Mistress Moira had sent a letter with detailed instructions on how to get rid of the tether curse that had left wide red bands on my wrists. The Tether Curse Removal Procedure had to be done during the right phase of the moon, and she wasn't going to be back in time to help me. It didn't look difficult, but everything had to be done EXACTLY RIGHT (her caps).

First, I had to collect some swamp mud.

I didn't want to go alone, but Frankie was busy with Dr. Frankenhammer and Darthin wouldn't go near the swamp because he was scared of swamp monsters, two-headed swamp cats, and Kevin. I didn't want to ask Boris or Eloni to skip hoopsmash practice because we had a game coming up at the Pravus Academy.

As I left class, I fell in step beside Meztli.

"Meztli, has anyone showed you the swamp?" I asked. I knew it was lame to lure him into coming with me, but Meztli was a were-jaguar. He could come in handy in a pinch.

"No, but we have *muchas* swamps in my country," he said. "I don't like them."

"Me, neither, but I have to get some mud." I lifted the bucket I'd left outside of class.

"You need *amigo*?" he asked. "I go with you."

"Really? Thanks!"

"No problem. On the way you can tell me about Minion Games. They're starting tomorrow, and I don't know what they are."

"Deal."

We took off, heading through the Memorial Garden. It was a nice afternoon, with a partly cloudy sky and no wind. Meztli climbed up onto the Wall of Heroes and walked along the top until someone told him to get off. He jumped down with the grace and agility of a cat—naturally.

"Do you always do stuff like that?" I asked.

"Like what?"

"I don't know, just do whatever you feel like doing? As long as someone doesn't tell you not to."

He shrugged. "How else do you learn the rules?"

I pointed to the sign that read, DO NOT CLIMB ON THE WALL OF HEROES.

"In my country, there are so many rules. Everywhere you go, signs saying 'Don't do this,' 'Don't do that.' But most of them don't mean anything. In one park, there's a sign that says, 'Do not climb the *árboles*.'"

"You don't climb trees?"

"Sure, we climb trees. You see a tree—how do you not climb it? Some rules, nobody is going to do anything if you break them."

"That's so confusing."

"We know which rules are important: do not steal, do not hurt others, do not eat the chili peppers growing on Telva hill. And we know which are not important: do not wear sandals in winter. Here, I don't know. So I have to figure it out."

"I just follow all the rules," I said.

"Yes, I can tell that about you."

Once through the Memorial Garden we took the route that cut past the cemetery and continued next to the necromancer's building. Along the way, I filled Mez in on the Minion Games.

"The teachers separate us into five teams," I said. "Over the course of the week we compete in different challenges, getting points for each win. The challenges change each year, which makes it fun. Nobody knows what to expect. It could be a physical game, or a treasure hunt, or something else. Last year, one of the events was a timed siege. The team that was able to breach the practice siege wall fastest won.

"Each team has at least one of each type of minion, because you never know what the challenge is going to be. Your team might need a flying minion, or one that can breathe underwater, for instance. There are also nonphysical events, like the Quiz Bowl, the Dissection Trials, and the Team Spirit competition."

"Is that to see who cheers the loudest?"

"No, it's a competition for ghosts. At the end of the week, we have a float parade and everyone dresses up to match their theme, and then the winning team is announced. The winners get a great prize too. Last year it was a free day off, spent at the Evil Overlord Adventure Amusement Park in Stull City."

We reached the edge of the lake and walked to where the marshlands spread out in a swampy, goopy mess that smelled like rotting wood and algae and death.

"Hey, Kevin," I said to the corpse-like alligator man bathing in the shallows.

"Hello, Runt," he said before slipping underneath the water. Kevin is shy.

We worked our way through dangling tree branches and slippery soil until we reached a small clearing. I put out an arm to stop Meztli.

"There's a swamp monster in there," I said. "Maybe more than one. They don't move too fast out of water, but they're really quiet, so they can sneak up on you."

"Like the *cocodrilos*," he said, nodding.

"Also, we're supposed to be on the lookout for some small trees with gray-green needles, about as tall as me."

"Like that?" Meztli said. He pointed to the edge of the water where, in a cluster of trees, one of the little buggers was splashing around. "That's not normal."

"It's an enchanted weeping blue atlas cedar," I said. "I'm going to see if I can reason with it."

I edged closer, not wanting to startle it. I used my softest voice, "Hey there, cedar, whatcha doing?"

It stopped moving and turned to me, limbs hanging limply. It looked like a gray-green mummy, only pricklier, because of the needles. But the shape of the tree was very mummy-like—round head, drooping branch arms, two thick trunk-legs.

"Wanna come see Tootles with me?" I said. "He's got a nice spot picked out for you."

The tree screeched, "Nooooo!" and then splashed water at me.

I wiped the water off my face. "Tree, you come with me *right now*!" I said, hoping my forceful tone would get it to cooperate.

"NOOOOOOOO!" it said, and then it ran off, pretty quickly for a tree, its branches waving above its head like a crazy person.

Meztli laughed. "That tree sounded like my little brother. He's three and so stubborn. Always 'no' this, 'no' that."

This was a disaster. How was I going to round up six stubborn little toddler trees when I couldn't go any farther into the swamp? Maybe I could tell Tootles that I'd spotted one, and he could send someone else to come get it.

I scooped up my bucket of mud, and Mez and I walked back to see if the Minion Games teams had been posted. As we walked, I asked him about his home, Galarza.

"Very dry in the winter. Hot and rainy in summer. We grow sugar canes on my farm. Many times the hill monsters come and eat what we grow, but we always manage to save some of the crop. When the winds come from Skelterdam, we have to stay inside. Very hot winds, full of the poisons.

"Is a difficult life," he said, beginning to tear up. "I miss it so much."

A huge crowd was huddled near the posting wall, where important announcements like dorm assignments and club sign-ups were posted. Most everyone had already found their names on the list and were busy comparing team strengths and weaknesses. There were five lists, each titled with a color. We'd arrived late, so we didn't have to push our way to the front. There were only a few kids ahead of us.

"I'm Red," Meztli said. "You?"

"Blue," I said, scanning the list to see who else was on my team. My happiness deflated like a leaky balloon when I saw Rufus's

48

name. I knew from experience that it was no fun being on his team, especially if you weren't a monster.

Back in my room, I sat on my bed. Things weren't looking so great—I was failing my junior henchman class, I hadn't been able to snag the toddler tree, I had no minions to lead, and Janet was leaving school for a while. I pulled out my Good List and a pencil and tried to find a bright spot in all that stuff.

I wrote, "I made a new friend—Meztli."

And then I braced myself for the work ahead, because tonight there was going to be a full moon.

CHAPTER 9

Tether curses are effective, but they aren't for everyone.
Cursing may cause temporary blindness, nausea, and insomnia.
Do not curse while pregnant or when operating heavy machinery.
—WARNING AFTER AN ADVERTISEMENT FOR MIRANDA'S
SPECIALTY CURSE KIT

According to my instructions, I had to perform the Tether Curse Removal Procedure during a full moon.

At midnight.

In the cemetery.

Naked, but covered in swamp mud, which smelled terrible.

I didn't mind the stinky swamp mud. Or midnight. Or even the cemetery. But the naked part terrified me.

I headed out at 11:30 p.m. I hadn't told anyone about this project, for obvious reasons. The cemetery was quiet, and the full moon made everything much brighter than I would have liked.

Luckily, it wasn't as cold as it might've been, and I was comfortable in my cargo pants and sweatshirt. We were finally easing out of winter's cold grasp, and the skies were clear.

I put the instructions on the ground, next to my DPS (Dungeon Positioning System and all-around helpful electronic device), stripped to my underwear, and slathered on the mud. It felt kind of good, actually. I spread it everywhere, even under my underwear, but I kept my underwear on. The mud covered every part of my skin.

11:55 p.m. Howling sounds drifted down from Mount Curiosity. For a second I wondered if this was a Night Prowl night, when monsters practice stalking pretend "prey," but then my DPS beeped with the reminder alarm I'd programmed.

11:59 p.m. I watched the seconds tick down. As the DPS clock switched to 12:00 midnight, I chanted, "Wentervix, carma, wentervix, newt. Glaffry, glaffry, quiplord, fint."

I repeated it four times, facing each cardinal point: North, East, South, and West.

Next came the spins. Arms wide, head back. Ten spins.

And then I heard laughing and lost track of my spins. A cold fear swept through my body, starting in my stomach and radiating outward. I closed my eyes and begged the world to tell me it was just the wind.

"Hey, look—Runt's still trying to change into a werewolf!" I heard someone yell.

"Oh, man, talk about pathetic."

A herd of monsters stood outside the cemetery fence, staring at me: werewolves, mummies, monkey-men, a couple trolls, and in front of them all, my nemesis, Rufus. If that wasn't bad enough, Bianca and a bunch of other siren girls had joined the Night Prowl.

If I hadn't been covered in swamp mud, I would've looked like a tomato, I was so embarrassed.

"It won't work, Runt!" Jud shouted through the bars. "You are what you are."

"Maybe we should bite him," Rufus said.

"That's a myth," Jud said. "It won't turn him into a werewolf."

"I know. I just want to bite him."

I wanted to curl up and sink into the mud.

"Whoa, who are *they*?" Bianca said, pointing to a group of skeletons rattling their way toward us from the road.

Rufus shrugged and led the group off. The skeletons followed them for a few steps, but then noticed me, standing in my underwear in the middle of the cemetery. They quickly turned my way, sensing easy prey.

"I know, I know—I look stupid," I said to them. "No need to rub it in."

There was something different about these guys. Around school, the skeletons wore the same uniform as the rest of us—black cargo pants, T-shirt, and grade-level colored jacket. These guys were all bones, their whiteness shining in the moonlight like glowsticks. And they weren't all human. One looked like a dog skeleton, one had horns growing out of a long head, and another was eight feet tall, with long arms and huge hands. A short one had a wide, thick rib cage and carried a club.

My embarrassment turned to fear as each skeleton focused on me with empty eye sockets that were darker than the night. I felt hypnotized, like those black holes were sucking me in with their powerful gravity.

I backed away, tripping over a mound of dirt and falling to the ground. Now they came at me faster, bones rattling in air that had gone still. Even the wind was afraid of these guys. As I scrambled to get up, the short one ran forward and grabbed my arm. He—or she—yanked me up, teeth clicking together, ready to take a bite out of me. Another skeleton grabbed my clothes and my DPS.

I screamed and pulled free, sprinting for the lake. I thought they would stay in the cemetery, but they followed me.

The lake was a dead end. I ran out to the end of the pier, and the skeletons still came after me, reaching for me with their bony fingers and taunting me with my stuff. Like I was stupid enough to go back to them just because they had my clothes.

I jumped. What else could I do?

The shock of icy water sucked my breath away, and I had to surface quickly for air before diving back under. I swam as fast as I could underwater, hoping the skeletons couldn't see which way I had gone. Maybe they'd keep walking out to the end of the pier, and I could come up behind them on the beach and then run back to my dorm.

Underwater, running out of air, I felt something latch on to my arm. I tried to yank out of it, but it held tight.

What's up, bro? Midnight swim?

Pismo.

Long story, I thought at my merman friend. *Trying to get away from some skeletons.*

Let me talk to them, he said, keeping hold of me so I wouldn't need air.

I stayed under while he peeked out of the water. In a flash, he was back under.

Who are *those guys?* he thought at me.

I don't know, but they're not your friends, are they? Pismo usually ate at the skeleton table in the cafeteria.

No. I guess we got some newbies. Why were they after you? And why are you only wearing underwear?

Mistress Moira gave me instructions to get rid of a curse, and I was covered in swamp mud in the cemetery. They saw me and started chasing me.

Pismo swam us over to a spot away from the pier, safe from the skeletons. My skin was completely numb from the cold by the time we made our way to shore. Pismo dried off with his towel and handed it to me. I wrapped it over my shoulders and we walked back together.

"P-p-pis-m-m-mo?" I asked, my teeth clattering from cold. "What's it l-l-like . . . b-b-being a p-p-prince?" Pismo was the fourteenth son of the king of the merpeople. It was unlikely he'd ever be king. Still, I wondered.

"Good and bad," he replied. "I like the perks, don't like the responsibilities."

"R-r-responsibilities?"

"Dressing up, attending boring dinners, showing up for events, and the lessons. Even though I'll never be king, when I'm home, I have to take all these lessons about economics and diplomacy and stuff. Bo-ring."

"What are the p-p-perks?"

"Well, we're rich, so there's that," he said. "I can have anything I want."

With that he shoved me into the bushes.

"Hey, Bianca, Verduccia, Grace. Nice Night Prowl?" he asked.

"Hey, Pismo," I heard Bianca say. "It was fun."

"Great warm-up for the Minion Games," Grace added.

I heard footsteps fade into the night, then Pismo's whisper. "Sorry, dude, but you're in your underwear, looking like a dork. Can't be seen with you. You understand. See you tomorrow."

After Pismo left, I sprinted back to the safety of my dorm.

CHAPTER 10

There's a sucker born every minute.

—MOTTO OF AUNT HOWIE'S LEECH MONSTER FARM

I went to the cafeteria early the next morning, expecting the worse. Sure enough, as I stood in line I overheard two ogre-men talking behind me.

"You hear about that kid who was dancing in the cemetery last night?"

"Yeah, hilarious! I heard he was howling at the moon, pretending to be a werewolf."

"That's just sad."

"Shut up, guys," an imp said. "He's standing right there."

I tried to sneak to my table, but lots of kids made a point of howling as I passed them, the howls then breaking into laughter.

I realized then that Syke had been my armor against these sorts of attacks. Kids could have teased me for a million things before this, but they were just doing it now. Why? Because before, if anyone teased me, Syke would throw some insults right back at them. Along with a fruit cup, and maybe a chair.

I missed Syke. So much.

Halfway to my table I detoured and snuck into the kitchen, blinking fast so the tears wouldn't spill down my face. Once safely there, I took a deep, shaky breath. I sat down at Cook's table in the corner and looked at my wrists for the twentieth time that morning. The angry red lines had faded to a mellow pink. I pulled out my Good List and added: "Tether Curse has been defeated!" And then tried to convince myself to be happy.

When Cook came over, I showed her my wrists.

"What does it mean?" she asked.

"Mistress Moira thinks that if the curser added a tether, her curse range must be weak," I said. "If it was strong, she wouldn't worry about me getting out of range. At the very least, I'll be able to escape the death curse by moving far away."

"But I don't want you to move far away," Cook said.

"Do you want me to die on my sixteenth birthday?"

"Of course not," she said. "This is really great news. And I will continue to hope that she finds out who cursed you and gets her to remove the curse altogether."

Cook placed a plate of muffins on the table. I showed her that my hands were clean, she nodded, and then I grabbed one. She returned to her pan of scrambled eggs on the stove top.

"Cook," I said between bites. "Have you seen any trees running around lately?"

"Excuse me?"

"Tootles raised some enchanted trees, but until their roots strengthen, they can run around. He's missing six weeping blue atlas cedars, about as tall as me."

"Well, that's a new one," she said. "No, I haven't."

"I saw one in the swamp, but when I asked it to come with me, it screamed 'Nooooo' and ran away like a toddler."

"You can't reason with a toddler," Cook said with a chuckle.

"That's the truth," Mrs. Gomes, the head of security, added. She'd just come into the kitchen with her assistant, Margaret. Between them, Mrs. Gomes and Cook had raised eleven kids, so they would know.

"And you can't win a struggle of wills, either," Mrs. Gomes added, grabbing a muffin. "Toddlers feel powerless most of the time. Saying no is the only power they have. You have to allow them to feel powerful, but in a constructive way."

"How do I do that?" I asked.

"Don't give him a chance to say no," Cook said. "If you say 'Come with me,' you've given him two choices—one, to come with you; the other, to say no. Instead, give him the power to decide between two choices *you* pick. Like, 'We can go to Tootle's tree house or to the field. Which one do you want to do?'"

"I'll tell Tootles," I said.

"One that always worked for me was turning what I wanted my kids to do into a game," Mrs. Gomes said.

Cook nodded. "And when all else fails, put them in charge of what you want them to do."

They continued to reminisce about their childrearing tactics. I left wondering if I really was in charge of handwashing in our family, or if that was just a trick. Jeesh.

I headed out to the new forest for my first-period mentor class and found Tootles pulling out weeds from a flowerbed near the river. I sat down next to him and helped while I told him about the tree I'd spotted in the swamp.

"And then he ran off," I said. "I couldn't catch him."

"When are you going to try again?" he asked.

"Um . . . ," I said, because I had no plans to try again. This was a job for someone else.

"Don't give up, Runt," Tootles said.

"It's just that . . . " I fell backward and lay on my back, staring up at the sky. "Nothing is going my way lately. Everything seems impossible."

"Would you look at these weeds?" he said, pointing to the pile he'd made. "I pull these weeds out all the time. And they keep coming back."

"That's annoying," I said.

He pointed to his toolshed, closer to the road. The small brick building was covered with ivy that seemed to drip from the wooden roof.

"I used to pull that ivy out too. But then I got busy and neglected to do it for a while. Now it's kind of grown on me, because I like the look of it."

"You like weeds?"

"No, I hate them," he said. "But I admire their persistence. I yank them out, telling them they can't grow here. They come back. I yank them out. They come back. I forget to yank them out, and all of a sudden—they win."

He helped me up. "Don't stop trying just because you don't succeed on your first try," he said. "Otherwise, you'll never know what you can do."

‡‡‡

At lunch, instead of stampeding to the cafeteria, everyone was racing to the front gate. I saw Eloni and Boris following some ogremen, so I jogged to catch up.

"What's happening?" I asked.

"Someone saw a giant gorilla outside the gate," Eloni said. "They think that Pravus is attacking the school for revenge, because he thinks Critchlore destroyed his gorilla enclosure."

"That can't be right," I said. "Pravus wouldn't risk attacking us. Plus, all his gorillas died in that cave-in."

"Maybe not," Eloni said. "What if Pravus faked the whole thing?"

We followed the mob to the gate. It didn't take long to see what the commotion was about. Giant gorillas are, well, giant. This one could have stepped right over our perimeter wall, but he sat huddled back between some trees. He seemed nervous and kept scanning the growing crowd, like he was looking for someone.

The guards at the gate were trying to get everyone to back away.

"Maybe he's a new student," I said. "Vodum sent two new recruits yesterday."

"Or maybe this is the minion that Dr. Pravus had to give us," Boris said.

"Why would he give us one of his best minions?" Eloni said. "He's probably going to give us that dorky human kid. You know, the one on their tackle three-ball team who never gets in the game and just sits on the bench?"

"Someone should get Janet," I said. "I bet she could get him to do whatever she wants."

Rufus knocked into me from behind. "Why don't you quit obsessing over Janet, Runt. She thinks you're lame."

"Runt's right, though," Eloni said. "Janet could talk to that gorilla."

"No, she couldn't," Rufus said. "She's not here. She went home because of a family emergency."

"Do you know what happened?" I asked.

"Of course I do," Rufus said. "And it's none of your business."

I had my theory about Janet. I was pretty sure she was a spy. There were just too many things about her that didn't add up. She claimed to be part-siren, but she couldn't sing. She'd avoided the Fashion Show when all the siren mothers came to visit, and none of them had asked about her. Clearly she was just pretending to be a siren. Plus, she'd acted very suspiciously in the capital during our field trip. I saw her talking to a very tall man in the library there, but she wouldn't tell me who he was.

And she knew I was a prince.

Security showed up, followed by Mr. Everest, the dean of students, who herded us away from the gate. Since I was close to the school's perimeter path, I decided to follow it to the swamp and see if I could rustle up some wayward trees.

CHAPTER 11

"Remember—safety first! No mauling allowed during the Minion Games."

—MRS. GOMES, ALL-POINTS SAFETY BULLETIN

I needed to get those trees back to Tootles so I could be assigned a new mentor and get some real minions to lead. If I could do something impressive in the Minion Games, maybe I'd pass Professor Murphy's class and stay in the Junior Henchman Program.

I approached the swamp carefully, hoping the tree was still there and not wanting to startle it. I rounded a clump of mangroves and saw the two giant leech-men napping in the shallows. Air hissed in and out of their gaping mouths. I've learned that most monsters leave you alone as long as you don't bother them, so I edged around them and headed farther down the path.

I saw two of the enchanted cedars splashing each other at the swamp's edge. As soon as they noticed me, they froze, like they were pretending to be normal trees.

"Hi, trees!" I said in a cheerful voice. "Looks like you're having fun." I could sense how much they wanted to run away from me. My plan was to take Cook's advice and turn it into a game. "Can I play?"

They slowly turned toward each other. I swear it looked like one of them shrugged.

"You like to run? How about a race?"

This got them bouncing up and down. I smiled. "Okay, let's race to that tree over there." I pointed to a cypress tree that was away from the swamp but equally far for all of us. "Ready? On your mark, get set—"

They took off, the little cheaters. I sprinted as fast as I could, but they beat me by a few steps.

"Good job, guys," I said. "But you have to wait until I say 'Go!' Otherwise, it's cheating." The taller one swiped a branch at the smaller one. Soon they were slapping each other like wimpy kids trying to fight. They made noises that sounded like the high-pitched whistles of wind through leaves.

"Hey, settle down!" I said. "It's fine—I didn't explain the rules first. Let's try again."

They stopped slapping and looked at me. Up close, I could see through the dangling pine needles that they had faces on their trunks. They were faint and hard to see, but they were there.

"Where should we race to next?" I said. "Let's go a bit farther this time. How about to that building over there?" I pointed to the Necromancy Building, which was on the way back to Tootles's tree house. "No cheating this time. Ready? On your mark, get set, GO!"

I sprinted. I wasn't sure they were going to follow, but soon they both passed me, waving their branches like crazy. The tall tree won this time, stretching his longest limb to reach the side of the building before shorty, who barreled into the building, rattling the windows.

"Wow, you guys are fast!" I said, panting, with my hands on my knees. "Are you even tired?"

"Nooooo," they both said, now sounding like a low wind howling through the forest.

"I am," I said. "I need to catch my breath." I sat down next to them. "Hey, what can I call you?"

"Googa," the tall one said.

"Fffthhhp," said shorty.

"Okay. Googa and . . . Fthip," I said. "I'm Runt."

"Ruunnnth," they said. Close enough.

"I have another game," I said, still sitting. "I'm going to cover my eyes. I'm just so tired from all that running. I wonder if you two will surprise me by racing to Tootles's tree house while I'm not looking. I just need to rest for a second. Here I go . . . closing my eyes . . ."

I covered my eyes and heard them scamper off with what sounded like tree giggles. I couldn't believe it—they were heading right for Tootles's tree house! I waited for a few seconds and then stood up.

"Hey!" I shouted. "Where did Googa and Fthip go?"

I watched their little tree limbs shake with glee as they sped up, sprinting for the tree house in the distance. I jogged after them.

Riga had spotted them coming and came down from the tree house with a watering can.

"Hello, darlings!" she said. "Look what I have for you!" She sprinkled them with water. She also attached little tracking bracelets to their branches and winked at me.

"Googa, Fthip," I said, "I can't believe you ran here when I wasn't looking. That was so funny. We'll have to play again later, but right now I have to meet my Minion Games team."

I waved good-bye as Riga herded them back toward the new forest.

Two down, four to go. And then I'd get a real mentor with some fierce minions to lead!

I changed into my blue team T-shirt and my black shorts for the opening ceremonies of the Minion Games, held, like every all-school event, on the giant boulderball field.

The teams filled the stands like a rainbow—groups of red-, yellow-, green-, blue-, and purple-shirted kids. Dr. Critchlore, Coach Foley, and other faculty stood on the track that circled the enormous field. Barry Merrybench hustled over with a microphone for Dr. Critchlore. After handing it to him, he wedged himself into place next to Dr. Critchlore, slightly pushing Professor Dunkirk.

She scowled at him but stepped aside. There was something very irritating about Barry Merrybench.

Once everyone had settled down, Dr. Critchlore called the captains down for the presentation of the symbols.

Even though Rufus was a third-year, like me, he was used to being in charge of games. He elected himself captain and ran down before anyone else on the blue team could say anything. We waited while the other teams voted for their captains.

"Looks like we're going to play Giants versus Villagers," I said to Penelope, a second-year human.

"Yep," she agreed.

Giants vs. Villagers is a lot of fun. Normally, a few minions of impressive size—not just the giants, but sometimes ogres or trolls—stand on the field while everyone else (the "villagers") lines up on one side. When the teacher says, "Villagers—flee!" we run across the field, trying not to get swatted by a giant. If you get tagged, you're out. Giant minions are kind of slow, but they have good reach. One giant can tag out ten villagers with a single swoop of his hand. The game's a riot of running and dodging and fun, unless a giant steps on you.

In the Minion Games version, there was one giant for each team, and he or she would try to tag out all the villagers not on his team. He could also protect his villager teammates by blocking the other giants.

They'd added some new obstacles as well. The normally clear field was now filled with trees in planter boxes, some of them as tall as the giants (these were probably part of Tootles forest restoration project), giant boulders, and even a few huts. These obstacles would provide some protection from the rampaging giants, but not much, and not for long.

At last, the other captains joined Rufus on the track with the faculty. Coach Foley arranged them in a line and Dr. Critchlore presented each team with a symbol: an ax, a sword, a scepter, a cup, and a crown. We got the crown. Each team had to protect its symbol carefully, because stealing another team's symbol was worth a bonus of ten points.

The captains then announced their team's evil overlord theme. Rufus decided on Fraze Coldheart and his realm of Riggen, which was a good choice. The games end with a float parade, and Riggen is filled with dangerous terrain and cool monsters. Perfect for a float theme. The red team chose Wexmir Smarvy (Lower Worb), yellow chose Maya Tupo (Delpha), green picked Tankotto (Voran), and purple went with Dark Victor (Bluetorch).

A sense of anticipation and excitement swept through the stands, and everyone cheered and stomped as Dr. Critchlore passed the microphone to Coach Foley to announce the first challenge.

"Today, you are going to compete in the War Games version of Giants versus Villagers," he said. "In addition to dodging the giants, there are a few more obstacles you villagers will have to navigate to make it to the other side of the field—namely, land mines and bombs dropping from the air."

Immediately hands rose up from us "villagers."

"No, not real ones," Coach Foley assured us. The hands went down. "The land mines are buried springboards that will pop you into the air if you step on them. The bombs are bags of flour dropped by flying minions.

"Each team will get two points for every minion who makes it to the other side. If any do, I'll be shocked, I have to say. The team that gets the most kids to the end earns a five-point bonus. In addition, any team that retrieves its flag from the hut in the middle of the field and carries it safely to the end line will get ten points. You have a few minutes to discuss strategy, and then we'll start on my whistle."

Dr. Critchlore took the microphone back. "I want your best effort out there," he said. "Those who perform well will be eligible for a special bonus game! Nothing suspicious, just a new, fun adventure! So go get 'em!"

Excited, we all headed for the end line.

Everyone except Frankie, who sat alone in the now-empty green section.

CHAPTER 12

"Teams can choose any evil overlord's realm for their float except Irma Trackno's Upper Worb. Dr. Critchlore forbids that one."

—RUNT, EXPLAINING FLOATS TO MEZTLI

As the faculty and staff took their places in the stands, I jogged over to where Frankie sat.

"Frankie? Why are you sitting here? You're on the green team."

He looked behind us and then whispered, "Daddy's here."

"So?"

He looked down. "I can't . . . I'll do something wrong, and he's watching." He was too sad to twist his neck bolts, which was his usual nervous habit.

I shook my head. "Frankie, that's just ridicu—"

"Runt!"

I turned and saw my team screaming at me.

"I gotta go," I told Frankie. "We'll talk later."

"Good luck," he said, sort of halfheartedly.

Frankie sitting there alone was kinda breaking my heart, but I had my own problems to deal with, and number one on that list was doing well in the Minion Games so I could pass my junior henchman class.

I wanted to show them all—but mostly Professor Murphy—that I could do well in a competition. I joined my team, ready to talk strategy.

"Let's spread out," an upperclassman said.

Rufus held up a hand. "Here's what we're going to do. You heard Coach Foley. Hardly anybody is going to make it across the field. If the giants don't get you, all that other stuff will. To win, we only need to get one or two of us safely to the other side. That's going to be either me or Jud. Our speed gives us the best chance of winning. We'll take the edge near Stevie." He looked up at Stevie, our giant. "Stevie, you protect us, no matter what—okay? Let the other giants tag out villagers."

Stevie nodded.

"You second-year kids will be the sacrifices. We'll let you go out first and draw off the other team's giants, and then we'll slip past."

"I don't want to be the sacrifice," Penelope said. "I'm really good at dodging giants. I'm from Burkeve, the land of giants."

Rufus pointed at her, scowling. "You'll do what I say or I'll eat your face." Then he turned to his minions, the mummies, and told them to stay with him as his own personal wall of protection. They looked a little droopy after Rufus told them that. Like the rest of us, they wanted to try and win themselves.

"What about me?" I asked.

"Just be your usual loser self, I guess," he said. "I don't think you can help here. In any way."

A whistle blew, and we all lined up. I stood next to Penelope in our "sacrifice" position.

Taking a long look at the competition, I couldn't help but be in awe of my classmates—monsters of all shapes and sizes. Werewolves, manticores, lizard-men, skeletons, imps, ogre-men, trolls—all of them. They were all so amazing, and strong, and indestructible.

I noticed some faculty members were down on the track, holding clipboards. They looked like the evil overlord recruiters who came to the games every year to evaluate our graduating seniors.

I put on my red helmet, feeling like a doofus. Mrs. Gomes made all the human minions wear helmets, and we stood out like monster zits.

Another whistle blew, and the game began. The giants cracked their knuckles and leaned forward, ready to swat. Kids paced up and down the starting line, trying to find good take-off spots. The two giant leech-men turned around and ran back to the swamp.

Darthin, on the yellow team, was the first to take off. He wobbled a bit, covering his helmeted head with both arms. He ran straight for a giant. Once close, he fell to the ground, curled up in a ball, and waited to be tagged out. Timmy, a giant who knew that Darthin was afraid of everything, tapped him gently. Darthin got up and ran to the safety of the sideline, where tagged-out kids had to sit. He looked like he was hyperventilating with fear.

In the early rounds, there's always someone who tries to charge up the middle, hoping his or her speed will surprise the giants and they'll be too slow to react. This time, it was Meztli. He was in his jaguar form, which, I was surprised to notice, wasn't the golden tan with black spots I'd been expecting. Instead, his fur was white.

Faint gray spots appeared when the sunlight hit him, but mostly he looked like he'd fallen into a bathtub filled with white paint.

He dashed straight at a giant named Hector, faked left, then bolted right. Another giant stood nearby, but Mez was quick and darted between his legs before the giant could reach down and swat him. He would have made it to the end, but he ran out of bounds to avoid the next giant and was disqualified.

"Wow, he's really fast," Penelope said.

"He's not that fast," Rufus scoffed. "And look at him. He's a freak of nature. That color is not normal."

As soon as the giants focused on Meztli, everyone else took off, and the field turned into complete mayhem. Kids and monsters dodged giants, flying minions dropped flour bombs everywhere, land mines popped runners into the air. Frieda yelled and swatted at her ogre-men troops, but they were just too big to dodge the giants successfully. Huts were smashed. Tootles screamed through a bullhorn, telling kids not to hurt the trees.

I watched Rufus and Jud head out in their human form, wearing their snap-free pants and team T-shirts. Rufus needed his human voice so he could yell at his mummies.

Once the giants looked like they had keyed in on their targets, I took off. I watched their faces, hoping their attention wouldn't switch to me. I ran, scanning the field for the little lumpy land mines. They were obvious if you were looking for them. Unfortunately, there was so much else to watch out for that kids were stepping right on them. And those "mines" were stronger than I'd expected. Frieda stepped on one, and it threw her into the air. Frieda! She landed with a thump that shook the ground.

"Runt!" a voice yelled. "Watch out!"

I looked up. Our team's flying monkey, Anubi, was pointing at Melissa, the shape-shifting eagle, who was about to drop a bag of flour on me. I dodged the bag and sprinted for the next bit of protection, an oak tree in a planter box.

As I ran, I heard something gaining on me. I turned around and saw three trees following me.

"Hey, what are you doing?" I asked when they had caught up. I recognized Googa and Fthip, but not the third one, who was a bushy little fella. Or gal. Or both? I'm not really sure about tree genders.

"Googa," Googa said, hopping up and down. "Race!" The end of "race" sounded like Dr. Frankenhammer stretching out his s's.

"Fthip too!"

"Swishhhh," the third one said. "Racessssssssss."

"Trees," I said. "This is dangerous. See Tootles over there? Go stand with him."

"Racessss," they all said, stamping their trunks. "Racesss."

"But no cheat!" Fthip said, smacking Googa with a branch.

"This isn't a race," I explained. "It's a game of tag. We can't let the big ones touch us."

"Tag," Fthip said. "Gooooooo."

They took off before I could explain anything else. I scanned the field while I ran to catch up with them. The air was cloudy with bursts of flour. I saw that Rufus had made it to the end line safely, but not Jud. The red team had two players at the end, and a third was getting close. All of my blue team's sacrifice players had been tagged out.

That left only me, and the only way we would get enough points to win was if I got the flag.

One of the giants, Wendy, noticed the toddler trees, and immediately the trees froze, just like they'd done with me in the swamp. Wendy looked confused, then shook her head as she refocused on other victims. I caught up with the trees and hid among them.

"We have to go to that shed in the middle, okay? Let's go, slowly. Make sure the big ones don't see me."

Nobody had tried for the flags because the giants were watching the hut carefully. The trees were stealthy, though, and froze whenever a giant noticed them. Slowly, we reached the hut, and I grabbed our flag from the side. Now all I had to do was get through a minefield while dodging flour bombs and then make it past a line of giants.

Tagged-out kids watching from the sideline bench had seen me take the flag. They screamed at the giants. "Get those little trees!"

Three giants turned their focus on us, hands flexing as they stepped closer.

"Split up!" I told the trees. As I ran to the left, I saw Anubi heading back for more flour bombs. Wendy chased after me. I ran around a tall tree in a huge planter box to avoid her.

"Anubi!" I screamed. He turned around in midair and watched me sprint after him with a giant on my tail and a flag in my hand. "Catch!"

As Wendy closed in on me, I sprinted straight for a landmine. I jumped on it as hard as I could, and it catapulted me into the air, much higher than I was expecting. I had meant for Anubi to catch the flag and take it to the end, but he caught me instead, saving me from a painful landing and lifting me away from the giant. Soon, the other flying minions swarmed on us, trying to make Anubi drop me. He swooped and swerved, but he tired quickly and dropped me about twenty yards from the end line, which was now blocked by Hector and his wide arms.

Hector was the largest giant in school. I wasn't going to get past him.

But then my little trees caught up with me. They started swatting me with their branches.

"No cheat," Googa said. "NO CHEEEAAAT!"

I was being pummeled by the trees, and Hector stood there gaping at us. I was about to ask him for a little help, because the branches were really scratchy.

"I didn't cheat!" I tried to explain. "We're a team. Together. Here." I tied the flag to one of Googa's branches. "Googa, tag that guy over there," I pointed to Rufus. "On your mark, get set, go!"

I ran to the right, taking Hector's attention with me. Googa ran for Rufus. I was tagged out, but Googa made it to the end. Rufus untied the flag and held it high.

"I got the flag!" he yelled.

CHAPTER 13

Winter sports offered at school include hoopsmash, combat archery,
dodge boulder, and mummy hunt.
—DR. CRITCHLORE'S SCHOOL CATALOG

At dinner, I was too angry to eat. No, that's a lie. I ate. But I was really, really angry.

"You guys saw me get the flag, right?" I asked everyone at my table.

"Not me," Eloni said. "I was dodging flour bombs."

Boris shook his head. "Frieda kept screaming at me. I don't know what her problem is."

Darthin shook his head. "I couldn't watch any of it."

"Frankie?" I asked. "You were in the stands."

"The field was so smoky, with all those flour bombs going off. I saw that monkey-man grab you. You made it really far. You should be proud of yourself."

"I *told* Anubi to grab me. I got the flag. Then I tied it to the tree, who gave it to Rufus. He's taking credit for my work."

They made murmuring sounds of sympathy, but it didn't make me feel better.

The big screen flashed on, showing Dr. Critchlore preparing to make an announcement. He looked exhausted, like he hadn't slept in days. His secretary, Barry Merrybench, stood behind him, giving him a neck massage.

"Students," he said. There was a pause while he rubbed his eyes and waved Barry Merrybench away. "Well done today. I have exciting news. Remember when I said that, based on your performance, some of you might be selected for a special bonus game? It's just like me to do unexpected things like this, don't you think? It's not unusual at all. Well, we've decided on the game, and we're calling it 'Treasure Hunt.'

"Some select students are going to venture outside Stull for this game. But here's the tricky part: Evil Overlords don't like minion schools to train minions outside Stull. So we're going to pretend that these excursions are just part of our normal 'Visit the Realms' program. Students go on this type of field trip during their final year so they can get to know the realms where they might be recruited. But the real task . . . er . . . game is to search for a rare mineral and bring it back here.

"We have been granted visitor visas for Bluetorch, Pinnacles, West Chambor, and Upper Worb. Each team will have a faculty leader, who will be assisted by a junior henchman trainee. In addition, we will have one student from each realm acting as a tour guide. This is an essential part of the 'field trip' ruse. The rest of the team will be made up of minions who have proved themselves worthy of the task, based on their performance in the Minion Games.

"The lists will be posted after dinner . . . Search hard! Don't let me down!"

I looked over at Darthin. He was the only kid at school from Upper Worb. I didn't think a person could get any paler than he already was, but he turned polar bear white in a flash.

"How hard can it be?" I asked him. "You won't be alone. You'll have a team with you. You'll travel on the EO express train and be there in a day. Search the crater, come back. Easy."

"The impact crater is located near Polar Bay. In the Polar Circle. That's practically at the North Pole."

"Pack some thermal underwear, then," I said. "Who knows, maybe I'll be going with you."

It turned out that I wasn't going with Darthin. I wasn't on the Upper Worb team, or the West Chambor team, or on any team.

At first I was angry, because I'd done a good job in the competition, but the more I thought about it, the more I wasn't really surprised. The thing is, my classmates were awesome. Even among my human and human-ish friends, I had the least to offer any team. Darthin was incredibly smart, Frankie had super-human strength, and so did Eloni. Even Boris had special skills (exceptionally high pain tolerance and strong teeth). Me? I had nothing.

Despite Dr. Critchlore's little act, the whole school knew what we would be doing—searching for something that was needed to make an Undefeatable Minion. We also knew that we were way behind Dr. Pravus. These were desperate times, and Professor Murphy told all the junior henchmen trainees that whoever found the mineral would earn an automatic A in his class.

Dr. Critchlore had chosen Professor Murphy to lead the Upper Worb team. Rufus and Jud would assist him. I was surprised that

Professor Murphy hadn't selected a more advanced junior hench-man for his team—from the sixth- or seventh-year classes. But then Frieda told me that the advanced junior henchmen didn't need his supervision, while his newer trainees did.

Even though I was frustrated that I hadn't been selected, at least I'd have a week or two without Professor Murphy and Rufus on campus, which I put in capital letters on my Good List.

"Take your time searching," I said to Darthin as we walked back to the dorm, both of us depressed. "Make sure you treat them to a tour of all the local sightseeing spots."

"This means I'm going to miss your first hoopsmash game," Darthin said. "Who's going to be scorekeeper?"

"I'm going to ask Frankie," I said. "Coach Foley loves him, and I think Frankie could use some praise from a grown-up right now."

"Good idea."

Normally, I'd be excited about our first hoopsmash game, but tomorrow's game was at the Pravus Academy, and the last time I'd seen Dr. Pravus, he'd threatened to kill me for turning Sara and the rest of the vaskor, his Girl Explorer minions, against him. Sure, the librarians had captured him and erased his memory of everything that had happened in the Great Library, but he still terrified me.

Our hoopsmash team took a slight hit when two of our players were sent out to search for sudithium. Dr. Critchlore said we had to play, though—he didn't want Dr. Pravus to know we were searching for the mineral.

The Pravus Academy looked like a prison to me, with huge

concrete buildings and angry kids dressed in green combat fatigues. At the center of the school was a massive gray building with a big circular glass window near the top, like a giant eyeball. I could feel Pravus's presence, watching, and I thought about hiding in the bus until it was time to leave.

We entered the gym, which was set up for hoopsmash. There were three scoring circles hanging vertically on each side of the court. You can score on any of them, but not with your hands. You have to kick, elbow, knee, or head the ball through the hoop. You can catch the ball with your hands, but as soon as you do, someone can tackle you. You can't move while holding the ball.

Coach Foley loved hoopsmash, and he was a good coach. He trained us to move and block and set picks and to time our tackles for maximum impact. While we got ready, he tossed balls to Frankie as fast as he could, and Frankie kicked every one through a circle. If only Dr. Frankenhammer would let him play on our team, we'd never lose!

Coach Foley whooped and cheered, and I smiled because Frankie looked so happy.

We were all feeling good, mostly because we had a new ringer—Meztli. The sport had originated in his country, and he was as quick and nimble as a jaguar, even in his human form. He could juggle a ball with his body like nobody I'd ever seen. During our first practice he had scored at will by shooting from far away or tossing the ball up to himself and volleying it through the hoop, bicycle-kick-style.

I couldn't believe he hadn't been chosen for a search team. I asked him as we warmed up.

"Same old story," he said, looking kind of sad. "I'm leucistic. My fur has no pigment, too *blanco*. It makes me stand out in the jungle. They never let me go on hunts or anything."

"Well, I'm glad you're here," I said. "We always lose to this team. See their center?"

"The tall one with the pointy nose?"

"Yeah, his name is Victus. Watch out for him. He loves to take cheap shots when the ball's on the other side of the court. Last year he gave Boris a bloody nose and bit Eloni on the ear. Their coach is scary too."

I pointed at Coach Reythor, who looked as mean as a hungry troll, with a thick neck and small, crazy eyes. He surveyed our team like he was figuring out which one of us to maim first. I was so focused on him that I didn't notice that they had a new player.

"Isn't that your *amiga*?" Meztli said, pointing to one of their players.

My mouth dropped to the floor, along with the ball I'd been holding.

It was Syke.

CHAPTER 14

*"The Most Intimidating Building Award goes to
'The Eye of Pravus' at the Pravus Academy. It's impossible
not to feel like you're being watched."*

—MAYA TUPO, AT THE EO AWARDS GALA

While Syke warmed up with the Pravus team, the guys on my team gathered around me to watch her.

"What's she doing here?" Eloni asked. "I thought you said she was taking classes at the Kobold Retraining Center."

"She was," I said.

"She can't play for Pravus," Boris said. "She doesn't go to the school."

"It looks like she does now."

They were warming up by moving through a series of passing plays. Syke looked completely serious, like the rest of their team. They were preparing for war, not for a fun game of hoopsmash. She wouldn't look at us, but I couldn't stop watching her. She had a dark bruise on her cheek, a bandage on her elbow, and her hands looked scratched up and raw.

Five seconds into the game she tackled me.

"Syke, what are you doing here?" I asked.

"Getting some real training, for once," she said.

Syke had never been a minion-in-training because Dr. Critchlore was planning for her to attend horticulture school in the capital after graduation. She'd always resented the fact that she couldn't take the same classes as the rest of us. She loved to be in on the action.

"Why here?" I asked.

"Pravus hates Critchlore. I hate Critchlore."

"Pravus is a psycho. He tried to choke you."

"Yeah, well, he doesn't remember that. And he loves me now. We have a good time sharing Critchlore stories. You would not believe how lame Critchlore was back in his school days."

Yeah—according to Pravus, I thought.

I got up, but she shoved me down as she ran after the ball. Meztli beat her to it and dodged her tackle, threw the ball against the wall, and headed it through the ring to score.

Mez was amazing. He darted between tacklers, jumped ridiculously high, and had dead-on aim every time. The Pravus kids couldn't even play dirty against him—he was too quick for their late hits and late tackles. At one point I stopped playing just so I could watch him move. But then that stupid Victus barreled into me from behind, sending me to the floor.

I tried to match up against Syke, so I could talk to her. I wanted to tell her about Tootles's forest, about how I thought the fire story was suspicious, and that everyone was hiding something. But after that first tackle, she avoided me.

And then, during the second half, I felt a sinister presence fill the gymnasium, like an ogre burp. I looked up at the seats perched above the court and saw Dr. Pravus standing next to a railing, staring down at me. He had a confused look on his face, like he wasn't sure if he knew me or not.

I knew that Dr. Frankenhammer had erased Pravus's memory of how I had turned his vaskor minions against him and stolen the Great Library from his clutches, but the way he was looking at me now made my insides feel mushy, like they were scrambling for a place to hide.

I ran back into the game, my heart racing faster than Meztli's feet. I shook all over as I remembered his deadly anger, his promise to kill me. Why had I come here?

I glanced up to see him still staring at me, and then I was tackled hard by Syke. She stood over me, blocking Dr. Pravus from my view. "That's for not telling me about my mom."

A few moments later she tripped me from behind and said, "That's for defending the man who murdered my mom." And finally, she hip-checked me into the side of the gym, "And that's the last of my hate for you, Runt Higgins. I'm done with you."

I won't lie, those words hurt. I had known that Syke was mad at me, but this hatred took me by surprise. Just like the elbow to the ribs that Victus gave me as I was lining up a shot.

My best friend hated me. I wanted to grab her, make her say she didn't mean it.

I finished the game covered in bruises. I had played the worst game of my life. I couldn't even get myself to be happy that we'd beaten that smug team 24–19, which normally would have been so satisfying. Syke ran off before the postgame handshake.

I tried to stay in the middle of my team as we left the gym. One quick glance told me that Dr. Pravus was still staring at me. It was the cold, intense stare of a predator right before it strikes. I pushed a few kids out of the way to get out of there and onto the bus. When we finally drove out the school gates, I'd never been so relieved in my life.

On the ride home I sat alone, resting my head against the glass and wondering why I hadn't just told Syke that Dr. Critchlore had burned down her mom's tree as soon as I'd heard about it. If I hadn't kept that secret from her, we'd still be friends. She wouldn't think I'd betrayed her, and we'd probably be working together right now, trying to find out the truth about that fire. She'd see, like I did, that people were hiding something.

I closed my eyes and listened to the rest of the guys talk about Syke.

"I asked about that bruise on her face," Eloni said. "She said she got it in the Gauntlet of Loyalty test."

"One of their forwards told me she got the highest score," Boris said. "She also passed the Test of Worthiness. And she did better than an ogre in the Pain Threshold Evaluator!"

"It's insane what Pravus makes his students go through," Frankie said.

"I heard she was near the sinkhole when it opened up," Eloni said. "She could have died. They don't even know how deep it is. It's that deep."

"Better than an ogre!" Boris repeated. He thumped his head against the window to prove how great ogres were at taking pain.

Did Syke really hate us that much, that she would put herself in that torture camp?

I had to find out the truth about the fire. If I did that, Syke would come back. She'd come back and see the new forest and we'd be happy again.

Driving into my nearly empty school reminded me about not being selected for a search team, that I still didn't have any minions to train, and that I was cursed to die on my sixteenth birthday.

Before getting off the bus, I took out my Good List and tried to wade through the mire of terrible things in my mind to find something to write. At last, I wrote, "We beat the Pravus team today!" I smiled and tucked it back in my pocket.

CHAPTER 15

"Growing up, Dr. Pravus never had an imaginary friend.
He had lots of imaginary enemies, though. He beat
them up after school every day."
—FROM AN UNAUTHORIZED BIOGRAPHY OF DR. PRAVUS

The next morning, I reported to Tootles at the FRP, eager to tell him about Syke and hoping the trees had somehow decided to return to their boxes on their own.

"She's at the Pravus Academy?" Tootles said, knee deep in a trench he'd dug for some bushes. "Oh no. Does Dr. Critchlore know about this?"

"I don't know. I can't get past Barry Merrybench to see him." I wasn't even going to try anymore. The last time he'd smiled at me and told me that Miss Merrybench left him something to give me. I ran out of there before finding out what it was.

"I'll talk to him," Tootles said. "Now, I have another problem I need help with."

"More missing trees?" I asked. I really, really hoped he wasn't going to send me after more trees. Anything would be better than that.

"I need you to feed that giant gorilla so he stops stripping the leaves off all the trees out front."

Except that.

"I'll go with you on this first trip," he said, stepping out of the trench. "But then I'd like you to do this each morning on your own. I just have too much work to do here."

Tootles had an electric cart that he used to get around school, with an attached trailer for his tools and supplies. He'd already filled the trailer with fruit and leaves, so we headed for the front gate.

I was beginning to think that Tootles didn't really care about my wellbeing. First swamp creatures and now a giant gorilla? Why did he think I could take on these monsters?

"I don't know if you've noticed, Tootles," I said as we rode along. "But I'm kinda small and weak. I'm not really the best person for all these jobs you're giving me. Maybe if I had more helpers, or if I was part troll."

He stopped the trailer and pointed in the direction of the maintenance buildings.

"You see that oak tree over there?"

I nodded. It grew at the far end of the tackle three-ball field and was so tall that the top was visible over the buildings.

"It's probably the strongest tree on campus," he said.

"Don't tell me," I said. "It didn't give up."

"It survived, despite being alone," he said. "All alone in that big field, it had to face the wind and weather without any protection. Now, you know the oaks by the dorms? They protect each other in a nice little clump, don't they?"

"Sure, I guess."

"But none of them has grown as big and strong as the lone oak.

Not one. That lone oak has had to fend for itself, and its struggles have made it stronger."

"You're not giving me any helpers, are you?"

Instead of replying, he took a bite of his apple, which I guess was his answer. Then he offered me one.

"Trees have very few needs, Runt. With enough water, nutrients, and sunlight, they thrive. And they give us such wonderful things." He lifted his apple. "I just love trees."

Which made the sight at the gate all the more heart-wrenching. The gorilla sat nestled in a forest of ferns, surrounded by the dead carcasses of all the trees he'd pulled up. He was chomping on one now, like it was corn on the cob, which made Tootles cringe.

"What's he hanging around for?" Tootles wondered out loud.

I had my theory, and it was this: He was looking for Janet. This had to be the gorilla that she'd tamed—the one that had made Dr. Pravus look bad at the EO Council meeting. That gorilla had been living in Delpha, not at the Pravus Academy, so he hadn't been killed in the sinkhole. The big ape had fallen in love with Janet and had followed her here. It's what I would do, and really, it was the only possible explanation.

"Pravus probably sent him here to spy on us," Tootles said. "He's so big, he can see the whole campus."

Or that. That was a pretty good theory too.

Tootles drove the cart through the gate and slowly approached the gorilla. I gripped my door, ready to make a break and run for safety. The gorilla spotted us and became completely still, except for his eyes, which watched our every move.

Tootles swung the cart around, detached the trailer, and motioned for me to help him push it toward the beast. "It's better if the food is in front of us," he whispered.

The gorilla frowned. He lifted his pointer finger and shook it back and forth, then he pointed to the right.

We pushed it closer. And then a little closer.

The gorilla kept making those motions with his finger.

"Get ready to run," Tootles said, "as soon as he makes a move."

We were about to reach the edge of the ferns when the gorilla jumped up and roared. We turned around and sprinted for the cart. I ran right past it and kept going for the gate. Sorry, Tootles, but it's every man for himself, especially when I didn't sign up for this job.

The gorilla didn't chase us, but soon the air was filled with flying fruit as he hurled all the food back at us. Tootles drove past me and didn't stop until he was inside the gate. I caught up to him, and we turned around to see the gorilla sit back down and pull up another tree, munching on it while he glared at us. "Take that!" each bite seemed to say.

I told Tootles to go ahead without me, because my Minion Games team was working on our float nearby, at the PE field. I wandered over and saw the yellow team there as well. The air was filled with hammering and music and laughter.

For our float, we were going to re-create Fraze Coldheart's mountain fortress, complete with zombie guards, the Cave of Dangers, and the Devil's Cauldron, which was a boiling tar pit where he threw his enemies. Someone, probably Rufus, would play Coldheart, and the rest of us would dress up as his army of the dead. It was going to be so cool!

Boris and I hauled mud for the simulated tar pit until I had to go to my free-period class with Professor Zaida. Every other class had been canceled because of the field trips, but not mine.

I headed back to the castle, kicking a rock and not really paying attention to what was around me, so I didn't see them until it was too late.

Those freaky skeletons. And they were coming for me, again.

CHAPTER 16

"I left my heart in Santo Lisco."
—POPULAR SKELETON SONG

The skeletons still weren't wearing uniforms. They were all white bones walking down the main road from the castle toward the front gate. They were heading right for me, and I froze, panic spreading through my body.

Seeing me, they burst forward. I turned to run, but the ground shook beneath my feet, making me stumble. In a flash, a group of giants came around the corner from the dorm road and barreled right toward me.

I was caught between a pack of menacing skeletons and a troop of giants. I dove for the side of the road, barely escaping the giants' trampling feet.

"Stevie!" I shouted, waving my arms. "Hey!"

Stevie stopped running and looked down.

"Give me a lift, okay?" I said.

He reached down and picked me up.

"Gently!" I shouted when we were face-to-face. "Hey, Stevie, do you see those skeletons over there?"

They'd stopped coming at me and were now huddled in the trees, watching. The dog was running in circles, agitated at not having caught me.

"Yeah, I see them," he said. "Why aren't they in uniform?"

"I don't know. They freak me out. They chased me in the cemetery a few days ago, and they were just coming after me here."

"Why were you in the cemetery? That place is creepy."

"I was doing something for Mistress Moira," I said. "Can you give me a lift past them to the castle steps?"

"Sure," he said.

There was a pause, and then he added, "You know, my uncle worked in necromancy."

"Really?" I said, because that wasn't the normal course of study for a giant.

"Yeah, he kept trying to get me interested in it, but I didn't like it. Being dead changes a person, you know?"

"Makes sense," I said. "I just wish they'd leave me alone."

"Maybe those skeletons saw you in the cemetery and thought you were rising from the dead or something."

"That's possible. I was covered in mud," I said. Hmm, interesting idea. "Thanks, Stevie, I owe you one."

"Can you help me with my Battlefield Instruments homework later?" he said. "You took that last year, right?"

"Sure," I said.

He smiled and placed me on the steps, then turned and ran for the boulderball field. I stood there wondering if I was going to need giant protection to get around the school from now on.

I got to the library before Professor Zaida, so I used the time to look up information about giant gorillas. All I could find online was a brochure from the Pravus Academy that talked about how great they are.

"Strong and ferocious, they can squish the insides out of a full-grown ogre," I read. I skimmed over the rest of that section, because I was sure it would give me nightmares. "Fantastically smart too." Ooh, this was interesting. "They understand commands and can communicate with over two thousand words in Gorilla Sign Language (GSL). They are actually easier to communicate with than trolls."

Maybe that's what he'd been trying to do with all that finger waving.

Professor Zaida arrived, hustling down the spiral staircase in the corner.

"Sorry I'm late, Runt," she said, handing me a very squished, very tiny piece of paper. "That's a note from Mistress Moira. She sent it with one of her trained carrier ravens."

I had to squint to read it.

Am in East Chambor. There are three witches here capable of casting a tethering curse. Also—have seen two Pravus kids interviewing people here. Tell Derek XOXO MM.

"I've informed Dr. Critchlore of the Pravus Academy kids," Professor Zaida said. "It just set him off in another fit of panic, though. 'Why didn't she message me directly?' 'Do you think she's avoiding me?' 'Can I send her a message back?'"

"Are there meteorite-impact craters in East Chambor?" I remembered that Dr. Critchlore had sent a team to West Chambor.

"No."

"Then why is Pravus searching there? Do you think he's going after another resource?"

"Yes, he is. We've just finished translating *The Top Secret Book of Minions*. We now know the four requirements needed to create an Undefeatable Minion. The final one is a spell of obedience, because why create a powerful monster if you can't control it?"

"Like the vaskor," I said.

"The vaskor weren't created, but yes. The spell that binds them to your command is centuries old and could only have been cast by an extremely powerful witch. There are very few capable of doing it today."

"And Pravus is looking . . . ," I said. "That means we still have time to catch up."

"We *have* to catch up," she said, looking extremely worried.

"Why? What will happen if we don't?"

"An Undefeatable Minion means ultimate power. If Dr. Pravus were to create them, what do you think would happen?"

"He'd drive other minion schools out of business?"

"Yes, but there's a worse possibility."

"What?"

She leaned forward. "Think, Runt. Ultimate power! The EOs will be falling over themselves to get them. Pravus could make a pact with a select few evil overlords and only supply the UMs to them. Then those EOs will quickly take over every other realm, further consolidating and broadening their power and their oppression of everyone else."

Yikes.

"Or something worse could happen," she added.

"What?"

"It would be madness, but it's possible: Dr. Pravus could use the UMs himself and take over the entire continent. The man is driven and brutal. If you think the EOs are bad, imagine a world run by that sadistic egomaniac.

"Both scenarios would be catastrophic for millions of people, and the only way to stop them from happening is to create the UMs ourselves. There has to be a balance of power. If Pravus wants to use them, we must threaten to use ours against him. If he lets Wexmir Smarvy recruit them, then we supply Smarvy's enemies with the same force. This is the only way to ensure that they are never used."

I sat there biting my lower lip, terrified.

"Now, to work," she said. "Did you finish your history assignment?"

"Huh?" I said. My mind was racing with thoughts of a few overlords controlling everything—or worse, Dr. Pravus ruling the world. I had no idea that the stakes were so high.

But if anyone could stop him, Dr. Critchlore could. He'd done it before, many times. I took some deep breaths and tried to convince myself of this.

"Your assignment?" she repeated.

I handed her my essay about the collapse of Erudyten two hundred years ago. I'd titled it "The Fall of a Great Society." It was a sad tale. A peaceful, prosperous, library-loving country had been torn apart by the greed of its neighbors and then turned into four realms filled with poverty and despair.

"Great," she said. She glanced at it quickly, then put it aside.

"For your next essay, I want you to research the similarities and differences between the fall of Erudyten and the fall of Andirat."

"I already know this," I said. "Peaceful and rich Erudyten fell because it thought it could appease its enemies with gifts, but they attacked anyway. Two hundred years later, their descendants, now ruling in Andirat and fearing the same outcome, built a strong army for defense, but then the army attacked them."

"There's more to it than that," she said. "Read this book. I want you to pay close attention to the people involved in the coup in Andirat. One of those people was a trusted advisor to your father."

I gulped. *My father.* It still seemed so strange to imagine King Natherly as my father. He was a figure in history now, as distant from me as all the other historical figures I read about.

In all my studies for Professor Zaida, I'd paid the most attention to him. He was so . . . fair. He believed that all laws should apply to everyone. If he asked his people to do something, then he did it too.

And then he'd been betrayed by someone he thought was his closest friend.

CHAPTER 17

*Anyone traveling to West Chambor must first be
vaccinated for wyvern pox.*

—MRS. GOMES, ALL-POINTS BULLETIN

At lunch the cafeteria was more than half empty because so many kids had gone on the Treasure Hunt Challenge. I saw Pismo across the room, sitting at his usual first-year table with some skeletons. I decided to ask him about the new guys.

I sat down across from him and a skeleton in a first-year purple jacket. KATE was stitched on the front.

"Hi guys, can I ask you a question?"

"Sure, Higgins," Pismo said. "What's up?"

"Have you seen the new skeletons around campus? The ones that don't wear a uniform. And there's a dog skeleton with them."

Pismo looked at Kate, who nodded. Then her fingers moved in rapid flicks, and Pismo laughed.

"What was that?" I asked.

"Skeleton sign language," Pismo said. "Kate said the new guys are"—he laughed—"something rude."

"Skeleton what now?" I said

"Sign language," Pismo said. "How else are they supposed to

communicate? I don't know if you've noticed, but they don't have vocal chords."

Kate seemed to shake with chuckles at that.

"But she can see without eyeballs? And hear without eardrums?" I said. "That doesn't make sense."

"Haven't you taken Necromancy 101? Sense data can go in, but it can't go out. It's science—your basic reanimating dead stuff . . . stuff."

I really needed to take that class, but I'd always avoided it in the past because it was taught by Professor Vodum.

I remembered the brochure about the gorillas, and that they spoke using sign language, so I asked Pismo, "Does this mean anything?" I made the motions the gorilla had made at me. The wagging finger and the pointing to the side.

"Yeah—'Where is it?'" Pismo said. "Or 'Where is he?' Or she."

Kate nodded.

"'Where is she?'" I repeated. "He's looking for someone. A 'she' someone. I knew it! It's got to be Janet. She made friends with him in Delpha, and he followed her here."

"Could be."

"You guys have to come with me to talk to the gorilla. Please, it's important. He's destroying the forest out there."

They agreed to come along. As we walked down the main road, I asked Pismo how he knew SSL.

"It's similar to TSL," he said.

"TSL?"

"Turtle sign language," he answered.

Kate's head tilted back with silent laughter.

"I'm kidding," Pismo said. "But as a prince, I have to be conversant in many forms of communication. Merpeople use telepathy with each other, but it doesn't always work with other species."

We went through the open front gate and carefully approached the gorilla. Like before, he sat in his patch of ferns, stripping leaves off a tree he had uprooted. He chewed slowly as he watched us approach.

"Kate, can you ask him his name?" I asked.

Kate nodded and stepped forward. The gorilla stopped chewing and stared at her with a gaze that made my insides feel squishy with fear. It was the exact same feeling I got when Cook served leftover goulash surprise. *Don't go any closer!* that feeling was telling me.

Once she had the gorilla's attention, Kate stopped. She made a sideways salute, then put her hand on her chest, tapped her hands together with two fingers, and made some more finger motions.

"She just said, 'Hi, my name is Kate,'" Pismo whispered to me.

The gorilla saluted back.

"The gorilla said hi back," Pismo said.

"Yeah, I picked up on that one," I said.

"And now Kate's asking his name . . . The gorilla just spelled out Kumi."

"Kate," I said. "Tell him we brought him food. Ask him to not eat the trees."

Kate nodded.

They had what seemed like a long conversation with their hands until Kumi abruptly stood up and roared. He pounded the ground with both fists, which shook so violently that we were knocked off our feet. Kate raced back to the front gate. Pismo and I followed.

"What happened?" I asked.

Kate signed to Pismo, who translated.

"She says that Kumi likes to eat trees, and he got angry when she asked him to stop. He also kept signing 'Where is she?' and when Kate told him 'She's gone,' he went berserk."

"Janet had better come back soon," I said. "Or we aren't going to have any trees left."

I'd been hoping the quiet campus would allow me to make progress on my projects, but that wasn't happening and I was frustrated.

Days passed and the gorilla wouldn't eat the food I brought him, the toddler trees were still running around out of control, and nobody would talk to me about the fire that had burned down Syke's mom's forest. And those creepy skeletons were following me, I was sure. It seemed that every time I turned around they were lurking behind me.

On the Good List side, I did not miss Professor Murphy's angry glares or Rufus's taunts. I was worried about Darthin, though. I really hoped he was doing okay.

On my way to the castle I saw Frankie heading back to the lab. I was going to pretend not to see him, because I didn't have the energy to deal with his emotional neediness. But he spotted me and ran over.

"Darthin's back," he said.

"Did they find anything?" I asked, not sure which answer I was hoping for. I wanted Dr. Critchlore to find this mineral, but I didn't want Rufus to be the one who did it.

"I don't think so," he said. "Darthin wouldn't say anything. He's hiding under his bed and won't come out. I was hoping you could talk to him."

"Me? Why not you?"

"I have to report to the lab. Dr. Critchlore just yelled at Daddy, saying he's spending too much time trying to figure out what's wrong with me and not enough trying to figure out what sudithium does. Dr. Frankenhammer kept telling him that he could fix my flaws, that he just needs some time, because"—he sniffed—"I have a few more flaws than he expected, and, yes, he's disappointed in himself for creating something below expectations, but he knows he can do better."

I put a hand on Frankie's arm, because those seemed like some pretty damaging words to hear.

"Dr. Critchlore told him to stop. He's to work on sudithium and nothing else. So now Dr. Frankenhammer needs me to read some more journals for him."

"He really has no idea what it does?" I asked.

"He thinks it might harden the skin, so that it becomes an impenetrable shell of some kind. Still flexible like skin, but super strong. He really needs a sample of it, so he can perform some tests, but nobody can find any."

Frankie wiped his eyes and took a deep breath. "Good luck with Darthin," he said.

Darthin wouldn't come out from under his bed. A part of me wanted to join him and hide from all my problems.

He wouldn't talk to me, either. He was completely terrified. Whenever I tried to ask him what had happened, he just shook his head and curled more tightly into a ball. I stayed with him all afternoon, until Frankie came back, just before dinner.

"Frankie, did you find out anything?" I asked.

"I did. I heard from Jud that the trip was a disaster. They found the crater, but no sudithium. Rufus got in a fight with a yeti, and something important got destroyed. After that, Professor Murphy wanted Darthin to talk to the locals, who are really mean and uncooperative. Darthin wouldn't leave the house where they were staying. Rufus got mad and dragged him outside, strapped him to a snowmobile, drove a few miles from the village, and left him there. Darthin had to walk back. Alone. He was nearly eaten by a giant creature."

"A snow crawler?"

"He won't say."

"What was it?" I asked Darthin.

A faint whisper seemed to say, "A polar bear."

"A polar bear?"

"No," he said, stronger now. "Not bear. *Hare*."

"A bunny?" Frankie asked, and both of us had to clamp our mouths shut to keep from laughing.

"It wasn't a bunny," Darthin said, his voice muffled. "It was an enormous polar hare, and there were five of them, I'll have you know. They stampeded right at me, coming from nowhere. I only escaped by playing dead."

"Bunnies?" I mouthed at Frankie.

He shrugged.

"It was the worst experience of my life," Darthin said. "I thought I was going to die every second I was there. And then as soon as we got back here, I was running to my dorm and some weird mushroom monster tried to eat me."

"Yeah—the Matango," I said. "Professor Vodum recruited him. He can't hurt you. Just don't eat anything he offers you, or you'll turn into a mushroom man yourself."

"Maybe Critchlore is trying to get out of training human minions and is going full-monster," Frankie said.

"Maybe," I said, remembering the leech-men, the new skeletons, and now the Matango. But I really hoped not.

"I'm not leaving this room," Darthin said. "Ever. They can search for sudithium without me."

"Nobody's found anything," Frankie said. "Critchlore is sending Uncle Ludwig and some other people out to find a sample of sudithium on the black market. He's getting really desperate."

So the rest of the teams had come back empty-handed as well. There didn't seem to be a trace of the rare gray-green mineral anywhere.

CHAPTER 18

To the next student who leaves a paper bag filled with dragon dung on my desk: You'll be in for a rude surprise.

—BARRY MERRYBENCH, ALL-POINTS BULLETIN

With everyone back at school, classes resumed. I was ready to go to breakfast, but Darthin wouldn't get out of bed. He had the covers pulled up over his head.

"Darthin, you have to go to class."

"Can't. There are too many monsters out there."

"What about food? You have to eat."

He pointed under his bed. The space was crammed full of little boxes marked MRE—Meals Ready to Eat. "They gave us those for our expedition. I'm starting to like dehydrated chicken loaf."

Something had to be done. I went outside to the Dormitory for Minions of Impressive Size. It was a busy time of day, and I had to dodge quite a few huge bodies as I made my way to their front steps. I grabbed one giant's leg thinking it was Stevie, but when he looked down, I saw it was George.

"Oops," I said. "Wrong giant. Have you seen Stevie?"

"Yeah, he's inside," George replied. "I'll get him."

In a few minutes, Stevie was holding me next to his face so I could tell him my plan.

"Got it," Stevie said. "And thanks for reminding me about that assignment."

I ran back to my dorm. Darthin hadn't moved, but there was an empty container on the floor and the room smelled like tinned food.

Soon we heard a tap on our window. The tap was a little harder than it should have been, and the glass shattered onto the floor.

"We're under attack!" Darthin screamed. He jumped up and ran to the far corner of the room.

"No, it's just Stevie," I said. "Hi, Stevie. How's it going?"

"Hi, Runt." Part of Stevie's big head appeared at the window, one eye glaring into our room. "Sorry about your window. Is Darthin in there?"

"He wants *me*?" Darthin said, shaking in the corner. "Why?"

"Oh, there you are," Stevie said. "Travis told me you aced Battlefield Instruments and that you might be able to help me figure out what's wrong with my seismograph."

"Y-y-you're in Battlefield Instruments?" Darthin asked.

"Yeah, and it's really hard," Stevie said. "I didn't do so good on my first two tests, and the final project is due tomorrow. I made a seismograph to measure the shaking power of different giants' steps. But the paper comes out with a flat line. It's not detecting my power." He stomped his foot in an unnecessary display of his stomp's power.

"Hmm . . . that's interesting," Darthin said. He stood up, his eyes seeming to focus on something far away. "Could the pen be stuck in one position?"

"No, that was the first thing I checked."

"Hmm . . . maybe your weighted beam is too heavy," Darthin said. "Can I see it?"

"Hang on."

Darthin got up and scooched closer to the window, brushing the glass shards to the side

When Stevie came back, Darthin got so caught up in the problem that he forgot he was talking to a giant.

With that intervention complete, I focused my attention on another problem: the stubborn little toddler trees. I'd just gotten Stevie to help with Darthin; maybe I could get Fthip, Googa, and Swish to help me find their missing friends. I saw them near Tootles's tree house and called them over. They weren't afraid of me anymore because we always played games. We raced to the kitchen, where Cook had left some fruit for the gorilla.

"Boy, those other trees are really good at hide-and-seek," I said as I threw some bananas on a wagon. "They're making us look bad."

"Hidey seek?" Googa said, turning to the others to see if they knew what I was talking about, but the other two just shrugged.

"Hide-*and*-seek," I said. "I was 'it' and I found you two in the swamp. When you find someone, then he or she . . . or both? . . . is on your team. So we're a team now." I pointed to each of them, then back at me. "But we can't find the other three. Gosh, and I really hate to lose. I've looked everywhere—in the forest, the swamp, by the river, by the boulderball field. I just don't know where he could be." I kicked a rock.

Googa hopped up and down. "Googa! Googa! Hidey seek! Seek Woooosh!"

"Is Woooosh a tree?" I asked.

All three started bouncing and saying, "Woooosh." Then they turned around and raced for Mount Curiosity.

"Nicely done," a voice behind me said.

I turned and saw Riga, holding a can of paint. She'd been really busy lately, helping all the teams with their floats.

"Thanks," I said. "Four down, two to go."

"Tootles really appreciates the help," she said, continuing on toward her tree house.

I fell in step beside her, pulling my wagon of fruit. "I wish he'd return the favor."

"What do you need, son?"

"Answers," I said. "About Syke's mother, and the fire, and everything. Tootles told me that Dr. Critchlore knew Syke's mother. How could he burn down her tree, if he knew she lived there?"

Riga stopped walking and touched my arm, a look of sadness on her face. "Runt, I want Syke to come back as much as you do. Maybe telling her the truth will bring her back, but Dr. Critchlore has forbidden it."

"I *knew* there was a truth to find. But why? Why would Dr. Critchlore let Syke believe that he killed her mother? What could he possibly gain from that?"

"Think, Runt. He wants to protect her."

"Protect her from what?" I asked.

"Just let it be, Runt," she said, and then she turned to go.

I gasped as something came to me. "Did Syke burn down the forest?" I asked, but either she didn't hear me or she chose to ignore me.

The more I thought about it, the more it made sense. The fire had to have been an accident.

Dr. Critchlore loved Syke. I knew he did. He was the kind of guy who would be noble and take the blame to keep Syke from living her life filled with guilt.

But if that were true, how would I get Syke back? I couldn't tell her that she'd accidentally killed her own mother. I needed to talk to Dr. Critchlore. But Barry stinking Merrybench was always in my way.

In junior henchman class, Professor Murphy was distracted and impatient.

"We've missed so much class time, and we have a lot of territory to cover. But Dr. Critchlore wants another Minion Games challenge, so I can't start a new subject. Instead, I've prepared a series of lectures on leadership, starting with—"

His lecture was interrupted by a giant roar coming from outside. Kumi had started roaring these last few days.

"WILL SOMEONE SHUT THAT BEAST UP!" Professor Murphy yelled in frustration.

I raised my hand.

"What?" he said.

"I was wondering . . . um . . . if someone got the gorilla to quiet down . . . could that person possibly earn some extra credit in this class?"

Professor Murphy sighed. "You want extra credit, do you?"

"Well, it just seems like it's going to be really hard for me to pass this course since I don't have any minions to lead in the Minion Games, and—"

"Runt," he said, raising his hand to stop me. "Let's be honest for a moment, because I don't think you get it. And I have to wonder . . . Do you really think you're junior henchman material?"

"Um . . ." How do you answer something like that? "I think I could do—"

"Take a look at your classmates," he said. He came around the desk and pointed to Frieda, at the opposite end of the row from me. "Terrifying power," he said.

Then he started walking toward me, pointing at my classmates as he came closer. Jud, "Terrifying werewolf." Rufus, "Terrifying werewolf." Janet's empty chair, "Terrifyingly intelligent and cunning." Meztli, "Terrifying were-jaguar." He stopped in front of me. "And then there's you, Runt."

"Terrifying incompetence," Rufus muttered.

I felt my face burn with both humiliation and anger. Mostly humiliation. I kept my head down for the rest of the class, just wanting to get out of there.

CHAPTER 19

To the kid who was trap-doored into a pit filled with dragon dung:
Don't say I didn't warn you.

—BARRY MERRYBENCH, ALL-POINTS BULLETIN

Humiliation like that doesn't go away quickly. I continued to feel like absolute garbage every time the scene replayed in my head, and it never stopped replaying. All the embarrassing things from that class would be etched in my memory forever, no matter how much I wanted to forget them: Professor Murphy's hurtful words; Meztli's face, full of pity; Rufus's gloating. Every feeling roared back like a firestorm when I remembered the scene—from the red-hot embarrassment that burned my face to the bottomless chasm of shame in my belly, and the shaky weakness I felt through my body.

I slunk down into the dungeon, passing a trio of humans—a very stinky fifth-year named Jeremy and two of his friends.

"Don't worry. We'll get him back," one of them said. "He's not getting away with trap-dooring a fifth-year!"

I found a dark corner, sat down, and cried. It all came out in shaking sobs. I'd been able to bottle up all the sadness I felt over everything that had happened to me lately, but Professor Murphy's words were the smooth minty candy that, when added to my soda bottle of sadness, made it all gush out of me. All of it—my frustration in his class, my loneliness with my best friend gone, the hurt I felt because she hated me, and the feeling that I wasn't going to do anything right, ever.

Why did all this bad stuff have to happen to me? Was Professor Murphy right? Did I not belong in his program? Was I really as useless as he constantly told me I was?

I grew too tired to cry anymore, so I just sat in that dark dungeon, and as I sat there, I realized something. This must be exactly how Frankie felt every day, because of Dr. Frankenhammer. The hurt, the humiliation, the feeling like a failure. But Dr. Frankenhammer was so wrong about Frankie. I could see that—everyone could. Maybe Professor Murphy was wrong about me too.

With red, swollen eyes, I got up and went to the secret library for my next class with Professor Zaida.

The place was empty. Uncle Ludwig had been sent on a secret mission by Dr. Critchlore to find some sudithium on the black market where he'd bought a copy of *The Top Secret Book of Minions*. If he could buy a sample of the mineral, then maybe Dr. Frankenhammer could figure out how it was used.

Professor Zaida showed up for our session with a pile of books for me to read. She slapped my essay on the table.

"Nice work," she said. "But you're just repeating facts. Think like a leader! What could the rulers of Erudyten have done to prevent their defeat, or at least to minimize it? They managed to save the books from the libraries—but what else could have been saved? Artwork? Historical sites? Important people? An entire culture was lost, Runt. A culture rich with values and ethics and traditions." She seemed to be overcome with emotion for a second. "Dig deeper, and give me five more pages."

"That sounds like a lot of work," I said, grabbing a book. "You know, I'm going to fail my junior henchman class. I might as well work on prince stuff for both periods now."

"You'd better not fail," she said. "That class is the only reason I'm letting you stay here."

And then she continued to casually take notes on her pad, like she hadn't just dropped a two-ton ogre on me, squishing me flat.

"What?" I said. "What do you mean by 'letting me stay'? You can't make me leave if I don't want to. Dr. Critchlore won't let you."

"Runt. Do *not* forget who I am," she said, pointing a finger at me. She leaned forward and whispered, even though we were alone, "I am an Archivist of the Great Library. I can break powerful people with a word. You've studied Egmont Luticus, the banished overlord of Riggen? Why he was overthrown?"

"It started with the Great Aspirin Shortage," I said. "The people had finally had enough, so they overthrew him."

"Yes, that was how we librarians rallied the population's anger. But the real reason was that he was close to finding the Great Library, and something had to be done. We took him out through the careful dissemination of information to the populace. *We* stoked their anger, *we* convinced other overlords not to help him."

For a brief moment she looked smug. But the moment passed, and a sadness came over her.

"And then we sat back and watched as that tyrannical chicken farmer took over." She shook her head, like it had been her fault.

"Fraze Coldheart," I said. One of the most ruthless men ever to rule.

"His real name is Gilbert Cank. We made a terrible mistake. One I will not make again. Power cannot rest in one person alone. Revolutions have to come with a plan to share power, so that the people are not oppressed. There must be a balance of power. That's why I'm teaching you to lead, Runt. You are going to be the kind of leader who will do the right thing."

There she went again, thinking I could be a prince. It had gone from ridiculously funny to downright terrifying.

"Knowledge is power, Runt," she said. "And I am more powerful than anyone at this school. Understand? If I say you're going to be privately tutored in a secret, remote location, then that's what's going to happen. I've often thought this school was too dangerous for you. But you *have* to learn to lead.

"I know you don't like Professor Murphy, but Dr. Critchlore hired him for a reason—he's the best junior henchman instructor in Stull. If you fail his class, I'm taking you to the Great Library's new location, end of discussion."

She returned to her note taking, and I couldn't stop staring at her. To me, Professor Zaida had always been the nice, sweet teacher. The one who was a bit of a pushover because she loved kids. The one who was a little crazy, because she thought I could be a prince.

But in one conversation she'd morphed into a completely new person. I don't know how to explain it, but I felt her power and self-confidence, and with it, a shift in our relationship. She was more than a teacher I wanted to impress, more than a tackle three-ball coach I had to patiently explain the rules of the game to. She was a force to be feared, and respected.

I didn't know the new location of the Great Library, but I knew I didn't want to live there. Sure, the library was amazing, filled with the largest collection of books and knowledge anywhere, and being inside had been awe-inspiring. But living away from here would feel like solitary confinement.

I read and took notes until the period was over, but it was hard to concentrate. I was filled with dread at the thought of leaving the only home I'd ever known. The only way to stay here was to pass Professor Murphy's class, and to do that I not only had to be chosen for a search team but I had to be the one who actually found some sudithium.

It was impossible.

Our next hoopsmash game was at the Westvolt Academy, and I was really looking forward to burning off some of my frustration on the court. I convinced Frankie to come along again. I figured he needed a break from hearing about his faults, and Coach Foley could once again provide the ego boost he needed.

When we reached the Westvolt Academy, I was surprised to see two other schoolbuses in the parking lot: one from the Center for Minion Excellence and the other from the Pravus Academy.

"What's up?" we asked Coach Foley.

"The gymnasium at the Center for Minion Excellence is still being renovated," Coach Foley said. "Due to sabotage."

"Pravus," we all muttered.

"Right. So they're playing their home games here. Their game against the Pravus Academy should be over shortly."

We filed into the gymnasium and waited for the game to end.

Syke was playing hard, as usual. I watched her give-and-go with Victus, the tall obnoxious kid. I watched them high-five each other after one of them scored. I watched them cheer for each other. That used to be me. I was the one she cheered for and passed to and high-fived. I felt a whole new level of hurt watching them. Not only did she hate me, but she'd already replaced me. With a complete jerk.

Their beady-eyed coach, Reythor, yelled at the referees over every call and noncall. He yelled at his players. He picked up a chair and squeezed it to pieces when one of his players missed a shot.

The game ended. I had to talk to Syke, so I ran to the exit before she got there. She was walking off the court with Victus, who smiled when he saw me. It wasn't a nice smile.

"Syke, I have to talk to you," I said.

"She's done with you losers," Victus said, putting a hand on my chest. "Let it go, already."

"Syke," I said. I had to lean around Victus to talk to her. "I've learned more about the fire. I know Dr. Critchlore is protecting someone."

She sighed and shook her head, then pushed by me to leave.

"Syke, please listen," I said, following her out.

"Dr. Critchlore only protects himself," she said without turning around. She walked rapidly toward their bus. I jogged to keep up.

"If he only protects himself, then why not get someone else to take the blame? He's done it before—you know he has. If he wanted to, he could have blamed it on anyone."

She didn't have an answer for that.

"I'm telling you, Syke, that fire was not his fault."

She stopped and turned to face me, poking me in the chest, hard.

Her whole face blazed with anger and hatred. "Here's what I know. The fire killed my mom. Even if he didn't start it, he didn't stop it, either. It happened on his property. He should have protected the forest, but he didn't. That means it's his fault. The other thing I know is that you are ridiculously gullible. So whatever you say, I'm not going to believe it.

"You're on the wrong side, Runt. Pravus is doing big things. Things that will make the world a better place. I'm never coming back, so get over it."

Victus bumped into me as I stood there gaping at Syke. I hadn't realized he'd followed me. "You guys are so lame," he said. "And so far behind us. In every way."

"Oh, really?" Man, this guy bugged me. I felt like I had to defend my school. "We know about the sudithium."

"Sure you do. But do you have any? Do you even know what it does?" He must have noticed my blank look, because he added, "Thought so."

Then he howled like a wolf, right in my face.

I stood there, unable to move. A herd of trolls could have trampled me then, and I don't think I'd feel any more hurt than I was feeling. My gut clenched with hurt.

Syke had told Victus that I used to think I was a werewolf—she'd told him my most embarrassing secret.

Hurt turned to anger as I watched them leave, laughing together. I'd been betrayed by my best friend, in the worst way possible. How could she have done that?

CHAPTER 20

"Who selected these teams?"

—OVERHEARD IN THE TEACHERS' LOUNGE AFTER THE GREEN
TEAM WON THE SPIRIT COMPETITION, THE OGRE PIE-EATING
COMPETITION, *AND* THE SWAMP CAT TOSS

The second all-team Minion Game was called Find the Flags, a giant treasure hunt where each team races to decipher clues and be the first to find the flags hidden at different spots around school. Giants versus Villagers had tested our agility against monsters. This game would test our cunning and our ability to find things that were hidden.

It was an all-day event, and by late afternoon three of the four hiding spots had been found. The yellow team had been the first to the flags in Frederick Critchlore's crypt. The green team had outraced everyone to the flags in the hawk's nest on top of Mount Curiosity. Then the red team used Kate, the skeleton, to go into the swamp, because she was safe from the leech-men there. Skeletons don't have any blood to suck.

There was one hiding spot left, and we were determined to find it first and get the blue team on the scoreboard. After the third spot was found, we regrouped by our home base on the sports field. We stood around our float, on a field littered with wood, paint cans, and props we were using to re-create Fraze Coldheart's realm.

Rufus took over, as usual. He had a red mark on his arm where a leech-man had grabbed him before he could morph and fight it off.

"Give me the last clue," he said to a sixth-year skeleton, who handed it over. Rufus read it out loud:

"Knives overhead, darkness below.
To capture your flag, you mustn't be slow.
You'll have to get by a monster's protection.
And danger awaits, in the wrong direction."

Delray, a mermaid, said, "It could be the lake—the knives overhead could be the piranha enclosure, over by the School for Aquatic Minions. 'Darkness below,' because it's really deep. It could be protected by the lake monster."

"Or it could be the armory room," said the sixth-year human, "with the dungeon underneath."

"It's the Caves of Doom," Rufus said. "The knives are the vampire bats' teeth. The darkness below is the bottomless pit. The claw worms are the monster's protection." He tapped the paper. "It all fits."

"It could be the underground grotto," I said. "The 'knives above' could mean the stalactites."

"That's stupid," Rufus said. "Stalactites don't look sharp . . . Okay, let's go to the Caves of Doom. Anubi will fly high to spy on what the other teams are doing.

"The Caves of Doom are notoriously difficult to navigate," he went on. "That's what the riddle means by danger waiting 'in the wrong direction.' I'll station one mummy at each cross section."

The mummies didn't seem too thrilled about this job.

"And the rest of you will make sure the other teams don't follow me and Jud."

The rest of us weren't too thrilled with our assignment, either. Rufus was being a glory hog once again.

We headed out as a group. As I followed, I twisted my ankle on a two-by-four and had to hobble for a few steps.

"If you can't keep up, just stay here," Rufus said to me. "I don't want you slowing us down."

Fine. I waved good-bye to him. What else could I do?

I could check out my own idea, that's what. Why not? I knew it would take them a while to get to the caves, which were around the back side of Mount Curiosity. I limped toward the castle, walking off the pain in my ankle.

My senses were on high alert all the time now because of all the strange monsters that Professor Vodum had recruited. I always had that feeling that someone, or something, was watching me.

This time, when I turned around, I saw someone duck behind a tree.

"Mez?" I called.

He stepped out, looking guilty. "Sorry," he said. "I'm the team spy. Not a very good one. As usual."

"Well, my team just went that way, if you want to catch up."

"Not really," he fell into step beside me. "So why does that dog hate you so much?"

"You heard that? I don't know. He's always picked on me. I thought he'd like you, though. He usually gets all the cool kids to join his group."

"I'm a cat. We don't hang with dogs. Where you going?"

"To the kitchen," I said. "I have an idea."

Mez followed me to the back entrance to the kitchen, which was empty. I grabbed a big plastic freezer bag and filled it with some raw squid that Cook used to make fried calamari for Dr. Critchlore. The rest of us got seafood tetrazzini.

"A little snack?" Mez asked.

"Not for me," I said.

Mez and I headed out of the kitchen and through the cafeteria.

"Where you going now?" he asked.

"The underground grotto," I said. "Don't you have a job to do?"

"I'm doing it," he said.

"Following me?"

"*Sí*. Drangulus says you know this school better than anyone. He said that you'll figure it out before that stupid werewolf."

I laughed. "I wish he'd tell that to Professor Murphy. Come on, then."

We made it to the grotto, which was dark, except for a string of dim lightbulbs. Water dripped off stalactites into an otherwise calm and very dark lake below.

"There they are!" Mez said. The brightly colored flags floated just below the surface of the water. Before Mez could rush to the edge, I grabbed his arm and held him back.

"It's a trap. The fish monster will get you if you step too close," I said. "Look." I pointed to a dark shape underneath the water.

"Ooooh. It's *grande*, no?"

"Muy grande."

I pulled out my bag of squid. "I'm going to put this in the water over there, and then we can grab our flags, okay?"

I walked around the edge of the water, as far from the flags as I could get. I went slowly, looking out for those tentacles. I placed the squid in the shallows and nearly jumped in fright when I heard a sound like branches creaking in the wind.

I looked over to a dark corner and saw a little tree with gray-green needles that sparkled in the dim light. The tree was shivering.

"Hello?" I asked. "Are you Googa's friend? I've been looking everywhere for you."

"Creeeeaack," the tree whispered.

I stepped toward him, or her, or both. (I still hadn't learned how trees handle the whole gender thing.) The tree shook harder and moaned, pointing behind me, where a giant tentacle as thick as my leg rose out of the water, stretching to the ceiling. I jumped out of the way.

"Yikes!"

The tentacle snatched the squid.

"Meztli—grab the flags!"

Meztli reached his hand into the water, but as soon as it got wet, he pulled it out, shaking it vigorously.

Cats, sheesh.

I ran over, waded in, and grabbed our flags.

"Sorry," he said, shrugging.

The tree had hustled after me and now stood behind Meztli, still shaking.

"Creak, let's get you out of here."

"Well done," a voice from the shadows said.

I turned and saw Professor Dunkirk, with a bag of fish and a grappling hook, just in case. She pushed a button on her DPS, and we heard the alarm bell blast one time. This was the signal to the other teams that the flags had been found.

At the entrance to the grotto, Creak didn't know which way to go. Aww, the poor little sapling had been lost down here. I grabbed a branch and led the way out of the dungeon.

Once outside, I handed Mez his red flag, but he wouldn't take it.

"Why not? We could both earn a point."

"You earned that, not me. Plus, you need to get on a search team. It would be better if only you got the flag."

"Thanks, Mez." I reached out to pat him on the back, and as I did, a furry shape charged between us, snatching my blue flag with its mouth. Jud, in werewolf form.

"Hey!" Mez yelled. In a flash he morphed into a jaguar and chased after Jud.

Creak followed too, yelling, "Cheaterrrrrr!"

I watched the tree chase the cat, who chased the dog into the hedge maze. Other students wandered back to the field, looking dejected. I saw my team near the end line, and walked over.

"Stupid mummies," Rufus said. "They slowed me down. I couldn't go fast enough, I kept having to wait for them, so I could place them as markers."

"Who got the flag?" someone asked.

"I did," I said. "It was in the grotto, like I said. Jud just stole it from me."

At that moment, Jud sped over, having lost Mez in the maze. Rufus grabbed the flag from his mouth.

"Good thing *I* sent you there," Rufus smiled. "Hey, Professor Murphy!" He yelled to where the teachers sat in the stands. "Dr. Critchlore! I got the flag!"

I shook my head. In one move, Rufus managed to blame the mummies for making him lose *and* steal the credit I deserved for finding the grotto flag.

"Blue team wins the final flag," the announcer said. Nobody cheered, not even the blue team, which annoyed Rufus, I could tell. The rest of the team looked at me in that pitying way, as if they were saying, "Why don't you stand up to him?"

"Professor Dunkirk knows I found the flag," I told them. "She'll tell Critchlore."

At least, I hoped she would. Creak toddled over to me and pointed to Rufus. "Cheeeeaaterrrrrr."

I nodded. "Yep. Rufus is a cheater."

CHAPTER 21

"The Red Team has been penalized two points for sportsmanlike behavior."

—RULING AFTER THE FIND THE FLAGS COMPETITION

The next morning, Dr. Critchlore announced another Treasure Hunt competition, with a new set of teams.

Everyone huddled around the lists, talking about how much fun they'd had on their previous searches, and how exciting it had been to travel outside Stull.

I'd beaten everyone to one of the flags. Professor Dunkirk saw it. Mez told me he would tell Professor Murphy. I was sure there was no way I'd be left off a team now.

I checked the lists.

Not chosen—again.

My heart fell as I stood there. It fell and bounced off the ground and rolled down the steps and across the cemetery, until it splashed into the swamp. I felt a gaping hole in my chest where it used to be. Why hadn't I been chosen?

I looked at the lists of names that were not me, and it hit me again. Of course I wasn't on a list. I had to face facts—my classmates were powerful, terrifying creatures. What could I offer a search team? Sure, I could search this school—I knew it better than most—but out in the real world? I had nothing to offer.

I sighed and headed for the FRP to pick up Kumi's food. I was so lost in my thoughts I didn't notice them until it was too late.

The skeletons.

And their creepy skeleton dog.

Dogs are so much nicer looking when they are fully fleshed and furred.

They stood near the entrance to the Aviary, which I'd have to pass on my way to the FRP. I thought about turning around to avoid them. Cowardly? Sure. But I'd seen the short one pick up an imp and throw him into the hedge maze, just for fun. They were mean.

I saw one of them tap the leader, the short guy. Or gal. Who could tell? The tapper nodded in my direction.

It's hard to imagine anything other than a sinister expression on a skull. Those empty eye sockets, that huge, gaping mouth. They're creepy.

I turned to jog back to the castle, but right as I did, I was tackled, hard. A heavy body landed on top of me, shoving me into the ground.

Rufus. In his human form, blue eyes flashing with hatred. He'd been following me, and I'd turned right into him.

"Not tagging along with that lame gang of humans today?" he asked. "Like the friendless loser you are? Maybe I should do everyone a favor and eat you before I leave on my next assignment."

"What's your problem with me, Rufus?" I said. "I've never done anything to you."

"You're so annoying. Janet keeps saying you saved the school, but you didn't do anything. You just luck into being in the right place at the right time."

He shoved my chest down, and it felt like my ribs were breaking. "She defends you, like, all the time. I pick on lots of losers, but suddenly she's all 'Leave him alone,' and 'If you harm one hair on Runt's head, I'll dump you faster than you can morph.'"

She said that? Really?

"Maybe she's trying to help you be a better person," I said. "I'd take her advice, if I were you."

He pulled his arm back, and I winced, because I was sure I was about to be hit. But suddenly his weight shifted off me. I opened my eyes and saw him lying on his back, surrounded by skeletons. They had their bony hands all over him.

"Hey!" Rufus shouted. "Get off me!" He struggled to get up, but the skeletons pushed him down. Sure, they had no muscles, but they were animated by a powerful spell.

With a roar, Rufus morphed into a wolf. He bit off one skeleton's arm, and charged at another. But when he dropped the arm to bite another skeleton, the arm zipped back to its owner and reattached. Those skeletons were unstoppable! It looked like Professor Vodum had finally found some impressive minions for the school.

Two skeletons grabbed me, holding my arms. The rest were busy fighting a raving werewolf lunatic. Rufus fought free, and the two that were holding me ran to help their friends. I took that opportunity to sprint away as fast as I could.

Once I realized they weren't chasing me, I slowed down and turned around. Bones were flying through the air, getting ripped off their owners and returning to them. It was like a snowstorm of bones.

I thought about running back to the safety of the castle, but instead, I continued on to the FRP.

Tootles could tell I was upset as I loaded up food for Kumi.

"Everything okay?" he asked.

"Sure," I said, throwing a melon onto the cart. "Just great. Everything's great."

"I can tell that it's not," he said. He pulled off a glove and grabbed my arm. "Talk to me, Runt. Please. You're reminding me of Syke. I knew she was upset, but I gave her space, and look what it got me. I've lost my daughter."

"I'm sorry," I said. "I'm in a bad mood because I can't do anything right, and when I finally do something good, I never get the credit."

He nodded sympathetically and then looked over at some trees.

"Are you going to tell me another tree story now?" I asked.

"I was just going to say . . . trees don't need to be told they're doing a good job. They don't need a pat on the back to keep growing and making fruit and providing shade and oxygen and doing all the wonderful things they do."

"But I bet trees don't get laughed at by their classmates," I said. "I can't walk by a group of kids without them howling at me, making fun of the fact that I was trying to turn myself into a werewolf—which I wasn't. But looking at them, it's hard not to think maybe I don't belong here. It's what Professor Murphy has been telling me too. Maybe they're right."

"Are you done?"

"Yes."

"Do you have any fight left in you?"

"Sure I do," I said. "I just don't think it matters."

"Do you see that pine tree?" He pointed to Mount Curiosity, where a pine tree grew out of the rocky cliff face. Its trunk twisted out of the granite and rose past the top of the cliff.

"Of course," I said.

"That tree started in the wrong spot—away from soil and in the shade for half the day. But did it give up? No. Plants never give up. They climb and climb and climb until they reach the light. Their roots dig and dig and dig until they reach water. And now look at it! It's glorious!"

I sighed. He was right—it was.

"Anyone looking at the rocky mountain would think, There's no way a tree could survive there. But that tree thought, Why not?

"It's what trees do—they fight until they can fight no more. They don't care what people say about them. They don't care if they were planted in the wrong spot.

"If you have any fight left in you, and you quit? Then your classmates are right, you are a loser. Keep trying, and you'll grow."

As I drove the food trailer past the side of the castle, another group of creatures blocked my way. This time I was happy, because it was the toddler trees. All six now. I looked at the new one, and it said, "Russssss."

"Trees, I'm heading out to the front gate. When I come back, I'll read to you, okay?"

"Storiesss!" they all said, hopping up and down. Tootles had been reading to them since they'd sprouted. He told me it was an important requirement in raising enchanted trees.

"I'll be right back," I said again, holding my hands up so that they would stay put, but of course they didn't. They followed me down the road, which was okay because I really wanted to vent about all my frustrations, and they were good listeners.

I drove the cart slowly, and the trees walked beside it on both sides. I felt like I was in a moving forest.

"The school's going to be empty again when everyone leaves on their special missions," I said. "You know, I should have been picked for a team too. Don't get me wrong, I like hanging out with you, but I wanted a chance to find the sudithium."

I was sure they didn't understand a thing I was saying. On the slow journey to the front gate I complained about everything—that Professor Murphy hated me, that Professor Zaida had crazy expectations of me, and that nobody would talk to me about Syke's mother.

"And don't get me started on Rufus, the big cheater."

"Noooo cheat," Googa said.

"That's right, Googa," I said. "We do not like cheaters."

The rest chanted, "Nooooo cheat," and I smiled.

We reached the gate and went through. I parked the trailer a safe distance from the gorilla and braced myself for the coming onslaught of fruit.

"I'm going to try and tempt the gorilla with this food," I said. "He's got to be sick of eating all those trees."

"Eaaaaat . . . treeeeessss?" Googa said.

Oops.

The trees huddled together, shaking.

"I meant *leaves!*" I said quickly. "He's eating lots of *leaves.* You guys lose your leaves every winter anyway, right?"

"Noooooooo." They continued to shake.

"Right—of course not. You're not deciduous. Stupid Runt." I hit my head. "Well, he only eats the leaves of trees that lose their leaves in winter. See?" I pointed to the bare trees now surrounding the ape, hoping they wouldn't notice the discarded trunks.

I pushed the cart in front of me. We had a routine, Kumi and me. I offered food. He signed, "Where is she?" I said, "I don't know," and then he threw the food at me.

"Hi, Kumi," I said. "I know you're lonely out here, and I'm sorry about your family. I brought you some food. Those trees have got to be tasting pretty bland by now, right?"

He grunted at me.

Something about him looked different. He was sitting in his nest of ferns, but he looked smaller. No, that was ridiculous. It was probably a visual trick because the pile of tree trunks surrounding him had grown.

"Where is she?" he signed.

"She's not here," I said. "I'm sorry. I miss her too."

Most times I could tell that Kumi understood what I said. Our communication problems came from me not understanding sign language. This time he used sign language that communicated his frustration perfectly. He scowled at me, knocked the cart over, and yanked a tree out of the ground.

High-pitched shrieking filled the air. I turned and saw all six trees rushing at Kumi, their branches flapping up and down in anger. They screamed and screeched. Kumi looked shocked, as anyone who had a bunch of five-foot-tall trees charging at him would. They made a sound filled with both pain and anger.

They only came up to his calves, but they kept whacking him. Kumi didn't know what to do.

"Put the tree back!" I shouted. "You killed their . . . their . . . cousin!"

The gorilla looked at me, eyes wide. He could have swiped them away with one swish of his arm, but he didn't. He put the tree back, tapping the soil around the base so it would be okay.

The toddler trees stopped hitting him. They ran over to the tree and hugged its trunk.

"Thank you, Kumi," I said.

He nodded and then reached over to the spilled fruit cart. He put a handful of melons in his mouth and crunched, then reached for another handful. The toddler trees turned to Kumi and threw some body-language glares at him before they walked back to me. I think one of them made a rude gesture with his branch.

"Don't be mad at him," I said. "He's sad. He misses someone he loves."

The trees looked back at Kumi, who nodded again. They ran over and tried to hug his leg. Kumi let out a soft grunt but didn't move to hurt them. One of the melons slipped out of his grasp and rolled back toward me. The toddler trees all ran after it, getting tangled up in a big pile as they fought to see who could grab it first. Kumi shook with laughter. Googa brought the melon back to him, and they waited like puppies for him to throw it again.

I sat down and watched Kumi finish the food on the cart while playing fetch with the trees. He seemed to bounce with laughter each time they fought to get the melon.

When he finished eating, I said, "Come on, guys. I need to take the cart back to the FRP. You can ride in the trailer this time."

"Stayyyyyy!" they screeched.

"Is that okay with you, Kumi?"

Kumi nodded. It almost looked like he smiled a little bit.

"Okay, stay. See you later!"

"Byyyyye, Ruuuuuunth."

CHAPTER 22

"They must be read to every day. You simply cannot expect your forest to be enchanting if the trees haven't been told many stories. The greater the variety, the better."

—*PLANTING AN ENCHANTED FOREST FOR DUMMIES*

I rode back happy that Kumi had made some friends, because he always seemed so lonely sitting in the ferns. But my happiness was short-lived. As I rode toward the castle, I couldn't help but realize that I'd be leaving the school soon. I'd never get on a search team, and if I didn't, I'd never find any sudithium, which was the only way I was going to pass Professor Murphy's class. And as soon as I failed his class, Professor Zaida was going to take me away.

My whole body felt heavy with sadness. I would miss my home so much. I took a detour to visit one of my favorite places—the grotto behind the castle. (Yes, we were a two-grotto school. One above ground, one below.)

Between the back of the castle and the Aviary, there was a clump of hazelnut trees with a clearing in the middle for two benches. At the end, two trees had grown up next to a large memorial stone, their branches stretching around the monument as if they were hugging it. KARYA, the stone read. Syke's mother.

Syke had often come to sit in the clearing when she was sad, touching the tree trunks and wondering about the mother she never knew.

Today, someone else was there. Dr. Critchlore.

This was the third time I'd found him sitting in the clearing. The first two times he'd pretended he was on his way to the Aviary and had just happened to stop and sit for a rest after walking for a minute and a half.

"Sorry," I said, as he looked up at me. "I didn't mean to interrupt, I just . . ."

"You miss your friend," he said.

I nodded.

"I miss her too."

I'd always suspected that his gruffness with people was an act. The iron-hearted headmaster—nobody could hurt him. But I knew he cared.

I sat on the bench opposite him. "Why don't you tell her the truth about her mother? You could convince her to come back."

"You've become much more direct lately," he said. "I'm not sure I like it."

I looked down.

"I could never tell her the truth."

I looked up. Dr. Critchlore stood and placed a hand on one of the tree trunks. This was the first time he'd even hinted that there was a truth to be told.

"Why not?" I asked.

"It would hurt her," he said. "I would rather she hate me than be hurt."

"Did she start the fire?" I asked. Was he protecting her from her own guilt?

"Don't be ridiculous—she was a baby," Dr. Critchlore said.

Oh, right. I should have realized that. "Then what are you protecting her from?"

He didn't seem to hear me. "We get so much of our identity from our parents," he said, stroking the tree trunk. "Sometimes a child is injured more by attacks on his parents than on direct personal attacks. It's funny but true. When I was younger, someone could call me names, and it wouldn't bother me, because I knew they were wrong. But if someone said something hurtful about my mother or my father, I had no defense for that. 'Critchlore, your mother hates you. That's why she left.' 'Critchlore, your father's insane. Does it run in the family?' And even though I told myself that they were only trying to hurt me, that what they said wasn't true, I wondered. I don't want Syke to suffer like I did."

"So you're protecting her from knowing something bad about her parents?"

He stared at me for a moment, then shook his head. "I'd rather not say more, because I've been told you can't keep a secret. But I'm asking you to respect my wishes, Prince Auberon."

Dr. Critchlore knew I was the missing prince? I smiled, feeling kind of proud and important all of a sudden.

"Dr. Critchlore? Can I ask you another question?"

"You can ask," he said.

"Why haven't I been picked for any of your search teams? I mean, field trips?"

"You have been," he said, sitting back down. "Professors Dunkirk, Travers, and Twilk all selected you, but Professor Murphy denied their requests. Said you needed more one-on-one tutoring."

One-on-one tutoring? What a joke! Professor Murphy was doing everything in his power to kick me out of his class, including keeping me from being on any team that might find sudithium.

"Now I have a question for you," he said. He looked around, to make sure nobody could overhear, then leaned forward. "Have you had any more ravens from Mistress Moira?"

I shook my head, still fuming about Professor Murphy. "Just the one she sent Professor Zaida about the witches in East Chambor," I said.

"And did she . . . uh . . . she didn't by any chance . . . mention me?" he asked.

"Yeah," I said, reaching into my pocket. I had a pile of scrunched-up pieces of paper. I unfolded them, looking for the note from Mistress Moira. I found my Cursed List (a list of bad things that had happened to me—I'd made it before I'd found out that I was, in fact, cursed). I found my To-Do List and my Good List. Then there was a note I'd written to Janet, even though I'd probably never give it to her, and finally, Moira's tiny note. I passed it to Dr. Critchlore, who seemed to light up as he took it. He read it and smiled but then turned his head to the side.

"Hmm. That's confusing," he said.

"I know. Why would Pravus send people to East Chambor?"

"What? No, I mean the end here: 'Tell Derek XOXO Moira.' That could be read two ways. XOXO is shorthand for 'love.' She could mean 'Tell Derek about the Pravus minions. Love, Moira.'" But there's no period after Derek, so maybe it means, Tell Derek XOXO. Which is like saying, send my love to—"

"Probably the first one," I said, maybe too quickly because he looked a little hurt. "But I could be wrong. I'm sure she'll send you a raven soon."

"She has," he said, handing back the note. "With a terse message: 'This is what you're looking for.' No greeting, no . . . XO. No indication as to when she'll be back."

"That's it? 'This is what you're looking for'?"

"The raven was carrying a sample of sudithium," he said. "Dr. Frankenhammer has it now."

"That's fantastic!" I said.

"Yes. Although I wondered about the message."

"There's not a lot of room to write," I said.

"True. I hope she's not in trouble. She's a wonder, that Moira. I don't know what I'd do without her." He looked over at me. "I mean, the school. What the school would do without her."

"She's awesome," I agreed.

"And I hope I'm not installing an elevator for nothing. Fantastically expensive. I do hope she returns. For the elevator's sake."

At lunch I sat with Frankie, Darthin, Boris, and Meztli, who was a regular at our table now. I told them what Critchlore had said about Professor Murphy keeping me off the search teams.

"That's so unfair," Frankie said.

"You should report him to Dean Everest," Darthin said. "Dr. Critchlore holds professors to a high standard, and he's falling short of it."

I was about to agree when Drangulus, a tall lizard boy, slinked over to our table and stood over Darthin. I'd met Drangulus in detention. He wasn't the best student, and I had mentioned to him recently that I thought Darthin might be able to help him with his science homework.

But Darthin, hunching down as low as he could get, looked ready to wet his pants. Drangulus was a frightening sight, and his breath was so raspy it made me think something was stuck in his throat. Like a large slice of pizza, or maybe a cat.

"Darthhhhin," he said. Slobber leaked out the side of his mouth, but he didn't wipe it away.

Darthin hunched even lower, looking at us for help.

"You know anythhhhhing about strength elixirs?" Drangulus asked.

"Y-y-yes?" Darthin answered.

"Do you know how to make lake serpent antivenom?"

"Uh-huh," Darthin answered, nodding his head. "Well, that is, if someone else milks the lake serpent for its venom."

"Could you tell me the steps?"

"Why don't you sit down?" I said.

Drangulus sat across from Darthin. He pulled a piece of paper out of his backpack. "Sorry about the stains," he said.

Darthin looked at the paper, and as soon as he started reading, he seemed to relax. "Oh, I see your problem. For the strength elixir, you don't start with the hair of giant. First, you have to soak the hair in the strength-extractor chemical bath. You're going to want to do that for at least fifteen minutes. Then you . . ."

I nudged Frankie, who gave me a thumbs-up.

CHAPTER 23

Please stop asking. The answer is no. Floats are absolutely forbidden from attacking each other during the parade.
—SPECIAL ANNOUNCEMENT FROM MRS. GOMES,

HEAD OF SECURITY

The school emptied, as nearly every kid went off on an assignment again. Groups headed out for West Chambor, Riggen, Euripidam, and Bluetorch. I really wanted to be on one of those teams.

There was nothing do, so after feeding Kumi one morning, I decided to talk to Uncle Ludwig. I'd try one final time to get someone to tell me about Syke's mother. I was past wanting to convince Syke to come back. I just wanted to know the truth. I knew people were lying, but I didn't know why.

On my way I passed the boulderball field, where I saw a mummy sitting on a bench. Someone was kneeling before him, rewrapping the loose bandage on his leg. As I got closer, I smiled, because it was Darthin.

"—and if you use a waterproof adhesive," he was saying, "your bandages won't unwrap so easily when you get wet."

The mummy nodded its head. I would have stopped to say hello, but I wanted to talk to Uncle Ludwig before I lost my nerve.

I found him in his secret library, updating his enormous spread-sheet that listed possible sites of the Great Library. I felt the usual stab of guilt that I had the knowledge he'd been searching for his whole life.

I sat down opposite him.

"I don't have time for your nonsense, Runt. I'm busy," he said. "I've missed days of work searching for sudithium in Corovilla."

"Did you find any?"

"No," he said. "It's impossible. And then I get back and find out Critchlore already has some."

"If he has some, then why are we still looking?"

"One little bit of the mineral is not enough to create an Unde-featable Minion. We need much, much more. Fortunately, it was enough for Dr. Frankenhammer to create a Sudithium Detector, which will help us in our search. He's also trying to figure out what the mineral does. Now, please. I'm very busy."

"Can I just ask you a couple questions?" I pleaded. "Please? I'll reshelve all your books upstairs."

"Deal," he said very quickly. I should have asked him how many he had up there. I hit myself in the head. Rookie mistake.

"Did you know Syke's father?" I asked.

"Anders?" Uncle Ludwig scowled. "Unfortunately, yes."

All I knew about Syke's dad was what Syke had told me (and I assumed it came from Dr. Critchlore)—that he had worked at the castle in the stables. He was strong and handsome. He loved Syke's mom, and she loved him. He was away when the fire happened, looking at some foals that were for sale in Yancy. He'd been trag-ically killed when a bunch of harpies swooped down and carried him off to Skelterdam. He died before he learned of Syke's mother's death.

"Why do you say, 'unfortunately'?" I asked.

"Did I? Hmm." He focused on his notetaking, not looking up at me.

"You know more than you're telling me," I said.

"About everything, yes," he said with a smirk. "You need to accept that some knowledge is only meant for certain people."

"Really? What if I knew where the Great Library was, and I didn't tell you because some knowledge is only meant for certain people? What if the reason I was away after the fashion show was that I'd found it?"

What was I doing? I'd said too much. But here's the thing—I think Professor Zaida *wanted* him to figure out that she was the Archivist. She dropped clues all the time, but he was too dense to pick them up. At this point, it was almost like she was playing with him.

"Sure you did. You, a third-year, found the most secret place in the world. Right, and I'm the prima ballerina of the Stull ballet." He chuckled, then refocused on his notes.

A part of me knew I should just walk away. But I was so tired of grown-ups treating me like I couldn't do anything right. I couldn't take it anymore. I really wanted to wipe that smug condescension off his face.

"It's not in Hagritano," I said, pointing to his notes. "The mountains there aren't big enough to hold seven stories of books, plus the living quarters of the librarians, and the shrine to the Natherly family."

He stopped writing. "How do you know about the shrine?"

"Because I've seen it."

He scowled. "You're not joking, are you?"

I shook my head slowly and emphatically. "The Archivist swore me to secrecy. But I hate secrets."

He gasped, then leaned over and grabbed my arm. "Tell me."

"First, I want you to tell me about Dr. Critchlore and Syke's mother, Karya."

"Derek was in love with her."

I gasped. Of course he was! All those times I'd found him in the grotto by her memorial—he wasn't resting. He was visiting a lost love.

"Your turn," he said.

"The Great Library is in Stull," I said. At least, it used to be. They'd probably moved it by now.

He gasped.

"If Dr. Critchlore loved her," I asked, "why did he burn down the forest?"

"He didn't. His mother did," he said.

I gasped.

There was a lot of gasping going on.

"Who is the Archivist?" he asked.

"A teacher," I replied. "Why did his mother burn down the forest?"

"She was tricked by Syke's father, Anders. When Anders found out that Karya was in love with Dr. Critchlore, he became enraged. He was a scoundrel of the worst sort. He had other women in every corner of Stull, but he didn't want to lose Karya to that 'spoiled kid who grew up having everything.' It's Dr. Frankenhammer, isn't it?"

"No. What did Anders do?"

"He convinced Dr. Critchlore's mother that it was wrong of her son to break up a family. Anders and Karya had a baby, after all. He said Karya was just confused and angry and wanted to get back at him for his affairs. She was using Derek—that was all."

"Was she?" I asked.

"No, she loved Derek. But Anders told Dr. Critchlore's mother that he wanted to make things right with Karya, and the only way he could do that was for the family to leave the castle. Hamadryads aren't bound to one single tree. They can move to a similar type anywhere, but they can't be away from a tree for very long. It disorients them and can eventually lead to death.

"Anders told Dr. Critchlore's mother that if she wanted to do the noble thing, she would burn the forest after they left, so Karya couldn't return to Derek. And since Derek's mother never approved of the relationship between her son and the hamadryad, she did it.

"It's Coach Foley," he said. "Right?"

"No. Then what happened?"

"Anders faked their departure. He never left. He watched as Dr. Critchlore's mother killed the woman her son loved. Derek thought she'd killed all three, but Anders had Syke with him. And then Dr. Critchlore got a letter from Anders, who mocked him. 'Anyone who tries to take what's mine will pay, and pay big,' Anders wrote.

"I wouldn't put it past Dr. Critchlore, or his mother, to have sent those harpies to get him. They rescued Syke, but Anders was dropped into Skelterdam. And good riddance! He was, by far, the most despicable person I have ever met. Is it Professor Inglenook? Murphy? Caruthers? Nguyen?"

"It's Professor Zaida," I said, feeling grateful to finally have the story.

"I knew it!" Uncle Ludwig said.

I gave him my sarcastic "Sure you did" look.

"I should have, right?" he said. "I mean, she's here all the time. Oh! What a fool she must take me for."

"She doesn't. She's just worried you can't keep a secret. And don't you think it's weird that all of your guesses were men?"

He looked slightly ashamed at that. And then we were silent. We stared at each other, both of us thrilled to know what we wanted to know, and both of us just realizing that we had broken a sacred trust.

"Um . . . ," I said. "Professor Zaida is going to kill me dead, and then kill my ghost."

"Right . . . ," he said. "And Derek is going to kick me out of the castle."

"We are both going to be in so much trouble," I said.

"Unless . . ."

"What?"

"What if we pretend to discover these things on our own?" He rubbed his chin. "It will require cunning and subtlety and careful planning."

He looked at me.

"We're doomed," I said, reading his expression.

‡‡‡

It all made sense now. Dr. Critchlore didn't want to harm Syke's memory of her father. He as much as told me so in the grotto. We get so much of our identity from our parents. If she knew that her father was the worst person in the world, how would that make her feel about herself?

Still, I couldn't stand by while she turned her back on people like Tootles and Riga. People who loved her. Plus, what Uncle Ludwig said about hamadryads had me worried. Syke was part hamadryad. He'd said that hamadryads get disoriented when away from trees.

There were no trees at the Pravus Academy.

I had to save her. I knew if I could just get her away from that place, she'd return to normal.

CHAPTER 24

*Fine, I'll allow T-shirt cannons. But if anything other than a
T-shirt is fired from them, detentions will follow!*
—ANOTHER SPECIAL ANNOUNCEMENT FROM MRS. GOMES

Over the next few days, search teams departed, came back,
and departed again. I spent my time studying with Professor
Zaida, playing with the toddler trees, practicing hoopsmash
with Meztli, working on our float (the tar pit had a new fire fea-
ture!), and worrying that I was going to get kicked out of school as
soon as someone came back with some sudithium.

I sat with Mez and Frankie at lunch. Darthin was over at the
ogre-man table, with his yellow team. They were plotting a revenge
operation on the green team after the green team had stolen their
symbolic sword.

It looked like my "Make Darthin brave" experiment had been a
success. After word got out about how he'd helped Stevie, Drangulus, and the mummy, other monsters sought him out. At first, this
terrified him, but gradually, as he got to know them, he realized that
they were just like everyone else. In other words, they all wanted his
help on their homework.

There was a new girl sitting with Frieda. Her name was Tingrid, and she was the "minion in recompense" from the Pravus Academy. Word had it that she was an ogre-woman, and like Boris, she'd gotten the looks of a human and the smarts of an ogre. I'd asked her about Syke, and she told me that Syke was, by far, the smartest person she'd ever met in her life and that she was doing really well in school. Well, bully for Syke.

"Our float will win," Mez said, pulling me out of my thoughts. "We have Lower Worb. Wexmir Smarvy. Wait till you see it."

"How's the green team's float going, Frankie?" I asked.

"I don't know. Dr. Frankenhammer won't let me work on it. We're too busy trying to fix me."

"Fix you?" Mez asked. "Are you broken?"

"No, he's not," I said.

"That isn't right," Mez said. "Nobody should work all the time. What does he let you do for fun?"

Frankie shrugged. "I organized his specimen cabinet yesterday. He says fun and games are distractions from our pursuit of excellence."

Poor Frankie. It made me sick to my stomach how unfair it was. But not so sick that I couldn't eat, so I got up to get a second helping of macaroni and cheese. When I passed the ogre-man table, a few guys howled at me. I ignored them, like always.

But then I heard something that made me turn around. A chair squeaked backward, and a high-pitched voice spoke out loudly over the din of the crowded cafeteria. "Cut it out!"

It was Darthin.

He stood up and looked at each ogre-man straight in the eye, since they were still sitting and they're very tall. He pointed at each of them in turn.

"Runt Higgins was not trying to turn himself into a werewolf!" he shouted. "He's cursed to die on his sixteenth birthday, and he was performing a chant to get rid of part of the curse. So you can all just shut up with the howling. It's mean. And it's not fair."

The ogre-men—the whole cafeteria, really—watched Darthin with their jaws hanging open.

"Are any of you cursed to die?" he went on. "Are any of you facing certain death a few short years from now? Doomed to never know what it means to live? No! All of you will be able to see how they're going to resolve the love triangle on *All My Overlords*, but not Runt. SO GIVE HIM A BREAK!" I didn't know whether to feel better or worse. I'd never realized I might not be around to see who Adrianne would pick to lead her army against the greedy Fabrizar. Aww.

But look at Darthin! Standing up to a room full of monsters. I grabbed his arm, because some of them were a little put off by that last bit and I was worried we might have overcorrected.

"Thanks, Darthin," I whispered, "but I wouldn't yell at ogre-men. They are wired to react violently to people yelling at them. Just ask Frieda."

We returned to our table while everyone got over the shock from Darthin's performance.

"Darthin!" Mez said, lifting a fist for him to bump. "Nice."

"That was brave," Frankie said. "I wish I could stand up to Dr. Frankenhammer like that."

"You should," I said. "At least tell him that his constant criticisms aren't going to make you better."

"Yeah, I've been thinking about that," Darthin said. "You know, I spend a lot of time with Dr. Frankenhammer as his lab assistant, and I've noticed something in the way he talks about you. You're not a kid to him. You're something he built. When he criticizes you, he doesn't think he's criticizing a kid. He thinks he's criticizing himself."

"What's the difference?" Frankie asked. "He's right either way."

"No, he's not," I said, but Frankie didn't believe me. Again.

"It's sad, but some scientists view their creations as extensions of themselves, and not as beings in their own right," Darthin said.

The bell rang. Lunch was over.

"Hey, guys, come help me feed the gorilla," I said. Frankie still had his head down, so I gestured at him, hoping the guys would get my meaning. We needed to help Frankie.

We all got up and headed out. As we walked down the main road, we tried to convince Frankie that he was awesome, but no matter how many examples of his awesomeness we gave him, he wasn't convinced.

"Dr. Frankenhammer's not perfect, you know," I said. "Why don't we think about what we'd fix about him. Starting with his lack of empathy."

"He's a neat freak," Darthin put in. "And his knowledge of classical mechanics is sketchy at best."

"How about those eyebrows?" Mez said, laughing.

"You are stronger and faster and have a photographic memory, and you already do half his work for him," Darthin said. "You're better than him, and you're only thirteen."

"Next time he criticizes you," I said, "just ask him when was the last time he ran a mile in two minutes."

We were all laughing by the time we reached the gate. Kumi was in his usual spot. He trusted me now and didn't roar when I arrived with food. He still terrified me, though.

I tossed a melon to him, but there was a big difference between how far I could throw a melon and the distance at which I felt safe from the giant beast. The melon hit the ground closer to me than to him. He reached out and picked it up, while I edged back behind the cart. Frankie picked up a melon and threw it right into Kumi's mouth. Kumi seemed to like that, so Frankie threw a few more.

"Is it me, or is Kumi shrinking?" I asked, because he really did look smaller. I wasn't imagining it.

"Not likely," Darthin said, but he wouldn't know, because he'd always been too frightened to come see Kumi.

"No, Runt's right," Frankie said. "He always sits like that, and when he got here, his head was as high as that tree."

I grabbed Frankie's arm. "Are you sure?"

"Photographic memory, remember?" he said.

"If that's true," Darthin said, "then I'd say he's lost . . . oh, about nine feet in height."

"Why?" I asked. "How?"

We pushed the trailer of food closer to Kumi's clearing.

"I've been listening to Dr. Frankenhammer try to figure out what sudithium does," Darthin said. "One of the theories he's come up with is that it enlarges organic tissue."

"Huh?"

"It makes things bigger," he explained. "What if this giant gorilla

154

came from a realm where there's lots of sudithium? What if the gorillas are big because they had access to the mineral? Ever since he's been here, eating our trees, he hasn't gotten the mineral that makes him big, so he's shrinking."

"That would explain why Dr. Pravus got rid of the gorillas. If they were shrinking, nobody would want to recruit them," I said.

"The gorillas that Wexmir Smarvy recruited are still huge," Frankie said. "Wouldn't they be shrinking too?"

"That's true." Darthin thought for a second. "Unless they were still getting sudithium. Here's another thought: What if Pravus has had sudithium all this time? Remember that kid who taunted you before the hoopsmash game? You told us he said, 'Do you even have any? Do you know what it does?' They have it, and they know. Pravus used it on the gorillas. He could have given Smarvy sudithium to feed his recruited gorillas, like a vitamin supplement."

"If sudithium makes things bigger, it should be easy to find, right?" Frankie said.

Darthin slapped his forehead. "It's in Upper Worb. Of course it is. Those people were hiding something. We all knew it. And the bunnies there are huge! They really are. I know you guys think I'm a coward, but they're so much bigger."

"So, if Pravus has it, like that stupid Victus implied, and if it comes from Upper Worb, then Pravus must have gotten it from Irma Trackno," I said. "I saw them talking together in the capital. At the time, I thought it was odd, because Irma doesn't recruit minions, so why would they be talking together?

"She seemed really angry with him. If she cut off his supply of the mineral, then he'd have to save whatever sudithium he had left for the UMs, and not give it to the gorillas. Destroying his gorilla enclosure solved two problems at the same time: He made it look like he'd been sabotaged, and he got rid of something that was about to make him look bad."

Darthin nodded.

"We should tell Dr. Critchlore," I said. "But Barry stupid Merrybench won't let kids into his office. He says we have to go up the chain of command."

"Which means you have to tell Professor Murphy," Meztli said.

"Which means he won't give you credit for figuring it out," Frankie added.

Darthin grabbed my arm. "Better to let him have the credit than let Pravus keep us from catching up."

I knew this was true, but it felt so unfair. And then I imagined Tootles's head floating around me, saying something like, "Trees don't care who gets credit for their fruit."

I was beginning to hate trees.

CHAPTER 25

"When the going gets tough, get used to it, because it's not going to get any better."

—POPULAR SAYING IN UPPER WORB

Professor Murphy returned the next day. I skipped my mentor period to see him. He didn't teach a first-period class, so he was alone in his classroom. I strode in and stood in front of his desk. He sighed heavily when he looked up.

"You said that whoever finds the sudithium will get an automatic A in the class," I said, my heart thumping. "I know where it is."

He shook his head. "Runt, I don't have time for your games. Dr. Critchlore is panicking, and he's running us all ragged. I have three more trips to coordinate. Now, please, go to your mentor."

"Remember when we went to the Overlord Council, and we saw Dr. Pravus talking to Irma Trackno? He gets sudithium from her. He's been using it for the past year."

He held up his hand like he wanted to stop me from talking, but then let it fall. "That's . . . what?"

"Sudithium makes things bigger. Pravus has been giving it to his gorillas. The one outside hasn't been fed any for a while, and now he's shrinking. When I was at the Kobold Academy, we were chased by one giant gorilla and two smaller ones that must have shrunk. Irma won't give Pravus any more, so he's saving what he has for his Undefeatable Minions. He destroyed his gorilla enclosure to hide the fact that they're shrinking."

Professor Murhpy blinked a few times. He looked at me, then looked down. "It's possible . . . ," he said. He rifled through some papers on his desk, selecting one. Then he stood up and walked past me, leaving me standing there alone, without so much as a "Good job, Runt."

It was what I'd expected.

The next morning I walked into my junior henchman class to see a note from Professor Murphy. "The following students will report for an emergency field trip to Upper Worb: Rufus Spaniel and Jud Shepherd."

Another punch in the gut.

I found Professor Murphy by the vans. He carefully placed a box labeled DETECTORS on top of a pile of bags.

"Professor Murphy," I said.

"Runt, I'm very busy. We're leaving this morning. Please, I left you an assignment in the classroom."

I jumped in front of him. "I'm just wondering if I'm going to get an A, since I told you where to find the sudithium."

"Having a guess is not the same as finding the mineral, Runt," he said. "That promise of an A was for someone who actually has the sudithium in hand."

"How can I do that when you never assign me to any teams? You have deliberately kept me off every single one."

"Runt, teams were picked based on who is the best qualified—"

"That's not true. I know that three team leaders have requested me, but you scratched me off their lists." I felt the anger rise in me, and I didn't want to back down. "You're making it impossible for me to pass your class. I'm going to file a complaint with Mr. Everest. I bet deliberately failing students is not part of your job description."

He squinted at me. "Do you really think you can do anything that Rufus, or Jud, or Frieda can do? They are junior henchman material, you are not."

"How do you know that, when you never give me a chance?"

"You want a chance? Okay, fine. Come on this trip. If you find the sudithium, I'll give you that A." He pointed a finger at me. "But if you don't? You're out of my class. For good this time."

"Deal. But I want to bring Meztli. And Frankie. They deserve a chance too."

"Fine. We leave in two hours. Make sure each of you gets a travel kit for Upper Worb in the supply depot and meet us back here."

Rufus strode up with his bag. "Runt's coming? Are you kidding me? He's going to get us all killed."

I ran off. I had a couple things to do before we left.

First, I went to say good-bye to Kumi, who was playing hide-and-seek with the trees. He didn't move from his spot, just covered his eyes while they hid. The toddler trees weren't very good at hiding. They shook with giggles as Kumi grunted little questioning sounds. Kate, Pismo, and I watched as they finished the round.

"Googa ooh ooh ooh?" Kumi said.

I could see Googa trying to hide behind the food cart. Kumi picked up the cart and said, "Ahhh ooooh!"

159

Googa slunked over to the tagged-out spot, where Swish patted him on the back with a long branch.

When the game was over, I walked up to Kumi, greeting him with the hello sign that Kate had taught me.

"Kumi, I'm going to be gone for a few days," I said.

"He's asking where you're going," Pismo said.

"To the snow," I said. "But don't worry—Tootles will bring you food every day. And the trees will come visit."

Kumi nodded, then reached down his giant hand so I could hug his finger good-bye. I looked at Kate and Pismo, who gave me a "Go on" nod, so I did. I quickly hugged the giant finger and waved good-bye.

After that I rounded up Darthin, Frankie, and Meztli. "I want you guys to come too."

"Professor Murphy said I didn't have to go this time," Darthin said. "They don't need me as a local guide, because Upper Worb welcomed us to come back to Polar Bay anytime."

"That's weird," I said. "But I still need your help. All of you. Darthin, you know the place better than anyone. Frankie, you're like a secret weapon—nobody knows what you can do. And Meztli, you deserve to go on a mission. Just like me."

"I'd really rather not," Darthin said.

"I'll pass the class anyway," Meztli added with a shrug.

"What if I do something wrong?" Frankie said.

I looked at them: Darthin, afraid to make a daring choice. Meztli, satisfied with doing just enough and no more. And Frankie, terrified of failure. I had to show them all that they could do better.

"You guys, we can do this. Together," I said. "I know we can. Look,

I know each of you feels exactly like I do. Like a failure. Like we're not good enough."

I turned to Darthin. "Darthin, you still feel humiliated by what Rufus did to you up there. Now's your chance to replace that memory with a better one. A successful one."

I looked at Frankie. "Frankie, if you continue to be too scared to try, you're never going to prove to Dr. Frankenhammer—and to yourself—that you're *not* broken. It doesn't seem to matter how many times we tell you. You have to try, and this is the perfect chance."

And finally, I turned to Meztli. "Mez, I think this would be good for you too. Together, we can go for the win. Why not us, instead of Rufus? Plus, I'm going to need your help," I repeated, looking at each of them. "I'm going to need all your help. Please."

"Okay, I'll go," Meztli said.

Darthin and Frankie looked at each other.

"Yeah, we'll go too," Darthin said. Frankie nodded.

It was make-or-break time for all of us. But mostly me. If I could find some sudithium, I could help Dr. Critchlore in his battle against Dr. Pravus, and maybe save the school. If I failed, I'd be banished to the Great Library to study in solitary confinement for the rest of my life.

I cannot put into words how absolutely bleak that made me feel. I couldn't fail. I just couldn't.

CHAPTER 26

"If your last name begins with a letter between A and M, you can buy food on alternate Wednesdays."
—ANDIRAT GENERALS' RESPONSE TO A FOOD SHORTAGE

The journey to Upper Worb was a long overnight trip. We took the protected Evil Overlord Missile Train, which all EOs agree not to attack. It allows them quick, safe passage from their realms to the capital. Most people aren't allowed to leave their realms, so the train was not crowded, which meant I didn't have to sit with Professor Murphy and Rufus. Darthin, Frankie, Meztli, and I sat in the empty dining compartment, at a table with bench seats.

Mez and I tossed peanuts into each other's glasses while Frankie slept and Darthin sketched in his notebook, looking nervous.

"What's that, Darthin?" I asked.

"Huh?" He looked up. "Oh, I wrote down everything last time." That wasn't a surprise, because he wrote down everything all the time. "Here's my map of the crater. It's huge—over five kilometers in diameter. When we were there, we mostly searched by the southwest end, but it had already been picked clean. There was evidence of abandoned mining operations there."

"Why does Irma let us in?" I asked.

"If you ask me," he whispered with a hand covering his mouth, "she's watching us." He nodded at the cameras mounted on the ceiling. "Checking us out. You said yourself that when you saw her in the capital, she seemed to be looking for information about the minion schools. She's lost too many homegrown troops and now needs to recruit from outside."

"Maybe. But what would she learn from watching us?"

"Polar Bay is the most dangerous area in her realm. What better place to test us?"

"What do you mean by 'most dangerous'?" Meztli asked.

"I told you, the animals there are huge. Growing up, we Upper Worbians always assumed it was the result of some accidental radiation leak. We know radiation causes genetic mutations, like the giant lizard monsters in Chent. But now I suspect it's the sudithium. It must have leached into the soil and affected everything in the food chain—from the foxes to the hares to the woolly bear caterpillars."

"The what?"

"They're huge. As big as my arm. Black and reddish brown, with spiky fur. Fortunately, they only come out in summer, so we won't see any. But the other animals? They're everywhere."

Darthin saw Meztli and me exchange a look, and he got defensive. "Oh, you'll see soon enough. The locals are mostly humans, but there are also some yeti, and they're really, really mean. They look like polar bears walking upright, but with blue faces and hands. And they hate outsiders. Then there's the giant gyrfalcon that nests in the mountains above town. The locals leave food for it on a tribute spot every day, so it won't attack people.

"Be careful," he continued. "Don't go outside without your bear bangers, your falcon flares, and your bunny hoppers."

We both laughed.

"Shut up! They make the hares hop away."

I pulled out my protection kit. The bear bangers and falcon flares were red and blue canisters, respectively, each about the size of my thumb. They were shot off the end of a pen-sized launcher. The bunny hopper was a separate device, but the same size, like a thick pen. It was green, and the end opened like an umbrella and spun around making a really annoying high-pitched sound and erupting in lots of sparkles.

"And pay attention to the rules," Darthin continued. "The locals have developed a cooperative, live-and-let-live relationship with the giant animals. They don't want that relationship damaged by outsiders who are quick to kill anything they're scared of. Rufus nearly got us all killed when he morphed into a wolf and attacked a polar fox that was the size of a horse."

"Follow the rules. Got it," I said. If there was one thing I was good at, it was following rules.

After the train reached the Upper Worb capital of Nostopako, we had to take a shuttle dragon north to Polar Bay because there were no roads into that isolated, mountainous region. There wasn't enough room on the first shuttle dragon, so Professor Murphy went ahead with everyone except Meztli and me, the two guys who had never been there before. We were told to wait for the next dragon.

But the next shuttle dragon didn't feel like flying, so we had to wait for the one after that, which wasn't leaving until the following day. Fortunately, the shuttle dock had sleeping bays available, because flight cancellations happened all the time. Dragons . . . Sheesh. They're such a temperamental way to travel.

Nothing seemed to bother Meztli. He had such a great attitude, and I tried to gain confidence from him as we finally flew north on a huge polar dragon, the kind with thick white fur and scaly wings. We relaxed in a twelve-person cabin on its back. Some locals returning from the south traveled with us.

"Hey, Mez, is this your first trip outside your realm and Stull?"

"No, I go to many realms in my *continente* and across the ocean too. My parents, they try to find someone to fix my color, but nothing worked."

"Have you ever been to the Currial Continent? To the country that used to be called Andirat?"

"The broken place, *sí*," he said.

"I think that's where I'm from."

"*Lo siento, amigo*. I'm sorry. That place, it's in very bad shape."

"What do you mean?"

"The people there, they are so poor. Unless they work for the generals, and even then, mostly poor. Every month each family gets a book of coupons to buy food, but it only lasts for ten days. That's twenty days of hunger.

"The generals are very paranoid. The people, they can do nothing because you can be arrested for meeting with more than two others. You can be arrested for talking bad about the generals. You can be arrested if they *think* you might be thinking about revolution. If you look angry, you'll be arrested. Nobody trusts nobody else. Even family members are afraid that one of them may turn on the others for a reward. It's loco."

"That sounds terrible," I said. I checked my wrists for the twentieth time.

"Why do you keep looking at your hands?" he asked.

"I'm just checking these marks. I've been cursed, and whoever did it added a tether, to keep me from traveling outside the curse's range. But Mistress Moira figured out how to get rid of it. You can kind of see where the marks used to be. I have to make sure they don't return. If they do, I'm going straight back to Stull."

He nodded. "There was a master curse *bruja* in my village. She did curses like that. Very nasty lady. Always thinking everyone was against her. She cursed many of the people in my village, that *bruja*. Pretty soon, everyone wanted her dead, because if she dies, curses die too. She went into hiding, people say, where nobody can follow."

"Mistress Moira is going to find out who cursed me. She told me that she's got connections."

"She knows people?"

"No—psychic connections. She thinks they'll help her find the curser."

And so we flew to the northernmost area of the planet. I watched color seep out of the world, replaced by white. When

166

we began our descent into Polar Bay, I couldn't tell where the bay started, because it was frozen and covered with snow, just like the

land. One vast landscape of whiteness.

We landed next to an enormous hangar. The dragon hurried right into its welcoming warmth, and the doors closed behind us. The space was wide and tall, with enough room for at least five dragons to spread their wings. It was busy with people running about, caring for the two currently in residence—another jumbo polar dragon and a smaller jet-black dragon.

Our dragon walked to its tethering spot, and the ground crew unlatched the harness holding the passenger cabin in place on its back. Giant mechanical claws lifted the cabin up, and then the dragon was led forward to a spot where a team of humans waited with food and water and a small pile of treasure for the dragon to lie down with. Once the dragon was settled, the cabin was lowered to the ground.

Meztli and I put on our sky blue Critchlore expedition jackets with the fur-trimmed hoods and followed the lights on the floor that directed us to the baggage claim area in the next room.

We weren't the only ones visiting Polar Bay, it seemed. As we entered the baggage claim area, I noticed a group of people wearing matching red jackets. When one turned in our direction, I froze.

I had known that by coming here I might be coming face-to-face with vicious monsters, but I never expected to see him and his cruel, beady eyes.

Coach Reythor.

"Pravus's hoopsmash trainer," Mez said. "What's he doing here?"

"I don't know," I whispered.

The evil man spotted us and scowled. I couldn't look away from him.

"Your *amiga* is here too."

"My friend?"

I gasped again. Syke. Seeing her brought back all the hurt and anger I'd felt during our last meeting. But as I watched her, I couldn't help but wonder what had happened to her.

She looked . . . faded, somehow. Her iridescent hair had lost some of its sheen, or maybe it was the artificial lighting in the hangar. Normally full of energy and confidence, she looked tired and weak.

She stood with a group of students, most of them towering over her. Her new friend Victus stood next to her, a sneer firmly in place as he spotted us. All in all, they had a team of twelve. Same as us.

"They're after the sudithium too," I said. "This is bad. Maybe Darthin was right and this is a test. Maybe Irma wants to see us go head-to-head."

Their baggage had been unloaded, and they were preparing to leave. Syke fell behind as she stopped to repack something in her bag.

"Mez, can you get our bags? I want to talk to her."

Mez nodded and walked over to the conveyer belt by the far wall. I looked at Syke. I wanted to tell her that she was wrong, that she'd been wrong the whole time, that she should have trusted the people who cared about her and not run off to our worst enemy.

I knew that Dr. Critchlore wanted to protect her from knowing about her father, but I knew her better than he did. She wasn't some frail, delicate child; she was the toughest kid I knew. She could handle the truth. She deserved the truth. I walked over and tapped her shoulder just as she stood up.

"Syke, I have to talk to you," I said.

"Runt, just leave me alone," she said. "You're going to ruin everything. I can't believe they let you come."

I had been worried about her, but now I was angry. "Why?" I asked her. "Because I'm some loser who can't do anything?"

Her mouth dropped open. "I can't do this," she said.

She looked so weak, so tired. I handed her the twig I'd been carrying in my pocket since Uncle Ludwig had told me that hamadryads got disoriented without trees. "You need this," I said. "It's from your mother's grotto. You've been away from trees for too long. You're not thinking straight."

She looked up at me and laughed. "You are such an idiot."

Victus came back looking for Syke. When he saw us standing together, Syke punched me in the gut.

I collapsed, the wind knocked out of me. My lungs clenched up, and I couldn't breathe. She stood over me, her face now raging. "I thought I made it clear. I'm done with you," she said. "Touch me again, and I'll do worse."

She picked up her bag and left, Victus smirking as he followed.

CHAPTER 27

"King Natherly's advisor told the generals where the royal family was hiding. All were reported murdered, but the young prince's grave was later discovered to be empty."

—*ANDIRAT, A HISTORY*

Y ou okay?" Meztli asked. He held out my bag for me.

"Yeah, I guess," I said.

"How much you gonna take from her? She called you an idiot."

Yes, she did.

I smiled, because the old Syke called me an idiot all the time. And I'd seen her tuck that twig into her pocket.

A man approached us wearing an airline uniform. He nodded at our jackets. "Your teacher told me to give this to you," he said, handing me a note.

I took it and read it. "It says we're supposed to meet a guy who will take us to his inn. We'll spend the night there. They didn't want to wait for us, so they left to set up camp near the crater."

"Your ride is waiting for you outside," the man said.

Well, I was tired and hungry, but mostly tired. Too tired to care about being left behind yet again.

We shouldered our bags and went outside. It's funny. I'd been so worried about the cold, but when we first walked outside, it didn't even register because my brain was trying to figure out why I was blind. I stumbled over a mound of snow and fell to the ground. With my eyes closed, I fumbled around inside my backpack and pulled out my sunglasses. Even then, I had to squint to reduce the glare. It was unbelievably bright, with the sun reflecting off anything white—which was everything.

And then the cold hit me. I thought I was prepared for it, bundled as I was in layers of clothing and the fancy jacket I'd gotten from the supply depot. But the polar region lets you know in a hurry if you've missed a spot. I'm not used to cold, so it was shocking when the slightest breeze instantly numbed my nose. And breathing felt like swallowing ice cubes.

Once I had acclimated and brushed off the snow, I saw them: two huge black transports with truck-like cabins perched on top of long rolling tracks. The red-jacketed Pravus team sat inside. The vehicles took off with a rumble of power, churning up the snow and ice with those tracks. After they'd moved on, I could see the beat-up pickup truck that had been parked behind them. Standing in front of the truck was a large man holding a sign that read DOOFUS.

I shook my head. "Rufus's idea of a joke."

"You Runt?" the man said. He was dressed in the traditional clothes of the region—animal-skin garments, complete with a furry-edged hood that framed a face Welnick the Horrible would've been jealous of, it was so frightening. His dark eyes were barely discernible through his squinting glare, and his face was huge and round and sported quite a few scars.

I smiled nervously and held out my hand. "Runt Higgins," I said. "And this is Meztli."

He looked at my hand, made a sound like, "Hmph," and motioned for us to get in the truck. Mez and I threw our bags in the back. When I opened the front passenger door, a blue-faced, white-furred monster-child with huge teeth hissed at me. I screamed and fell backward into Meztli's arms.

The monster had a face that was somewhat girl-like, for a monster. It was etched with lines and framed by the white fur that covered her body. She had a scowl that matched the one the big guy was wearing.

"Hi?" I tried.

She turned her head forward, ignoring me.

Mez and I climbed into the narrow seats behind her, and we took off. We drove in silence down what looked like the only road around, which was just a smushed-down white as opposed to the fluffier white surrounding it. The bay stretched out on our left—flat and white. An iceberg was frozen in place near the middle of the bay. It looked like a giant fist breaking through the ice.

Ahead, I could just make out the small black dots of village houses lined up beneath the protection of the cliff wall.

The land was more varied than it appeared from the sky. The hills on our right were speckled with bare, rocky outcroppings. We drove past a larger mountain that was carved with grooves, probably from runoff. The grooves were filled with snow, but the bumpy parts between the grooves were bare: thin dark lines on a white background.

I leaned forward to talk to our driver. "It looks like that mountain has a barcode."

Silence.

"Like packages have, at the grocery store. They scan them to get the price."

Silence.

"Do you have those here?"

Silence.

"Price check on aisle nine, one large mountain." Pause. "Okay, I'll shut up now."

On the back of our instructions was a list of rules. I nudged Meztli so he could look at them along with me. The list read:

Stay inside at dusk and dawn.
Do not go into the crater.
Do not talk to the yeti.
Do not feed the polar hares.
Do not wear orange.
Any aggression toward the local wildlife will result in immediate removal from the area.

Meztli had a sly smile on his face. Something about that look made me wonder if he was thinking about putting on some orange so he could go into the crater at dusk to feed the hares. As if to prove my instincts right, he tapped the yeti girl's shoulder and said, "Hi."

She ignored him, and we continued toward town.

The village was a cluster of buildings stretching out in three lines, with larger buildings here and there. The roofs were frosted with snow, like little cakes, but the sides showed a variety of muted colors: blues and greens and reds.

We approached the inn, a light-green two-story building with a bold red stripe near the roof. It seemed to be propped up on stilts that lifted the base a few feet above the ground.

Our host parked. "Out," he said.

Mez and I grabbed our luggage and hopped out of the truck.

"Come," he added gruffly, heading up the stairs, not offering to help us with our luggage. Apparently, somebody had forgotten to take the hospitality lesson in hotel management school.

After pointing out our room, he said, "Dinner at six," turned around, and left.

We collapsed on the beds, and I didn't wake up until 6:45.

"Meztli, wake up!" I said, but he just grunted at me. "Dinner!"

"No *gracias*," he said, turning over.

Fine. I was hoping for his company, for some sort of cushion against the scariness of our hosts, but I was so hungry I was willing to brave it alone.

The inn's dining room was small, only three tables, each seating four people, as well as some stools by a counter that separated the kitchen from the dining room. One empty spot remained at the counter, so I sat there. I leaned forward and saw my host's massive back hunched over the stove.

"Um, excuse me?" I tried.

He didn't move.

"Hello?"

The guy next to me snorted and shook his head. In front of

him was a bowl of soup. It smelled yummy, a rich aroma I couldn't quite place, both sweet and something else, something that made my mouth water.

Finally my host came to the counter, but he wouldn't look at me. He picked up the bowls in front of the other two guys.

"Hi, uh, could I get something to eat?"

He turned around without acknowledging me but eventually returned and plopped a bowl of soup down in front of me. Then he disappeared into the kitchen again.

The soup was cold. It was tasty, but cold. I knew that it was my fault for oversleeping and arriving after I'd been told to come down. I began to think that I was not going to get on this guy's good side ever, not with a start like this.

As I ate my soup, the front door opened. I turned around and saw Rufus and Jud.

Great.

They wore their Critchlore snow parkas and had Critchlore beanies on their heads. I noticed the locals all scowl at Rufus and then turn their backs to him. He came right over to me. The man sitting next to me edged sideways.

"You made it, what a surprise," Rufus said. "Where's kitty?"

"Meztli is sleeping," I said.

"Typical cat," Rufus said. He eyed the guy next to me. "You look done, fella. Do you mind?"

The man got up and left. The yeti girl came out of the kitchen to clear his bowl. She seemed to scowl harder in Rufus's direction.

"Hey, Alasie," he said. "How's probation?" And then he laughed.

The yeti girl, Alasie, grabbed the bowl and returned to the

kitchen. No wonder she was so gruff. She must have been the one who'd fought with Rufus on the last trip.

Rufus took the man's seat. Jud stood next to him.

"Okay, here's the deal," Rufus said. "Apparently Dr. Pravus sent a team here, which is freaking Professor Murphy out. He wants us to split up into smaller teams. We're going to meet tomorrow morning at camp. Professor Murphy will come get you guys when he picks up our guides. We're each going to take a different section of the crater while Professor Murphy and Darthin try to get more information from the locals, but they're a bunch of backwards hicks and impossible to talk to."

He was so rude, my jaw dropped open. I looked at the others in the room, hoping they hadn't heard him.

"Hello?" he said sarcastically. "Do you think you and kitty can be ready tomorrow morning at seven?"

"Um, sure," I said.

With that, my dour host came out of the kitchen and stood behind Rufus. Rufus turned around, right into the big man's gut.

"Told you to stay away," the big guy said.

"Relax, Jimbo," Rufus said, standing up. If he'd wanted to face down the big man, it didn't work. Rufus, as big as he was, only came up to his chin. "I'm just talking to my friend here."

Jimbo grabbed Rufus by the jacket and turned him around. "You go. Now."

"I'm going, I'm going," Rufus said. "Runt, see you tomorrow at camp."

"Okay," I said.

He left, laughing with Jud. After the door shut behind them, conversations resumed. I could tell the people here did not care for Rufus. *You and me both*, I wanted to say.

And then I noticed that my jacket was the same as Rufus's, and their hatred of me made sense.

I finished my soup as the other diners gradually left, each one saying good-bye to the host. Most of the guests called him "Big Jim."

The yeti girl came out to clear and wipe down the tables. She wore an apron around her furry white waist. She was about my height, with huge hands and a scowling glare. No wonder Darthin had been too afraid to talk to them last time.

As she passed me, I said, "Big Jim? His name is Big Jim? And you're Alasie?"

She ignored me and went about her cleaning. Drowsiness seemed to seep into my bones with the soup, so I sighed and said, "Goodnight, Alasie. Please tell Big Jim his soup was delicious."

She didn't reply.

CHAPTER 28

"Mr. Yeti does not wear clothes. You'd think he'd be cold, yeti isn't."

—ELONI, MAKING A JOKE BEFORE WE LEFT

The next morning Professor Murphy picked us up at the inn, along with some locals he'd hired to be our guides, including the silent yeti girl, Alasie.

Mez and I should have given ourselves extra time to get ready, because we didn't realize how long it would take to put on all the layers of clothing. Over our tight-fitting thermals we both wore long-sleeved shirts, a fleece, another fleece, and then finished up with our waterproof jackets. Same for our lower half: thermal pants, followed by a fleece layer and a waterproof layer. We had gloves and hand warmers and mittens, layers of socks, and a face-covering balaclava to wear under our beanies.

We packed up our backpacks with everything we'd need according to the list that Professor Murphy had given us: MREs (Meals Ready to Eat), binoculars, goggles, sunglasses, extra batteries for our heated gloves, and, of course, the flare pens that shot the variety of protection devices. Once ready, we headed downstairs.

Professor Murphy was waiting in the van with the local guides.

He frowned at us, looking at his watch to indicate that we were late. Then we drove out to the crater, taking the road that led back toward the airport, but turning away from the bay just as we exited town. The road looked like it had been heavily traveled. After a short drive through some small hills it ended at a camp of tan tent-cabins nestled in a group within a fenced-off area. A line of snowmobiles waited just outside the fence.

As we walked into camp, Professor Murphy pulled the face opening of his balaclava down to expose his mouth so he could talk. When I did the same, my nostrils froze shut. It was c-c-cold.

"That fence is electric, to keep predators out," Professor Murphy said. "Don't touch it."

Meztli touched it. He pulled his gloved hand away with a shake and a pained look on his face.

Everyone stood in an open space in the middle of the cabins, a big group of sky blue jackets with fur-edged hoods and covered faces, along with the local guides clad in animal skins or snow parkas, carrying bows.

"Let's get to work," Professor Murphy said, stepping into the center of the group. "As you all know, Dr. Pravus has sent a team here, which tells me that we must be close to finding something. We haven't come across a Pravus team at any other site.

"We have to move fast. We can't let them find something before we do. And so, I've decided to split us up into teams. Each team will have a local guide and be assigned to search a specific section of the crater rim.

"Do *not* go into the crater. The floor of the crater was the site of a major mining operation that spanned many years. It's been picked clean. However, given the size of the animals here, there must be deposits of the mineral that were forced out by the impact of the meteorite. We'll be able to find these deposits with our detectors." He held up one of the devices, which looked like something Tootles used to check the water content of the soil: a long metal prong coming out of a square box that displayed a reading with a needle moving along a dial.

" fragments can be propelled as far as five miles from the impact site," Professor Murphy went on. "So we're going to be working from the rim outward.

"You know what to do: Dig through the snow to the permafrost beneath. Push the tip of the sudithium detector into the ground. Record your readings. Be methodical. Be persistent. We'll meet back here before dusk to share our findings."

He split us up into four teams: Rufus, Jud, and Pantha (a shape-shifter) were taking the far eastern section of the crater. Lapso, Ethan (ogre-man), and Sethi (shape-shifter) took the north. Frankie, Vinch (ogre-man), and Trinka (imp) took the south. He gave each team a sudithium detector and a notebook to record our findings.

"You and Meztli get the west," he said, handing us a map. "Everyone please be respectful of the dangers here. The locals have learned to coexist with the dangerous creatures. They don't need to take defensive measures, but in an emergency, they are expert marksmen with their bows, and they've developed a drug that will put these giant creatures to sleep within seconds. Darthin and I will continue to try and get information from the locals. Good luck."

I could only see Darthin's eyes through his layers of warm clothing, but that's all I needed to see. He was scared. I went over to him and whispered, "You'll be fine. You can do this."

He nodded.

We were all about to head off on our assignments when one of the guides whistled at us and held up a hand. He pointed at a spot just beyond the fence. There, hopping past a small hill, was a polar hare. It was very well camouflaged in the snow, being completely white except for little black spots on its ears. It was larger than a regular rabbit and had shorter ears and a thicker, fluffier body.

"Aww," I said. "It's so cute."

"It's big for a rabbit," Frankie said. "But I wouldn't call it 'giant.'"

"That's not the giant hare, you idiots," Darthin said. "The giant hare is behind it."

"Where? All I see is that hill," I said.

Oh.

The hill twitched. Then it grew, and grew, and grew as the giant polar hare rose up on its hind legs. Its front legs looked thin compared to its fluffy, elephant-sized body.

It plopped down with a thump. Professor Murphy, who didn't have time for delays, shot off a bunny hopper in its face, and it jerked away. One of the guides hissed at Professor Murphy, shaking his head.

"So cute," I said.

"Sí," Meztli agreed.

"You wouldn't say that if five of them were charging at you," Darthin said, "trying to trip you with their paws."

Professor Murphy and Darthin left in the van while the others took off on snowmobiles. Mez and I waited for our guide, Alasie, who was checking her gear. We watched the giant hare follow Professor Murphy's van. As the van accelerated, the hare hopped forward to match its speed. With a quick jab, it reached out a paw and knocked the van on its side. Professor Murphy crawled out the window, bunny hopper in hand, ready to fire.

Mez was laughing hysterically, and I had to clamp my mouth shut when Professor Murphy and Darthin walked back to camp. They took the snowmobile Mez and I were going to use. They sped off, but the giant hare was waiting for them, and took another swipe as they raced by. Professor Murphy dodged it and continued on.

Mez and I had to walk to our searching zone with our guide, Alasie, who followed us sullenly. This wasn't a big deal, because our spot turned out to be only a hundred feet away. I checked my instructions, because I was sure this was a mistake, but it wasn't.

Alasie didn't seem too happy with her assignment. That made two of us. This was ridiculous! We'd just been assigned to look for a rare and valuable mineral in the most traveled-on spot in the area.

I walked over to the edge of the crater, which was not very deep for a crater, maybe just twenty feet from the edge to the bottom. The drop was gradual and bumpy, with snow-covered rocks. Plant life was beginning to poke through the snow on the ridges, and I saw another giant hare nibbling on something farther away.

I watched the other Critchlore teams on their snowmobiles, getting smaller and smaller as they ventured into the unknown on their quest. I felt like I'd been left behind in the parking lot.

Alasie sat on a small hill and watched us work, her white fur blending in with the snow so that if I looked away and then back, it took me a moment to find her. Mez and I dug into the icy ground just outside the crater's rim and plunged the tip of the sudithium detector into the ground below, but the needle didn't move.

It was pretty dull work, I have to say. Dig, jab, record the reading, repeat. I dug and jabbed. Meztli recorded the zeroes. After a while I noticed him fill the whole page with zeroes and then throw the notebook to the ground.

"Mez, I haven't given you those readings yet," I said.

He shrugged. "They are going to be zeroes." Then he tilted his head at the yeti girl, who was facing away from us. "She can speak," he said. "I heard her talking to another yeti at camp."

"Her name's Alasie," I said. "And she's not going to speak to us, thanks to Rufus. He got her in trouble on their last trip here. I think she's here for punishment."

"I bet I can get her to talk." Mez wiggled his eyebrows beneath his goggles.

I shook my head and kept stabbing the snow, hoping to find some trace of sudithium. Mez focused on the more interesting challenge of getting Alasie to talk, but no matter how hard he tried, she wouldn't say anything. She never even acknowledged that she heard him.

At lunch I offered her some of my food, but she shook her head and stayed on the hill, away from both of us.

"Nice try," he said, "but I will win."

"Win what?"

"The contest to see who can make her talk. You, Mr. Nice Guy, or me."

"You should be so competitive in finding sudithium," I said.

"Ha! There's nothing here," he said, and I had to agree with him. What chance was there that we'd find anything in this spot that was so close to camp? None.

We looked over at Alasie. She had turned her focus to the bay. I climbed up the hill until I could see what held her attention. She was watching a group of kids zipping across the snow on skis as they held onto kites that looked like colorful parachute wedges against the blue sky. Some of the kids were dressed in ski parkas, but a few were white-furred yeti. When I looked at her, I could tell she'd rather be out there with her friends.

"You should go," I said to her. "I'm sure there's no danger this close to the campsite. We have our bear bangers and stuff."

She scowled and shook her head.

"Maybe she can't ski," Mez said, winking at me. "Maybe it is too *difícil* for her."

She screeched at him.

Mez laughed.

"Screeching doesn't count," I told him as I got back to work. "You haven't won yet."

After lunch a Pravus team rode by on snowmobiles. At the front of the group was that obnoxious kid, Victus. I could tell it was him by the arrogant way he drove his snowmobile. He stopped, lifted his goggles, and stared at us, taking in our little base of operations.

"Are you kidding me?" he said, shaking his head. "Oh, man, what a bunch of losers."

They rode off laughing.

‡‡‡

Our guides returned to the village while we ate dinner at camp, which was an MRE and a thermos of hot chocolate that stayed hot for about three seconds. We sat on folding chairs as the sun began its descent, and Professor Murphy asked about our findings.

"Rufus?" he asked.

"I got some blips on my detector," he said. "But nothing solid."

"Great start," Professor Murphy said. "This is exciting! If only we'd had these sudithium detectors last time. How about you Lapso?"

"Same. A few blips. We'll dig deeper tomorrow."

"Excellent. Frankie?"

"Nothing."

"Well, keep trying," Professor Murphy said. "Darthin, did you find out anything from the local children?"

"I talked to them!" Darthin said, as if this was the achievement that Professor Murphy had been waiting to hear. "I wore traditional clothing and greeted them the traditional yeti way, by scooping up some snow and rubbing it in on their cheeks."

Professor Murphy made a "Get on with it" motion with his hands.

"Um . . . well . . . I found out why they hate visitors," Darthin said. "They're afraid we'll do something that will bring 'Him' back. Or wake 'Him' up. I'm not sure which, but they are very afraid of this 'Him.' It might be the creature who destroyed the town two years ago."

"How does this relate to sudithium?" Professor Murphy asked.

"I don't know," Darthin admitted. "I did ask a few kids why the animals are so large here, and they all gave me the same answer:

a shrug and something about radiation. But we know that's a lie. There are no detectable traces of radiation here."

"Let's stay focused going forward, okay?"

Darthin nodded. I gave him a thumbs-up and mouthed, "Good job," because on the first trip, he had been too scared to talk to anyone. This was a huge accomplishment for him.

I waited for Professor Murphy to ask me if I'd discovered anything, but he didn't. I shouldn't have been surprised that his expectations of me were zero, but it still stung.

"Did you guys notice the Pravus teams watching you?" I asked.

"Yeah, they're watching us," Rufus said. "Not even trying to be sneaky about it, either."

"Good point, Rufus," Professor Murphy said. "When we do find some sudithium, we should expect the Pravus team to try and prevent us from taking it back to school. We have to be ready with an escape plan or two. Perhaps a diversion of some sort. I'll think of something. You all continue searching."

There wasn't a cabin for Mez and me at camp, so we hurried toward our snowmobile as soon as Professor Murphy was done. "Stay inside at dusk and dawn," our rules had said. The sun had just gone into hiding, and we needed to follow its example and get back to town.

The snowmobile's engine was as loud as fireworks in the stillness, a blaring announcement that rulebreakers were approaching. Mez drove while I checked behind us for hares. He had to dodge quite a few yetis that appeared out of nowhere, walking around like slow-moving mummies. They growled and swung their big, hairy arms at us.

"Very creepy, those yetis," Mez said when we got to the inn.

We went inside and were greeted by Alasie screeching at us. It wasn't as ear-aching as Pismo's screech, but close. Mez ran upstairs while I apologized for being out at dusk. She shook her head and pointed at the trail of drippy footprints we'd trailed in. I guess we were supposed to remove our boots at the door. Whoops.

CHAPTER 29

In Riggen, there are three sets of laws: one for the general population, one for minorities, and one for the rich. Riggen's EO, Fraze Coldheart, can do whatever he wants.

—TRUE FACT

The next day Alasie and I waited outside by the snowmobile. At last, Mez came down to join us, wearing an orange vest over his parka—one of those safety vests with reflector tape that construction workers use. Where he got it, I had no idea. Alasie hissed when she saw him.

"What? You don't like my vest?" he asked.

She shook her head and made motions for him to take it off.

"I'm sorry, are you trying to say something?" he asked innocently. "*Por favor,* use words, so I can understand." He looked at me for help.

"Mez, come on," I said. "Take it off."

"Why? Orange is my favorite color. Unless there is some reason? No?" When Alasie didn't answer, he shrugged. "Here I go. I'll jog this morning."

He took off. Alasie shook her head, then readied her bow and arrow.

"What can happen to him?" I asked.

She pointed to a spot on the ice near the cliffs. There, just in front of a long corrugated-metal building was a giant orange circle. It took me a second to realize that it must be the spot where they left food for the giant gyrfalcon Darthin had warned us about.

Mez passed a row of houses and reached the open space outside of town. Alasie gunned the snowmobile, and we followed. I held on with one hand and pulled out my falcon flare with the other, just in case.

We'd only gone about thirty yards when Alasie shrieked and pointed to the sky. There, gliding silently across the bay, was an enormous bird of prey. It looked like a giant white eagle, with gray flecks dotting its wings. I could tell that its keen eyes had latched onto Mez's orange vest.

"Mez!" I screamed. "Look out! Giant bird!"

Mez looked up and saw the bird homing in on him. Two thick, fluffy legs reached out with sharp, hooked talons that were each as long as my forearm. I fired my flare, which burst next to the falcon's face, startling it. Mez tore off his orange vest, threw it at the bird, and rolled away, just under those talons. He got up and sprinted for the nearest building, diving around the corner just as the bird swooped off with his vest.

Alasie and I rode over to him.

"You could have warned me," he said.

She scowled and shook her head, but I thought I detected the faintest twitch of a smile around her mouth.

A loud screech startled us and we looked up. The gyrfalcon was speeding back toward the cliffs, where a black dragon was circling. I pulled out my binoculars.

"There's someone on the dragon," I said. I passed the binoculars to Meztli.

"Wearing red," he said. "It's a *Pravus* kid."

I nodded. So that black dragon in the hangar had come here with the Pravus team. We watched as the gyrfalcon flew right at the dragon, who turned to spit fire at the bird. The gyrfalcon dodged the flames and kept heading for the intruder.

"Darthin said the gyrfalcon has a nest up there," I said. "She's protecting it. But what is the Pravus team doing?"

Mez didn't answer. We watched the short confrontation as the dragon quickly gave up and flew away. The gyrfalcon landed in its nest, victorious.

Battle over, Mez hopped on the snowmobile behind Alasie, and I climbed on behind him. We continued to the site, where we spent the day digging, recording, and getting laughed at by Pravus kids. After a dinner of MREs, we headed back to the inn, where another copy of the rules was waiting for us on our bed.

I pulled out my Good List, trying to come up with something to put on it. Everyone in this freezing town hated us. The area was filled with huge, annoying rabbits, terrifying yeti, and a giant bird of prey. The Pravus kids were mean, and it was obvious that I was being set up to fail.

After thinking hard for a few minutes, I wrote: "Travel to new places is educational. I've learned that I do not like the taste of raw whale blubber."

"I really need to find something," I told Mez the next day at breakfast. "Professor Murphy will fail me if I don't."

Meztli had finished eating and was resting his chin on the counter. With great concentration he pushed the saltshaker toward the edge of the counter with short little pokes.

"Is frustrating," Mez said. He watched the shaker as it reached the edge, where it teetered. "We won't find anything in our spot. He's definitely messing with you." One more poke, and the shaker fell to the ground.

"Why do you do that?" I asked.

He shrugged.

I sighed. "I just want to prove myself here," I said. I didn't say it out loud, but I wanted Professor Murphy to be proud of me for once, like he was of the other junior henchmen. I didn't want him to look at me like I was an embarrassment.

"Wouldn't it be great to be the ones to find something?" I added. "Instead of Rufus?"

"Stupid dog. He's the worst."

We bundled up and headed out for another day of digging in the ice, along with our guide, who was so silent we hardly noticed she was there. We found nothing. Again. I did learn a lot about Meztli, though. His family had sent him to Stull because there was a revolution going on in his home country, and they wanted to keep him safe. We laughed about this as we loaded our flare pens with bear bangers, just in case. Safety was relative.

"You're not going to do anything . . . rash, are you?" I asked him when I noticed he was getting bored. "You know, that orange rule was pretty important."

"Now I know," he said, smiling.

"Mez, breaking a rule can get you killed. Why take the risk?"

"In my country, big heroes in history are people who broke rules," he said. "Unfair rules—like the Chapuca tribe aren't allowed to vote or lizard-men aren't allowed in restaurants. And selfish rules—like nobody can swim in Lake Tarnolacco, because it belongs to Lord Dunga, who is never at his lake house anyway. So brave monsters voted, brave monsters ate in restaurants, and brave people swam in Lord Dunga's lake. Rules change after that."

A Pravus team approached, and I cringed when I recognized Victus. He was about to say something mean, I was sure, but before he could, I said, "Where's Syke?"

"She's sick," he said. "Guess she's not as strong as we thought she was. Typical weak Critchlore kid, after all."

Mez shot off a bunny hopper in his face. Victus accelerated his snowmobile to evade the flash and drove it into a snowbank. He had to get off to pull the snowmobile out, which was great because we got to laugh at him for a change. He pointed a threatening finger at us and took off.

Those guys weren't even pretending to look for sudithium. It seemed like their sole purpose was to make sure we didn't find anything, and if we did, to take it from us. They had teams positioned at each of our spots.

When Professor Murphy realized this, he decided to rearrange our teams. That afternoon, back at camp, Darthin told me that he and Professor Murphy had spent the morning huddled over his *Monster Desk Reference* book.

"The Pravus team has five trolls, two skeletons, two ogres, a tree nymph, and two humans," he said. "We have three werewolves, a were-jaguar, two ogre-men, an imp, two shape-shifters, two humans, and a Frankie. We figured out how to split up our teams so that any team of ours can take on any team of theirs. It was like working a complicated mathematical puzzle. I had so much fun!

"For instance, according to the Vlagnof-Spitzer matrices, one werewolf and one ogre-man should defeat two werewolves, but not a werewolf and a troll. We created the best monster match-ups."

And that was how I lost Meztli. Professor Murphy moved him into the camp (apparently there was an extra cot for one more kid, but not two) because they needed him for one of the other teams. I wasn't familiar with the Vlag-whatever matrices, but I was pretty sure one scrawny human kid wouldn't be able to defeat anything. When I mentioned this to Professor Murphy, he told me that I'd be fine. Since I was close to camp, if I found anything—I'm sure he chuckled here—I would be safe where I was.

The Pravus teams took one look at our new search teams and raised the stakes by messing with them as much as possible. They started by feeding the hares near where our teams were working. I had wondered why that was a no-no and quickly found out.

"There must be fifteen of the huge beasts surrounding our spot now," Jud complained. "I morphed to scare them off, but it's too cold for me to be in wolf form for long."

"We ran out of bunny hoppers," Lapso said.

The Pravus teams painted orange circles all over our digging spots. Our guides spent the morning trying to lure the giant gyr-falcon back to its normal food spot, and then our teams wasted valuable search time cleaning up the graffiti.

If the locals hated us before, by now they absolutely detested us.

All of us. To them, we were a bunch of disrespectful, rule-breaking hooligans, and they wanted us gone. Darthin told us so.

While all this was happening, I was alone with Alasie, who still wouldn't talk to me. Not when I asked her questions, or complimented her skills with the bow and arrow, or offered her food.

"Do you know what happened between Rufus and my yeti guide?" I asked Darthin that afternoon.

"Yes," he said. "Rufus was warned not to harass the local animals, but he kept doing it anyway. He tried to ride a polar hare, and then he fought a giant fox. Alasie had been trying to lure the fox away from town, and then Rufus messed up everything. She threw a snowball at him in frustration. When she turned around, he hit her with an ice-ball. This absolutely enraged her, and she picked up a boulder and threw it at him. She's incredibly strong, but her aim isn't the best, luckily for Rufus. She missed him but hit one of the stilts holding up the community building, and it partially collapsed."

"Yikes," I said.

"And so she was put on probation. I think she has to work off her debt to the community."

No wonder she was mad. Well, I was mad too.

Each day I felt a slow, boiling rage grow hotter and hotter inside me, but I kept working. Tootle's lessons about plants kept playing in my head, like a catchy tune you can't shake: Weeds keep trying, trees become stronger when they're alone, trees never give up . . .

And then I looked around and noticed something: There were no trees in the polar region. Maybe they *did* give up.

And maybe I should too.

CHAPTER 30

"A must-have reference book for EOs, minion trainers, and Mixed Monster Arts competitors."

—ADVERTISEMENT FOR THE *MONSTER DESK REFERENCE*

Every afternoon the other Critchlore teams passed by my spot on their way back to camp. Frankie always stopped to walk back with me, and this time we met Darthin as he returned from town.

"What's up, Darthin?" I asked, pulling down my face-covering and watching my words take flight with a cloud of fog.

"I haven't had much luck," he said, looking back at town. "The kids are relaxing a bit around me, but they won't talk about sudithium. A couple offered to teach me how to kite-ski. There's a competition coming up. It's kind of a big deal here."

"It looks like fun," I said. "Do they know what sudithium is?"

"They act like they don't," he said. "They know we're looking for it, but they play dumb and it's so obvious. I have noticed some interesting things, though."

"Like what?"

"Have you noticed that huge corrugated-metal building that faces the bay? Well, every day fishermen take snowmobiles out to the floe edge, where the frozen ice meets open water. Every day they come back and load the fish into that giant building. It must be stuffed full of fish. Why do they need so much fish?"

"For the bird?"

"It's way more than they need to feed the gyrfalcon. And they can't be storing it for winter, because it's spring. It's weird, but the adults clam up when they see me. They don't trust me. Also, they're getting really upset about all the stuff going on near the crater."

"It's the Pravus team," Frankie said.

"I know," Darthin said. "How about you guys? Find anything?"

"Rufus's team has collected a small vial of flakes," Frankie said. When he noticed me deflate, he added, "It's not much, really. But Professor Murphy is excited. He's moving me over there, to help dig. He told me I am the single best addition to the team."

"That's great, Frankie," I said, feeling a stab of jealousy at those words. Once, just once, I wish Professor Murphy would feel that way about me. "I hope you find more."

"Runt," Frankie said. "If I find some, maybe I can sneak it to you, so you can say you found something too."

I shook my head. "No, I don't want you to do that."

"But it's not fair," he said. "He's put you where you won't find anything. You're going to flunk his class, and it's not your fault."

"I've got to do it on my own," I said.

Inside I wasn't so sure. What if Professor Murphy had been right all along? Maybe I wasn't junior henchman material. Ever since Dr. Critchlore had called me "Prince Auberon" I'd wondered if he'd put me in the class because he knew I was a prince and not because he saw some potential in me.

Professor Zaida was right too. I didn't want to be given something I didn't earn, whether it was a bit of sudithium or a place in an elite training program.

Darthin, Frankie, Meztli, and I joined the rest of the group for the end-of-the day meeting in camp. The sun was close to the horizon, and the wind was kicking up little clouds of snow as it hurried through camp. We stood in a circle, close together, stamping our feet to stay warm.

"The locals are petitioning Irma Trackno to revoke our visas," Professor Murphy said. "They say that we and the Pravus team are disrupting local wildlife, that it will result in irreparable harm to life here if the animals start encroaching on the village again."

"That's probably what the Pravus team is hoping for, with all their assaults," Jud said.

Professor Murphy nodded. "Yes. It's become quite obvious that they aren't here to look for sudithium. They just don't want us to find any. I have to report to the village council tomorrow. I'm guessing we have a few days left, at best." Then he held up Rufus's small vial of sudithium. The flakes inside the glass vial practically glowed with a gray-green color. "And this is not an acceptable amount. It's less than we got from Mistress Moira. We need more. A lot more."

My rage bubble was about to pop. Normally, fear of embarrassment kept me from speaking in groups, but this was too much.

"I can help at one of the other sites," I said.

Rufus laughed.

Professor Murphy scowled. "I want you to stay where you are."

So I went back to the inn, alone. I tried to talk to Alasie, but she had perfected ignoring me. I had to sit at the counter, eating alone, with my lonely thoughts. I wanted to work with my friends, and stay in the camp with them.

No wonder Kumi had been so angry.

I pulled out my Good List, but could only think of one thing to write on it: "My wrists aren't changing color." Then I laughed, because that's not something most people would be thankful for. Most people take for granted the simple things in life, like fresh fruit and having un-cursed skin.

Again I thought about giving up. Why bother? I wasn't going to find anything. The whole trip had been rigged against me. I was a joke.

My chest felt tight as humiliation gripped me once again. I should have been used to the feeling by now. I tried to get rid of it by daydreaming about finding some sudithium. I imagined myself with a large chunk of the gray-green mineral. I'd hand it to Professor Murphy and say, "How do you like me now?"

And then he'd hug me and say, "You did it!"

The next morning, Darthin, Frankie, and Meztli came to the inn to tell me not to come to the camp. Professor Murphy had wanted the teams to continue searching while he was called before the council, but our local guides were part of the council, and we couldn't go out without them.

This made Alasie very happy, and after getting a nod from Big Jim, she left for the ice.

"We could go watch," I suggested. There was nothing else to

do, so we bundled up and headed for the shore of the frozen bay to watch the local kids kite-ski.

"The big race is tomorrow," Darthin said. "The whole village will be there."

We continued past the last line of houses facing the bay and reached a small ridge. There must have been thirty kids out on the ice, preparing their kites.

To the right, a group of men stood near the giant metal building that Darthin had told us was filled with fish. Some sat on snow-mobiles with attached sleds, ready to head out on the ice.

"Does Professor Murphy know what that fish is for?" I asked Darthin.

"He said that our mission was to find sudithium, nothing else. He said he doesn't care why they fish, where they fish, or who they're fishing for, and neither should I. So . . . no."

"I have an idea," I said, looking at the men. "Mez, you could sneak over there. They'd never notice you in the rocks and snow. Just listen in."

Mez nodded. "I go," he said. He ducked behind a building, stripped down to his snap-free thermals, and morphed into the white-as-snow jaguar that he was. He had a determined look on his face as he snuck down the rocky shore, edging closer to the men. He had always wanted to join a hunt, and now he was finally getting the chance. And he was good. He kept low to the ground and moved so carefully.

We walked down the slope, closer to where the racers were taking off on their practice runs. We were hoping to draw the attention of the men to us, so they wouldn't notice the white shape edging closer and closer to them.

The kids zipped across the ice. They headed for the iceberg fist in the middle of the bay and then cruised around it and back. Sometimes they rose in the air, breathtakingly high, before maneuvering back to the ice again.

"They're fast," Frankie said.

"It's not normally this windy," Darthin said. "I've heard there's a storm approaching from the south."

We snuck glances at the fishermen. After a few minutes, two others joined the group and they all headed out. We watched their snowmobiles pull sleds across the ice as kids flew past them with their kites. Mez came bounding back, shivering, so we hustled back to the inn and upstairs to my room.

Bundled in dry clothes and wrapped in a thick blanket, Mez took sips of hot chocolate while he told us what he'd learned.

"That was fun," he said, still shivering. "But so cold. My fur's not thick enough for this place."

"I could barely see you," I said. "You were practically invisible."

He shrugged. "It's unlucky for me," he said. "Here, I fit in, but I do not belong. At home, I belong, but I don't fit in."

We all murmured about how unfair that was, and then Darthin said, "Did you hear anything?"

"The men were angry," Mez said. "They said they'd just gotten the giant animals to leave the village alone, but now they're coming back, because of us. One bunny stays very close to town. It likes to follow Professor Murphy and swat at him."

This was true. Professor Murphy was getting very annoyed by it.

"They want us gone, all of us," Mez went on. "One of them said, 'Why don't we just give it to them?' but another said, 'Then they will keep coming back.'"

"I knew it!" Darthin said. "I knew they were hiding something."

"Not just something," I said. "They have the sudithium. They must be hiding it somewhere. But where?"

"I've been all over this town with the sudithium detector," Darthin said. "I've never even gotten a blip."

"Anything else?" I asked Meztli.

"One guy said something like, 'What if they wake him up? It's too early.'"

"Wake who up?"

"I don't know," Mez said.

"Something that eats a lot of fish," Darthin said. "I'm guessing."

"So they have it," Frankie said. "What now?"

They were looking at me, all of them.

"We have to find it," I said. "Not the flakes in the crater. We have to find the village's secret stash of the mineral."

CHAPTER 31

Treasure Hiding, Prisoner Watching, Advanced Sabotage,
Evil Overlord Flattery, and Blame the Other Guy

—PARTIAL LIST OF EXTRACURRICULAR SEMINARS OFFERED

AT DR. CRITCHLORE'S SCHOOL

W e were silent as we thought about where the villagers could be hiding the sudithium. Meztli finished his drink and put the mug on the edge of the table. After a few seconds, he swatted it with his hand, knocking it to the floor, but I was ready this time and caught it.

"Guys, what's the first rule of hiding treasure?" I asked.

"Use lots of booby traps," Frankie said.

"No, that's the fourth rule," I said. "The first rule is: Get a monster to protect it."

"A monster . . . like that giant bird," Meztli said.

"You think they could be hiding the sudithium in its nest?" Darthin asked.

"It seems like a good hiding spot to me," I said. "But how could we get it?"

We thought about that.

"I know how we could test your theory," Darthin said. "We could leave a sudithium detector on the bird's tribute spot. I saw it bring back an orange vest and leave it there. If it doesn't like something, it returns it, so the villagers will know not to feed it that again. It's a smart bird."

"So we could put the sudithium detector in something we know the bird won't eat," I said. "The bird will take the detector to its nest, realize it doesn't want to eat it, and bring it back."

"And if there is sudithium in the nest, the detector will come back with a reading," Frankie said.

Darthin nodded. "It's worth a try."

"Let's do it."

We put the sudithium detector in my pillowcase, wrapping it up with a cord. We headed back out to the bay. The locals were done practicing and had already packed up their kites. We were able to walk over to the long building and then hide behind the far end, where the villagers couldn't see us.

"Frankie," I said, "you're fastest. Go run it out there."

He nodded and grabbed the bundle. The ice and heavy clothes slowed him down a little, but still, he was back in a flash.

"And now we wait."

It didn't take long for the bird to pick up our gift. I grabbed Darthin's shoulder as she flew back to her nest. "It worked!"

We waited for her to come back. And waited. We were due back at camp to meet with Professor Murphy after the council meeting. I told everyone to go ahead, I'd catch up with them later. I couldn't leave the spot unattended. I told them to tell Professor Murphy that I wasn't feeling well.

After they left, I kept my binoculars focused on the nest. I could see the giant bird with her chicks. She looked like she was settling in for a while. Rats.

I scanned the ice. It was so beautiful at this time of day. The iceberg frozen in place in the bay was a brilliant white cutting into the blue sky with its jagged edges. Beyond it, way off in the open water, I saw an icebreaker. I wondered if the ship was one of Professor Murphy's escape plans for once we found the sudithium.

I noticed movement out of the corner of my eye and turned to see the bird swoop down from the nest. She dropped the bundle on the tribute spot without landing and swooped right back up.

I waited a minute and then ran out, snatched the bundle, and sprinted away as fast as I could. Once safe, I opened it up to look at the reading on the sudithium detector.

It was zero. The needle hadn't budged.

I caught up with everyone at camp. I'd been able to hitch a ride with two of the guides that Professor Murphy had hired. The guides joined Professor Murphy inside one of the cabins, and I found my friends in another one. Darthin sat at a table with his journal, while Mez lay bundled in his sleeping bag and Frankie stretched out on a cot.

"The villagers voted to kick us all out," Darthin said. "But a representative of Irma Trackno told them they had to give us one more chance."

"It's not a good situation, though," Frankie said. "Professor Murphy told us we have to work fast, because we could be forced to leave at any time."

I handed the sudithium detector to Darthin, who looked at it and said, "Not in the nest?"

"Nope," I said.

"Well, it was a good guess," Meztli said. "Now what?"

I sat down by Frankie's feet. "What's the second rule of hiding treasure?" I asked.

Frankie sat up. "Plant a decoy treasure and make a fake map with a giant X on it?"

"No, that's the third rule," I said. "The second rule is: Hide the treasure where people have already looked."

"The crater?" Darthin said.

"We've been told that the mining operation found everything in the crater," I said. "Wouldn't that make it the perfect spot to hide a pile of sudithium, if you had it?"

"Maybe," Darthin said. "It's not a bad plan."

"But it's a huge crater," Frankie said. "And our guides won't let us go inside. You should see them. They get very agitated if we even step near."

"Doesn't that prove my point?" I asked.

Professor Murphy yelled for a meeting, so we went outside and gathered around him.

"We can continue our work," he said. "I've told the council that the Pravus team is the one upsetting the local animals, and they have promised to deal with them. This means we may have a few more days to dig—ideally, without distraction. We must dig fast, just in case we are forced to leave. Let's make it count. Tomorrow I want all teams to report to Rufus's site, where we've had the most luck."

"Jud and I can handle it alone," Rufus said.

"Nonsense," Professor Murphy said. "We need all hands working there."

"Great!" I said.

"Runt, you stay put. We don't want the Pravus team to think we're focusing on that one spot."

Not great.

Everyone returned to their tents, and I stood up to join the guides going back to town in the van. Before I left, Darthin grabbed my arm.

"What are you going to do?" he asked.

I looked at my friends. My mind was made up.

"Tomorrow," I said. "I'm breaking a rule."

CHAPTER 32

"The swirls of dancing lights in the night sky, which most people call 'the aurora,' are called 'Nature's Tribute to Irma Trackno' in Upper Worb."

—GUIDEBOOK TO UPPER WORB

The next morning I sat at the counter eating breakfast. I was having second thoughts about my plan. But then I thought about what would happen if I kept doing what Professor Murphy wanted me to do, and I got mad all over again. While Rufus and the others were on a real archaeological dig, he'd assigned me to search in the equivalent of the playground sandbox.

I watched Alasie and Big Jim in the kitchen. They probably knew where the sudithium was hidden. If only I could get them to tell me . . .

There seemed to be quite a lot of tension between them. Alasie was slamming pots and pans and grunting at him. Big Jim grunted back.

"You have a job to do," Big Jim said. "There'll be other races. You're lucky you weren't sent back to Okkopiku after you knocked over the building. I put my reputation on the line to keep you here."

Alasie screeched.

Today was the day of the big race, and she was being forced to babysit me. It gave me an idea.

I finished my breakfast and coughed. They ignored me. I coughed again.

"Big Jim," I said, throwing a few more coughs in the air as I spoke. "Hey! Big Jim."

At last he walked over. Alasie kept up her slamming routine.

"Listen, I'm"—*cough*—"all alone today," I said. "And I don't"—*cough*—"think I'm going to go out to the site. I'm not feeling well. Going back to bed. So we won't need"—*cough*—"her today. Thanks."

Alasie looked over. The air stilled.

"I'm sure Professor Murphy will still pay you for your time," I added.

Alasie rushed over and grabbed Big Jim's arm.

I coughed one more time and then headed back upstairs.

My chest really did feel tight, and my nose was constantly running in the cold up here, but I had no intention of staying in my room. I waited about thirty minutes and then left, walking down the road toward camp. Brightly colored kites zipped across the ice in front of town. And then, as I neared camp, Pravus's dragon swooped overhead, heading for the cliffs.

I wondered if the Pravus team had come to the same conclusion as me. Did they think the village was hiding sudithium in the nest?

I pulled out my binoculars to watch. The rider, clearly a Pravus kid, was trying to keep the dragon above the gyrfalcon, but the gyrfalcon guarded the cliffs like a boulderball goalie.

The gyrfalcon was faster, but the dragon had a better weapon—

fire. One blast after another shot out at the bird, who flapped the flames away with her powerful wings. The dragon edged higher, now just above the cliffs. As the gyrfalcon rose for another attack, the Pravus rider fell off.

I gasped.

The dragon and gyrfalcon were still battling when a parachute opened. I focused on the rider and gasped again when I saw a flash of green in the rider's hair. It was Syke.

Syke had never ridden a dragon in her life. Critchlore wouldn't let her. And I knew for sure she'd never parachuted before. That was an elective for sixth-years.

She was heading right for the cliffs.

"Turn!" I shouted, as if she could hear me. *"TURN!"*

She landed on a small ridge above the gyrfalcon's nest, her parachute tangling in the rocks above her. How was she going to get down? Just as I was wondering if I should tell Coach Reythor about her, I saw the sun glint off her own binoculars. She was up there scanning the village below.

She'd landed there on purpose. From that spot, she could see the entire area, from the dragon hangar to the village. From the crater to the iceberg. It was the perfect lookout spot, if you didn't mind freezing to death.

I made it to our base camp, ready to march into the crater and finally search for real, but the rest of the Critchlore team was still there. Apparently, they'd called another council meeting. Professor Murphy had told everyone to sit tight, it wouldn't take long.

"Where are Rufus and Jud?" I asked.

"They said they didn't need protection and went to dig," Frankie said. "Two Pravus teams followed them. We were just trying to decide if we should go out or wait for Professor Murphy."

A loud bang ripped through the air. I pulled out my binoculars. I could see a line of Pravus trolls standing on a hill, firing bear bangers over Rufus's head.

If it were anyone else, I'd rally the troops to go out and help him, but this was Rufus. He was trying to steal all the glory for himself while the rest of us were stuck here, obeying Professor Murphy's order to wait.

A van sped toward camp, stopping just outside the electric fence. Professor Murphy and some villagers stepped out.

"What's going on?" Professor Murphy asked.

"Rufus and Jud went out to dig," Frankie said. "Pravus trolls are harassing them."

Professor Murphy frowned. "While I admire their dedication to the task, they disobeyed my command." He turned to the two guides, nodding at them to head out there. "The Pravus team won't risk attacking us when we have guides. Rufus and Jud should have waited.

"The rest of you get out there as well," he said. "We've been given an allowance to continue digging, but one more incident with the wildlife and that's it."

A white-furred body came out of the van—Alasie. She saw me and frowned.

"Everyone to their digging spots!" Professor Murphy called.

I shrugged my shoulders and headed out. Alasie followed, her usual scowl in place. This was an unfortunate development for me. I was sure Alasie wouldn't let me go into the crater.

"I thought if I pretended to be sick, you could go to your race," I said. "I'm sorry you missed it. They made you come out here anyway, huh?"

She didn't look at me or answer. She just hiked up to her spot on the little hill and sat down to watch me dig.

I wasn't going to dig anymore. I was trying to think up a way to distract Alasie when Meztli and Frankie approached on their snowmobile. They were the last team to leave camp, and before they reached me, I noticed two Pravus kids, Victus and a rather ugly troll, following them. Meztli turned and shot a bear banger at them. They returned fire.

Victus nearly hit Alasie. He might not have seen her, because she was all white fur sitting on a white hill. This clearly was the last straw for her, because she picked up a boulder, screeched, and chucked it as far as she could. Her aim wasn't great, but I was impressed with her strength. The boulder flew over my head and landed in the crater, hitting another rock with a loud crack that seemed to reverberate across the land.

She froze, her eyes suddenly wide with fear.

We all turned to look at where it had landed, wondering why she was so frightened.

And then the rock moved. The ground shook, and then seemed to moan. A low rumbling sound surrounded us.

"Do you hear that?" I asked Frankie and Mez.

And then I heard a softer moan behind me. Alasie, hands to her mouth, was shaking her head. She turned and ran for the village. Victus and his friend zoomed off on their snowmobile, heading for the other teams.

The ground shook again. The moan grew louder. It sounded like the kind of moan my foster brother Pierre makes when he's woken up in the morning, only ten times louder. I scanned the crater floor, but nothing had changed. There was nothing anywhere in the stupid crater except for a few kids near the edge here, and in the far distance, Rufus and Jud.

Then a bigger earthquake knocked us off our feet, and a giant crack split open the white floor of the crater.

The icy ground seemed to rise, slowly. Only it wasn't the crater floor, it was a giant creature who had been sleeping at the bottom of the crater. Its torso rose up out of the snow . . . and rose . . . and rose. The big rock that Alasie had hit was actually its toe, now wiggling. I didn't know what it was, but it was focused on Victus's noisy snowmobile racing away.

The monster stood up and shook its body. Snow flew off in all directions. It was huge and hairy, like a moving three-story building with limbs and fur. It roared and took two giant strides to get ahead of the snowmobile, then turned to look down on it with a long, angry face that was cut with scars. Its mouth had an underbite full of huge, sharp teeth. Four horns sprung out the top of its head, with two more curving down in front. Its fur was thick, like a woolly mammoth.

Someone in Rufus's area shot at it with something, and the beast turned on them. I pulled out my binoculars and focused on Rufus. He and Jud both morphed and ran for their lives. The Pravus kids were shooting bear bangers at the monster, and the beast roared again. It started toward them, each step shaking the earth so hard it would have broken Stevie's seismograph, I was sure.

Huge polar hares hopped up and fled in all directions. Enormous polar foxes ran after them. It was pandemonium.

"We have to warn the village," I said.

"I think they probably know," Frankie said, looking up at the incredible height of the monster.

Everyone seemed to be fleeing in our direction now, with the beast following.

"Let's get out of here!"

CHAPTER 33

"Woolly Gigantoths are thought to be the ancestors of the modern giant, but many giants refuse to believe that they could have evolved from something so ugly."

—PROFESSOR VIDLEY'S MONSTER HISTORY CLASS

The mountain of a monster roared. The Pravus team kept shooting at it, with arrows now, but it was like shooting a person with toothpicks. It only made him mad.

I ran for a snowmobile, with Mez right behind me. Frankie joined us, and we took off for town. "We have to find Darthin!" Frankie yelled over the rush of noise.

We headed for the village. Once there, we could see that the whole area was in complete mayhem. Many villagers were racing for the giant fish-containing building.

"I guess we know what they were saving all that fish for," Meztli said.

"But the fish is on the other side of town," Frankie said. "That monster is going to flatten every building before he gets there."

"Look!" I said, pointing to the metal building. "They're trying to load the fish onto sleds. Maybe we can help."

We drove over to the crowd, chased by the roar of the monster.

It stomped on their community building. I really hoped it was empty of people, because now it was flat.

Every snowmobile and every sled in the village had been driven or hauled to the fish-storage building. Darthin stood in the group, helping. Men and women raced into the building and came out holding armfuls of fish. Once a sled was loaded, the snowmobile took off for the beast.

He stood on top of the smashed building, swinging his arms in the air, as if he were battling imaginary attackers. Below, the first sled filled with fish had reached him. The villager unlatched the sled and left it in front of the monster. Then he got back on his snowmobile and sped away.

The monster didn't look down. He roared and stepped on top of the sled of fish. Another snowmobile put on the brakes, left its offering of fish, and turned around.

"He's too angry to eat," Frankie said. "He's ignoring the food. Or he hasn't seen it."

"Oh, no!" I said. "He'll destroy the village."

This was our fault. Not directly—Alasie had thrown the boulder. But she never would have if it hadn't been for us.

I imagined I was back in a game of Giants vs. Villagers and took off, straight at the monster. His motions were jerky and unfocused, just like Pierre's when he woke up after a long sleep. I was pretty sure I could dodge his feet, and I was too small to be a threat he would focus on. Someone had to make him see the food.

I reached the sled and grabbed a fish. It was frozen and slippery and as big as my thigh. I held it by the tail and spun around to heave it at the monster, but it only went about twenty feet, falling well short.

Frankie caught up with me. He grabbed a fish and did the same maneuver, and this time the fish flew like it had been shot from a canon, hitting the monster in the face. The monster shook his head, looked down at us, and roared angrily.

"Throw another one!" I yelled, and Frankie did. His practice with Kumi paid off, because he hit the monster square in the face again. This time, the monster caught the fish in his mouth.

"Again!" I yelled, handing him another fish.

We teamed up, me handing Frankie a fish, him throwing it. Grab and throw, grab and throw. The pile of fish got smaller and smaller. I turned and yelled for more fish. Two snowmobiles raced over, ridden by local men, who helped me hand fish to Frankie. Their mouths hung open as they watched Frankie work.

Frankie kept throwing, his aim worsening as he got dizzier and dizzier from all that spinning, but the monster had stopped his approach. The fish were coming too fast for him to do anything more than catch them.

Three sleds of fish later, Frankie collapsed, but so did the monster. He held his belly and curled up on the ground. It looked like he'd fallen back to sleep.

Gradually, the rest of the villagers came over to where we stood. Soon we were in the midst of a huge, relieved group. They all wanted to pat Frankie and me on the back. We'd done it—we'd saved the village.

Big Jim stood on the ridge above us. The air was crowded with

excited chatter, but when Big Jim's voice boomed out, everyone went silent.

"Who woke up Amaruq?" he said, glaring at us.

I looked at Alasie. She was trying to disappear backward into the crowd.

"I did," I said, raising my hand. "It was me."

The crowd that had been congratulating us a moment earlier immediately edged away.

Frankie grabbed my arm. "What are you doing?"

"Hoping I can get them to break the fifth rule of hiding treasure," I said with a shrug.

"Pack up, visitors!" Big Jim yelled. "You're leaving on the next dragon!"

CHAPTER 34

"The fifth rule of hiding treasure: Don't tell anyone where you hid it."

—FROM PROFESSOR FLAGHOTH'S SEMINAR ON TREASURE HIDING

I was hoping that Alasie's frozen demeanor toward me might thaw a little bit. Taking the blame was a long shot, I knew, but it was the only shot I had left.

I couldn't help but feel jittery as I returned to the inn to pack up. The rest of the group went back to camp. I'd just gotten us all kicked out, and we had nothing but a few flakes of sudithium. It would be my fault if we didn't get any more.

Villagers stumbled into the inn, looking spent from the battle we'd just waged—the panic, the desperate loading of fish, the fleeing for safety. Now, tired and relieved, they sat down to rest. They'd lost their community building, but fortunately it had been empty at the time of its destruction.

The villagers seemed happy, and I soon realized why when I heard Big Jim's voice from the kitchen.

"They all have to leave now," he said. "That was the agreement: one more incident and they'd leave."

He came out with hot drinks for everyone. I was heading for the stairs, but he grabbed my arm with his free hand and nodded to the counter, where a mug sat steaming at my usual spot.

"Aren't you mad at me?" I asked, because I couldn't tell.

"You woke Amaruq," he said. "That was the thing we were most worried about happening. But your bravery helped save the town. You didn't run. I admire that. And now all you visitors have to leave, and that makes me happy." He shrugged.

I nodded. "I'm sorry for everything we've done," I said.

A moment later, the front door burst open, and an enraged Professor Murphy stepped inside, with Rufus right behind him.

"Are you a complete idiot?!" he screamed at me. "I told you one thing—*one thing!* Do not go in the crater, and what do you do?"

"You set me up to fail. You gave me an area that'd been picked clean," I said.

"You could have killed us all. Do you realize that?" Professor Murphy said. Rufus clenched his fist and lunged toward me, only to be held back by Professor Murphy. "And we're so close. So close! I want you to pack your bags and get out of here on the first dragon. The rest of us will wait for tomorrow. It's bad enough that we have the Pravus team taunting us at every turn, but to be sabotaged by one of our own . . . We look like fools! Because of you."

I didn't know what to say to that. I knew it wasn't fair, but I couldn't come up with a defense.

"Go home. The shuttle dragon leaves this afternoon. Be on it." They turned and left, slamming the door.

The room was quiet after that. Nobody even picked up a fork. They were all looking at me, even Alasie. My face was hot with embarrassment and shame.

Alasie was leaning against the wall, furry arms crossed as she stared at me. After everyone had been served and Big Jim had returned to the kitchen, she crooked her finger at me, beckoning me to join her in the corner. When I did, she said, "Why'd you do that?"

My eyebrows went up. She was speaking? To me?

"Why'd you take the blame for what I did?" she repeated.

"I don't know," I answered, and I really didn't. "Look, I know you don't want us here, and we've attracted all those hares and everything. I feel bad about that. And then you missed your race, because of us."

She kept glaring at me.

"I heard what Big Jim said to you, about how the village wanted to send you away from here after you'd made a mistake. I know how you feel."

"You're not being sent away from your home," she said. "You just have to leave *my* home."

"It's not that," I said. "I made a deal with Professor Murphy. I have to find some sudithium or I'll be kicked out of school. And then he set me up to fail—making me dig in the stupidest spot, knowing I wouldn't find any.

"You know, I'm just as angry as you," I went on. "I would have thrown that boulder too, if I could've lifted it."

She nodded.

"Why didn't you just tell us about that hibernating snow beast?" I asked.

She surprised me by laughing. "Amaruq. That's his name," she said. "He's supposed to be a secret. We don't want the white woman to know that he's here. It's a long story. I'm sorry you got in trouble."

"It's okay," I said. "It was bound to happen sooner or later."

"Wait here," she said. She disappeared into the kitchen. I heard her talking with Big Jim. When she came back, she grabbed my arm. "Come with me."

"Where?" I asked.

"Just come," she said. "I want to show you something."

As she dragged me through the kitchen, Big Jim said, "Take a weapon."

Outside, she attached a sled to one of the snowmobiles parked behind the house and began loading it with equipment.

"Where are we going?"

"I'm going to give you some," she said, motioning for me to get on the snowmobile behind her. "Now that Amaruq is awake, the white woman will know we have it. We've been hiding it from her. But when word gets out about Amaruq, she'll know. And she'll come for it. She wants to make sure she has it all. She'll come and find it, no matter where it's hidden. It has to go. We knew this would happen sometime, but we were hoping we'd have a plan by then."

"You're going to give me some sudithium?"

"It's not going to be easy," she said over her shoulder to me. "There might be . . . obstacles."

Of course there would be. That was the fourth rule of hiding treasure.

"Can I get my friends?" I asked.

"No time."

And then we sped off.

‡‡‡

It was still early, though it was hard to tell because the clouds hung low in the sky, making it seem like dusk. Alasie took off a different way, along a track that snuck out the back of town and headed through the smaller hills there. We came down to a narrow bay that was also frozen over and started across. Riding on the sea ice made me nervous, because there were pockets of water on top, but Alasie rode through them without worry. The ice below must have been very strong.

The scenery was the same: white, white, and whitish gray with the occasional dark chasms where the ice was split and the sea below was revealed. We had to take detours around those cracks in the ice.

We rode across the bay toward a towering red cliff. It had a crumbly look to it, and chunks of rock had sheared off and fallen to the frozen ice below. A narrow opening divided the cliff in two, allowing passage through to the other side. Alasie headed for the opening but stopped just as we reached it.

"Almost there," she said, looking through to the other side.

"Where?"

"You'll see."

She drove up a smooth incline of snow and through the alley-way in the cliff. The rock walls on either side rose straight up and loomed over us, like skyscrapers.

Another frozen bay met us once we made it through. This bay was enclosed by a horseshoe of cliffs. We rode across the ice to the tip of the other side. Alasie stopped the snowmobile next to the cliff wall and got off.

"There's a mark here somewhere," she said, scanning the wall of rock.

This reminded me of the last rule of hiding treasure—don't forget where you hid it. It's surprising how many people do.

"There!" She pointed to a spot on the wall. Then she turned to the sled and removed a shovel and a pickax. She handed me the shovel.

She walked out onto the ice, measuring off ten paces. "We have to dig a hole right here," she said.

She stabbed the ax into the ice, but only a few flakes shot off. She kept at it, and so did I, right next to her.

"Amaruq is not so bad," she said, between jabs. "He wasn't supposed to wake up for another couple of weeks. We would have moved the food to the crater before then, because he wakes up really, really hungry. And confused—thinks he's back in the war. But after he eats and takes another nap, he'll be happy."

"Why is he a secret?"

"He is a deserter from the white woman's army," she said.

"Irma Trackno?"

"Yes. Irma wants him back. He came here last summer to hide from her. It was great at first, because he kept the other big animals out of town and we felt safe. Even after he hibernated in the crater, the animals stayed away. Until you guys showed up."

"Sorry," I said.

"We knew that as soon as he woke up, Irma would find out he's here. Her search teams didn't show up until after he hibernated, but we see them often now. Once she knows he's here, she'll come for him. And she'll punish us for hiding him."

"She does seem like the vengeful type," I said, remembering all the stories Darthin had told me about her.

"Yes. Some on the council think we should give Amaruq the mineral, so he stays big. Then he can protect us from Irma's revenge. But next winter he'll hibernate again, and we'll be defenseless, and Irma will come. Others on the council want to give her the mineral. Maybe she'll be so happy to have it, she won't be mad that we hid Amaruq."

"How did you get the sudithium?" I asked. "Didn't the miners get it all?"

"In the big crater, yes. That was many years ago. The white woman's army set up camp near where your cabins are, and they mined that crater for years."

Alasie gave a mighty swing, and the ax went through the ice. She swung it a few more times, until she had a little hole. She went back to the sled, grabbed a large sword, her bow and arrow, some rope, and a fish. She placed these next to her hole in the ice, and then motioned for me to help her widen it. As we dug, she continued with her story.

"The people here hated the miners, who were from the south and very rude and condescending, acting so superior with their fancy tools and weapons. They couldn't last one winter here alone, and they had no respect for the people who can, and have, for generations."

I nodded. "My foster mother, Cook, says that's the problem with people. Everyone thinks they're better than everyone else and they don't treat others with respect."

We gave the edges of the hole a few whacks, then rested. Dig and rest. Dig and rest. My arms started to ache.

"If the miners got all the sudithium, how did you end up with it?" I asked during one rest.

"Two years ago, long after the miners were gone, there was a big explosion in the sky. A meteorite broke up before landing, and the rocks with green flakes fell across the ice here, in this spot. Fishermen used to come to this bay for mussels, and two of them found the rocks. They remembered the mining people, so they collected all the rocks and hid them in a secret cave.

"We don't want Irma to have it, because she uses it for war. So when she asks, we tell her there's nothing left here. But all the animals are still so big. We tell her trace amounts must still be in the soil, or maybe they adapted to be that big. Who knows? She doesn't believe this. She thinks we're hiding it. So she lets intruders like you come to look for it. She wants to make life so miserable for us that we just give it to her."

I kept jabbing at the ice while Alasie talked.

"It's very sad, but her plan has worked," she went on. "We're ready to give up. Every group that comes causes more problems than if we just let Amaruq shrink back to size and leave. We're sad for him, but we can't protect him anymore."

"You guys are protecting *him*?"

"Yes. He was in many battles, and he doesn't want to fight anymore. You saw him. When he wakes up, he thinks he's back in a war. The fighting has affected him very badly.

"Big Jim says the council has decided to give Irma the sudithium, but before we do, I want to give you some. I told him what you did, and he said okay. Then you could show that Murphy and not be in trouble."

Aww, that was so nice of her.

"And the sudithium is under this ice?"

"Yes."

I looked into the hole and saw a gap below the ice. "Where's the water?" I asked.

"The tide is going out," she said. "When the tide comes in, the water hits the top of the ice. When it goes out, the ice stays frozen in place. Sea ice is very strong."

"How'd the sudithium get down there?" I shined my flashlight into the hole and saw dark, swirling water down below.

"We hid it here. Like I said, we didn't want Irma to find it. We know from Amaruq that most of the creatures she gives it to go straight to battle and are forced to fight huge armies by themselves. Most of them die, but she doesn't care. She says she can make more monsters.

"Some boys found a secret cave in the wall here when they were hunting for mussels. When the tide goes out, they can walk to the cave. When the tide comes in, the entry to the cave floods, but the inside is higher and stays dry. It's the perfect place to hide the rocks from Irma's soldiers. They come to the village with their fancy equipment to find the sudithium, but they don't find anything."

"That's amazing!" I said. We never would have found it—that was obvious.

"It's a good hiding spot to keep it from people," she said. "Unfortunately, something else found it."

As she said this, a giant tentacle slithered through the opening in the ice and grabbed my leg.

CHAPTER 35

"Polar bears eat seal meat, so they haven't been exposed to sudithium in their food chain. They avoid this area because of the other large animals."

—DARTHIN, EXPLAINING THE ABSENCE OF POLAR BEARS

I screamed. Alasie moved quickly. She grabbed her sword and swung it down hard on the tentacle, puncturing the thick hide. The tentacle released me in a flash and slithered back into the darkness below. I heard splashes echo from beneath the ice.

I scurried away from the hole as fast as I could. Alasie dropped the sword and picked up her bow and arrow, firing three quick shots into the darkness.

"What was *that*?" I asked.

"Ice squid," she said. "Very dangerous to the fishermen around here."

"How are we going to get past it?"

She kept her focus on the hole, but no more tentacles emerged.

"We wait for the tide to go out all the way."

I heard a crack behind me. Turning, I saw tentacles waving in the air, having burst through one of the crevasses we'd crisscrossed on our way to this spot. "It's huge!" I screamed.

The slithering tentacles rose up high and then crashed down on the ice, trying to break it. Alasie kept shooting until she ran out of arrows, hitting them five times before they slithered back down.

"I'm not sure our tranquilizer works on this one," she said.

As if to prove her point, a tentacle rose back up in the air.

"Should we get off the ice?" I asked. It seemed like a good idea to me. I nodded at our snowmobile.

Alasie shook her head. "The tide is almost out," she said. "He has to go to deeper water now."

We watched as the tentacle withdrew, and soon the thumping below the ice stopped. After a nervous few minutes spent watching and listening, Alasie edged back over to the hole. She gave the ice a few whacks, then backed away. She did this a few times, until she felt safe.

"The tide is out," she said. "The monster is gone. Come here."

She dumped everything off the sled, then motioned for me to help her lower it into the hole. The sled had a slat-like base, like a ladder.

"We must be quick," she said, climbing down the ladder.

I was thinking this might be a one-person job and that I could wait up here and not enter that hole of doom. But Alasie had another idea.

"You hold the flashlight; I hold the weapons." She'd reached the bottom. "Come on—hurry."

I climbed down and landed in a shallow layer of water. It was dark under the roof of ice. I shivered, thinking that a giant tentacle could reach through the darkness and grab me. It was so eerie and

231

quiet. No longer was the wind howling past my ears, but there were other sounds: drips and creaks that echoed in the enclosed space. I thought I heard something that sounded like a moan.

"This way," Alasie said. She started off, ducking under a low swoop of the ice roof.

If my heart wasn't hammering in my chest with panic, I might have taken a moment to think, "Wow, I'm walking on the ocean floor, beneath a roof of ice. This is so cool." Instead, all I could think about was how we needed to get out of there as quickly as possible.

The ice that was flat on the surface above drooped down on us when we were below, like when you build a blanket fort and the blankets aren't tight. Some of the drooping parts reached the sea floor, creating walls of ice that looked so smooth and shiny in the beam of the flashlight. Alasie followed a narrow passageway that curved between the bulges. Wider passageways split off in all directions.

"We have to hurry," she said, "before the tide comes back."

Every sound made me jump with fear. Clicks and cracks echoed in the tight space. I stayed as close to Alasie as I could.

"The people who gather mussels here must be very brave," I said.

"They are. I love the people here. So brave and strong and kind. They are the only ones who stand up to the white woman. I don't want to leave. That's why you taking the blame meant so much to me."

Little pools of deeper water dotted the ground. We made our way around them to reach a dark cave. I let Alasie go in first. She pulled herself up the steep slope while I shined the flashlight ahead of her. Then I tossed it up to her, and she scanned the cave with it. She turned and nodded for me to come up, which I did in a flash, because I was terrified of what might be waiting in the darkness behind me.

I crawled in next to Alasie and looked at the wide cave. The ceiling was low, claustrophobically low.

The container that Alasie's people had used to store the rocks sat in the back of the cave. It had toppled on its side, and the rocks had spilled out. "Let's grab some and go," I said.

"Take them all," Alasie said.

"Really?"

"Yes, I'll tell them I gave you some and the tentacle beast took the rest."

It took a few minutes to transfer the rocks to my backpack. My pack was heavy, but it felt great. Professor Murphy was going to faint with shock! Rufus would hang his head in shame! The guys were going to be so happy! And not only that, but this had to be enough for us to catch up with Dr. Pravus.

I couldn't believe how amazing this was, how awesome I felt. I bumped into Alasie, who had stopped at the entrance to the cave.

"Let's move," she said. "The tide's coming back in." It was true, a thin layer of water had snuck in to cover the ocean floor while we were inside. "Come, hurry!"

She left with the flashlight, and the darkness in the cave immediately smothered me. I watched the bobbing light disappear around a drooping wall of ice as she ran for the ladder.

I knew that if the water was coming back, something else was probably coming with it. Panic squeezed me tight as I hustled after Alasie. I couldn't lose her down here or I'd be stuck in the darkness with a homicidal giant squid.

"Alasie! Wait for me!"

I splashed through water, the roof of ice creaking above my head. I followed what I thought was the twisty path we'd taken to the cave, but things looked so different coming from the opposite direction. Alasie had heard me, though, and she turned around to shine the light. Once I caught up, she shined the flashlight forward. It was such a relief to see the ladder, hanging in its spotlight of sunlight coming through the hole.

But then I had to rub my eyes because I couldn't believe what I was seeing.

The ladder was moving. Somebody, or something, was lifting it out of the hole.

CHAPTER 36

Most mussel hunters post a lookout to watch for the returning tide.

—OOPS

The water was creeping up around my boots. We splashed through it toward the ladder, which zipped up out of reach just as we got there.

"Oh, hey—look who it is," Rufus said as he shined his flashlight beneath the ice. "I knew you were up to something."

"Rufus, put the ladder back," I said. "The water's getting higher." I thought I heard some splashes coming toward us in the darkness.

"Toss up your backpack first," he said.

I shook my head, grabbing the straps a little tighter. "Rufus, there's a monster down here! Put the ladder back!"

"Toss up the pack, and I'll put the ladder back."

I looked at Alasie. She shook her head and said, "We could go back to the cave and stay there until the tide goes out again, but this hole will freeze over. We'll be stuck down here."

I didn't want Rufus to take the sudithium, but I was not going to stay down here waiting for that tentacled monster to grab me. I heaved the backpack out. Rufus put the ladder back.

I climbed out and saw Rufus and Jud huddled over my opened pack. The sky had grown darker, and the wind was whipping up loose snow and ice, making it hard to see very far.

"I knew these villagers were hiding something!" Rufus said. He lifted a handful of rocks out of the bag. Out in the open, I could see how green they were.

"They're mine," I said as I climbed out. "I found them."

"Yeah, sure you did!" Rufus yelled over the wind. "Nobody's going to believe that. It's just so easy to outsmart you, Runt." He stood up and laughed. "So easy! Come on, Jud. Let's go show Professor Murphy what I found."

A thunderous rumble filled the air. It felt like the stormy skies were echoing my rage at Rufus, but it wasn't the approaching storm. Two snowmobiles rounded the far edge of the cliffs. The riders were wearing red parkas.

"The Pravus team," Rufus said. He smacked Jud. "You said they weren't following us!"

"They weren't," he said. "They followed Lapso, like we planned."

"It's that useless tree girl," Rufus said. He turned to me. "Your traitorous ex-BFF has ratted us out! She's their lookout in the cliffs. She must have seen us ride over here. Let's go!"

Rufus and Jud jumped on their snowmobile and sped off, but the Pravus snowmobiles were closing fast. Alasie and I watched the chase as we hustled back to our own snowmobile.

Rufus and Jud were getting farther and farther away. The snowmobiles following them seemed to slow down. From behind I could tell that they weren't trying to catch Rufus and Jud; instead, they were herding them. Rufus and Jud didn't seem to realize it. They kept speeding straight for the gap in the mountains that would take them back to camp. It was a narrow gap, the perfect place for a—

"Trap!" I screamed, but it was useless. Between the roar of the engines and the rush of wind, my words never reached them.

Just as they entered the gap, a giant net sprang up out of the snow. It must have been a really strong net, because Rufus's snowmobile didn't bust through. The Pravus snowmobiles approached carefully from behind, and so did we.

We watched as the Pravus trolls, who'd been waiting by the net, wrapped up their prize. Rufus and Jud were now completely trapped. They morphed into werewolves, using their teeth and claws to try and free themselves from the net. Unfortunately, when they did this, they no longer had hands with which to hold onto the sudithium-filled backpack, and while they struggled with the net, a member of the Pravus team managed to grab the backpack from beneath the net while the others distracted Rufus and Jud.

Victus.

Now stupid Victus had the backpack of sudithium. I was sure he was smirking beneath all those layers covering his face.

The two Pravus snowmobiles edged slowly around the squirming net. Victus jumped on the back of one snowmobile, and they took off through the gap, leaving my classmates struggling to get free. Alasie and I quickly pulled the net off Rufus and Jud before we chased after the Pravus team. Rufus and Jud, unable to remorph into humans because their clothes had been shredded, ran after us.

"We have to stop them!" I told Alasie.

Rufus stealing the sudithium was bad, but the Pravus team getting it was a complete disaster. I couldn't believe that Syke would betray us like that, but when I looked to the mountain, it made sense that she'd been the one who had spotted us, or had spotted Rufus and Jud, and sent the Pravus team after us. If my heart hadn't already been in pieces after losing the sudithium, it would've been shattered by that betrayal.

The snowmobiles had to slow down as they edged around crevices in the ice, but soon they'd hit the land and be able to zip away. And even if we caught Victus—then what? How could Alasie and I take on two snowmobiles and four Pravus minions? On the Vlag-whatever scale, we were clearly out-monstered.

Make that the whole team of Pravus minions, because as we approached land, I saw one of their big black snow vans coming our way. It was easy to spot, an SUV-type car churning up snow with its rolling track.

What wasn't easy to see was the white jaguar crouching on the ice. I didn't even see Meztli until he sprang. He crashed into Victus with enough force to throw him from the snowmobile.

Frankie popped up next, shaking off the snow he'd covered himself with. He ran straight for the SUV and knocked it on its side. Then he ran to help Meztli with the trolls on the snowmobiles.

"Grab my backpack!" I yelled at Meztli. He looked at me, gave me a short nod, then stared at Victus, who was hiding behind the trolls, clutching the backpack.

Frankie lifted one of the snowmobiles—with the troll still on it!—and threw it across the ice and into one of the crevasses. He charged the next troll while Meztli closed in on Victus and tore the backpack from his grip.

Other Pravus team members tried to climb out of the sideways van, but they took one look at Frankie, who now held Victus's snowmobile over his head, and ducked back inside.

"Take my backpack to camp!" I yelled at Meztli, and he took off. Frankie and Alasie and I stood ready to keep the Pravus team from following. I felt good, because their snow transport wasn't going anywhere, stuck on its side, and Frankie had broken both snowmobiles by throwing them. I relaxed, knowing we had this covered.

But then I saw Jud and Rufus racing after Meztli. Meztli was probably faster, but he was slowed down by the heavy backpack.

Frankie saw it too. He jumped on the back of the snowmobile, behind me and Alasie, and we took off after the rest of my team.

We made it back to camp and through the electrified fence. Meztli, Jud, and Rufus got there before us, because the snowmobile wasn't as fast over the rough terrain. I headed for Professor Murphy's hut.

Rufus and Jud were with him, smiling wide because Professor Murphy was holding a backpack filled with sudithium.

"This is incredible, Rufus!" he shouted. "More than I thought we'd ever get!" He jumped up to hug Rufus.

That was *my* hug. Rufus had stolen everything from me—the sudithium, the credit, and the hug.

"Runt, what are you still doing here?" Professor Murphy said. He wasn't even angry with me—that's how happy he was to have the sudithium.

"That's my backpack," I said, pointing. "I'm the one who found all that sudithium. Alasie, the yeti girl you hired to be my babysitter, showed me where it was after I took the blame for waking Amaruq."

"Pathetic," Rufus said. "Always trying to take credit for other people's achievements."

Professor Murphy waved a hand. "Right now we have to get this out of here—fast. Before the Pravus team gets back. We have to split it up. I'll head for the hangar with Frankie and Meztli for protection. Rufus, I want you, Jud, and Lapso to take a snowmobile south to the next town and see if you can catch a dragon from there."

"What's the third plan?" I asked. I knew that Professor Murphy would follow Dr. Critchlore's motto: Always have at least three plans.

"I was going to send a team to the icebreaker waiting in the open water," he said. "It's positioned at the edge of the floe, just past the iceberg, but Rufus told me we've lost a snowmobile."

"I'll take it," I said. "Alasie, can you kite-ski me past that iceberg?"

She nodded.

Professor Murphy looked doubtful.

"Let him go—but don't give him any sudithium," Rufus said. "He'll make a good distraction, because Syke will see him from her spying spot. They won't be able to chase all of us, because we've destroyed two of their snowmobiles and one transport."

"We?" I said, because now he was taking credit for Frankie's work.

Professor Murphy ignored me and divided the sudithium into three bags. He handed one to Rufus. "Go," he said. Then he handed one to me. "You never know." He shrugged.

"Alasie? Where's your kite-ski?"

"We keep it in a shed by the edge of town."

At the sound of Alasie's voice, Meztli's gaze shot over to me and his jaw dropped open. I wiggled my eyebrows in victory and laughed. He shook his head, mouthing, "You win."

I looked at my friends. "Good luck, guys. And thanks for coming after me."

"We saw Rufus take off and knew he was up to no good," Frankie said. "We had no idea the Pravus team was going to be there too."

"Let's get moving," Professor Murphy said, and we ran outside.

Professor Murphy, Frankie, and Mez raced for the van. Rufus and Jud were already far away, zipping along on the snowmobile. Two Pravus snowmobiles peeled out of their camp to follow.

Professor Murphy sped off before the van doors were shut.

Alasie and I headed for the ice, where a shed held the kite-skiing supplies. She unfurled her kite, attached the safety harness around her waist, and hooked the kite to the harness. She put on goggles and boots, then clipped the boots onto her skis. I climbed on her back, wearing the backpack with my bag of sudithium, and we took off. The gusting wind yanked us forward. I clung to her shoulders, trying to not get bounced off as we sped over clumps of snow.

"Hang on!" Alasie yelled. She held on to a bar, which she used to steer the kite, guiding us toward the smoother ice of the bay. As we neared it, we saw three Pravus snowmobiles moving to cut us off. It seemed like each Pravus kid had his own snowmobile. Jerks. Alasie turned the kite to catch more wind, and we picked up speed, swooping ahead of them.

The snowmobiles followed, and even though the wind was strong, they were faster. One got ahead of us, and the rider pulled out a knife. He was going to try and cut the kite free, but as he

swerved toward us, Alasie pulled back on the harness and we went airborne over him. We landed and zipped off, heading for the iceberg.

The snowmobiles closed in from both sides. One raced ahead of us, and I thought he was going to try to cut us off, but instead, he splattered a can of orange paint all over us.

I covered my eyes before the paint hit, so my goggles remained clear. Alasie couldn't do the same, and now she couldn't see through the paint. We jerked around a bit as she used one furry arm to clear her goggles.

We were nearing the iceberg. It looked like that giant fist was going to punch us hard. The wind roared in my ears. I held on, hoping Alasie could see. A Pravus snowmobile zipped in front of us again.

"Alasie!" I screamed.

Again she pulled back on the bar and we were airborne. We went higher this time, terrifyingly high. The wind was fierce and unpredictable, and I knew we could crash to the ice easily.

But then I felt something grab me from behind and yank me off Alasie's back.

"Alasie!" I yelled. She turned and screamed.

I was being lifted away by the giant gyrfalcon.

CHAPTER 37

"Giant gyrfalcons are lactose-intolerant. If one grabs you, try to look like a block of cheese."

—GUIDEBOOK TO UPPER WORB

Hey, there, buddy," I said. "Thanks for the lift. You can put me down by that ship over there."

A part of me was hoping that this majestic bird had decided to save me from the Pravus kids. But then I realized, as we rose higher and higher, that she was planning on feeding me to her chicks.

She dropped me into her nest, right next to the sleeping babies. There were three of them, each one as big as me, with sharp beaks and claws. The mother's twitchy head looked from them to me, as if she was wondering whether to wake them up or not. Realizing I couldn't go anywhere, she left to get more food.

I was high up—*really* high up. I could see everything—the bay, the hangar, the crater, even the gap in the cliffs where Alasie and I had gone. No wonder Syke had positioned herself here as lookout.

Syke! She had to be nearby.

"*SYKE!*" I screamed.

A head appeared above me, leaning over the cliff.

"Syke! Help me!"

She disappeared. I saw a rope fly over the edge of the cliff and dangle just out of my reach. Syke's body followed, as she rappelled down the cliff face. She dropped into the nest just as the baby birds were waking up.

"Thank goodness," I said. "Can you get us out of here?"

"Yeah, the dragon is coming," she said, lowering her balaclava. Her face looked ashen, almost ghostly. "We're all getting ready to leave this place."

"I knew you wouldn't leave me."

"Yeah, right. Just give me the backpack."

I didn't say anything. I stood there with my jaw hanging open. One of the baby birds edged closer, and Syke punched it on the beak.

"Back off!" she yelled. She seemed shaky and on edge.

I spotted the black dragon heading for us. Syke opened her backpack and pulled out a harness that she threw on over her head.

"You have to give me the backpack," she said.

"Syke, no," I said, my voice cracking a little. "This is the only way I can stay at Critchlore's. If I don't save this for Murphy, he'll fail me. And if I fail junior henchman class, Professor Zaida is taking me to the Great Library. I'll be all alone there. Please." How could she do this to me? "I know you're mad about what I did. But can't you remember the good stuff? That time we almost got caught spying on Dr. Frankenhammer and we had to hide in his storage cabinet? I saved you from that jelly-monster we thought was dead."

"They're going to take it from you when we land. It would be better if I had it."

The dragon was approaching, and so was the gyrfalcon, ready to protect her babies. Screeches filled the air.

"Now or never," Syke said, preparing her harness.

I handed her the bag. She stuffed it inside her own bag and helped me up. "We'll only have a few seconds. The mother is coming fast."

The dragon swooped down from above. The gyrfalcon was coming up to meet him. As soon as the dragon touched down on the edge of the nest, Syke jumped onto its back and clipped her harness to its sadle. I climbed up after her, just as the beast rose in the air. It turned to the gyrfalcon, blowing a blast of fire that forced the giant bird to stop its upward flight.

The dragon sped off for the hangar.

The icy wind was painful, and I turned my head to protect my face from the oncoming blast. Behind me I saw a dark sky filled with churning, heavy clouds.

We landed at the hangar, and the dragon rushed inside, where two transport dragons were being loaded with the Pravus team and its gear. Syke dismounted without looking at me. She strode over to the group and handed my bag of sudithium to Reythor, who looked smug. Then he turned to look behind him, where I noticed the Critchlore teams were sitting like criminals against the wall. Two Pravus trolls stood next to them, making sure nobody tried anything funny. Alasie sat next to Meztli, her white fur tinged with orange.

"We have it all now!" Reythor said loudly. "Ha!"

Professor Murphy glared at me and shook his head.

Hot anger flared up and consumed me. I had taken enough of

Professor Murphy's abuse, and I wasn't going to take any more. I strode over to the group. "If you're as smart as you pretend to be," I said, "then you know this is not my fault. If Rufus and Jud hadn't chased after me, the Pravus team wouldn't know about the sudithium I found."

"Again with the 'I found' bit," Rufus said. "Give it up, Runt."

"You know it, and I know it," I said to him. Then I grabbed my chest, because it felt like I was in the grip of the gyrfalcon again. Maybe the bird had broken my ribs.

"I can't breathe," I said.

Rufus rolled his eyes, but Professor Murphy stood up. "Let me see your wrists."

I held them out, and Professor Murphy examined them. The red marks hadn't come back. Then he pressed on my ribs, which didn't hurt at all, so broken ribs weren't the issue.

"Mistress Moira warned me about this," he said. "Take off your jacket."

I took off my parka . . . and also my fleece jacket, my sweater, my thermal shirt, and my second thermal shirt. I stood in front of him in my Critchlore T-shirt.

Professor Murphy lifted it up. "Oh, no . . . it goes all the way around," he said.

I looked down and saw a black band stretch across my chest.

I gasped as I realized what it was.

"My tether curse," I said. "It's come back. On my chest!"

Mistress Moira had told me that if I hadn't returned from the Great Library as quickly as I had, those red bands on my wrist would have turned black and tightened. Now that was happening on my chest.

Professor Murphy said, "She told me to get you out of here at the first sign of the curse coming back. How have you not noticed this before now?"

Okay, this is a little embarrassing to admit.

Yes, I had been in the polar region for a week, and no, I hadn't actually changed my shirt or showered that whole time. Hey, there are worse things a kid could do, right? I did brush my teeth once or twice. Wait, did I? I think I did. On second thought, did I even bring a toothbrush?

"I have to get back to school," I said. "Now."

Professor Murphy looked around. The Pravus team was almost packed up. He grabbed me by the wrist and dragged me over to their dragons. Two Pravus trolls blocked our approach.

"Reythor," Professor Murphy called.

Reythor turned around but didn't say anything.

"This boy has been cursed," Professor Murphy went on. "He needs to get back to Stull as quickly as possible, or he'll die. You've won the prize. Now please do the honorable thing and take him with you. Dr. Critchlore will reward you, I promise."

Reythor smirked at us. "This is some sort of trick to steal the sudithium," he said. "I will not take him."

"Tell him, Syke!" I shouted, because she was standing right behind him. "Tell him I'm cursed, that I have to get back."

She looked at me. I raised my shirt to show her the mark.

All eyes were on Syke. The entire Pravus team, the Critchlore kids, everyone. I begged her with my eyes. She looked around nervously, unsure of what to say.

"Syke, please," I begged.

At last she shrugged. "He might be cursed," she said. "Or it might be a trick. I really don't know."

And there it was: complete indifference.

She could have saved me, and then I'd have known that she really cared. She could have told Reythor it was a trick, and then I would've known it was out of anger. But no, she absolutely didn't care one way or the other.

The look she gave me—a look that told me I was nothing to her—felt like Stevie's fist around my chest, clenching tight. My best friend was turning her back on me in my moment of need, my moment of desperation. I felt crushed.

She looked straight at me. "He *is* tricky. He likes to sneak into places. He brags about it all the time." She turned and boarded the dragon, patting the storage compartment on her way inside.

"I trust that one," Reythor said, laughing. "No deal." He turned and followed her, closing the door to the passenger cabin behind him.

With the Pravus team loaded up, the dragons were led to the hangar door. They were leaving.

"You there," Professor Murphy called to a worker. "When's the next dragon shuttle."

"In this weather? We won't be getting a return dragon for a few days."

"I'll be dead in a few days," I said. "I can barely breathe right now."

CHAPTER 38

"You can really judge a person by how he or she reacts to impending doom."

—*100 THINGS ABOUT PEOPLE*

I ran to get my parka, then took off after the dragons. They'd stopped near the hangar doors, which were opening slowly. I caught up and studied the luggage compartment door. I was sure I could pry it open, but then the dragon started edging backward. Something outside was startling it.

The wind howled, throwing ice and snow into the hangar. Even louder were the workers shouting orders at one another. Some of them abandoned their lines and ran off, as if Amaruq was coming for them.

Professor Murphy ducked under a dragon's wing to reach the hangar doors, and I followed. The wind was incredibly fierce, snatching our voices and carrying them too far away to hear. With gestures, we managed to figure out what was happening.

The dragons were not going to fly through the storm. They wanted to go back inside where it was warm.

But the workers were shouting about something else. One of

them pointed in the direction away from town. There, cresting a hill, was an army.

"What are *those* things?" Professor Murphy asked.

Alasie appeared beside me. "The white woman is back," she said, cluthing my arm. "That's her army of seal-men. They ride snow oxen. Those beasts can go through anything. They are so powerful, so huge. And look at that fur!" Even from afar, the snow oxen looked bigger than elephants, with thick coats of white fur all over their bodies.

And at the head of the group was the biggest snow ox, draped in royal livery, and riding it, a very regal figure.

"Irma Trackno," I said.

The dragons hustled back inside the hangar. We waited, while the ground shook from the approaching army.

A small access door flew open, and ten seal-men rushed inside, their long pole weapons held in front of them. They walked like men but had gray rubbery skin and faces with long noses and whiskers.

"Everyone down!" they shouted.

Everyone obeyed.

And then Irma Trackno entered, brushing the snow off her white hood, removing her white balaclava, and shaking out her white hair. She surveyed the scene.

"I want those transport dragons searched," she said. "Nobody is leaving here with sudithium. Nobody. Anyone in possession of sudithium will be arrested and charged with theft of *our* natural resources."

She pulled off her gloves and strode toward the glass-fronted offices that stretched down one side of the hangar. She entered the biggest one.

The Pravus team had disembarked, and Professor Murphy threw a smug look in Reythor's direction. The man had paled significantly since the arrival of Her Greatness.

"If you'd shared, maybe you'd have some friendly company in jail," Professor Murphy said. "Too bad for you."

Professor Murphy then grabbed my arm and dragged me over to Irma's office, where two seal-men stood guard.

"I'd like a word with your Great and Wonderful Leader," he said. "It's a matter of life and death."

One of the seal-men guards turned his head toward the office. The door stood open, and I was sure that Irma Trackno had heard Professor Murphy. We could see her through the glass wall, sitting behind a conference table, giving orders to her men.

"It's fine—send them in," Irma called out. She turned to one of her guards. "Get the oxen to safety in the cove. The storm is going to be big." She looked at us as we entered. "What do you want?"

"Runt, show her your mark," Professor Murphy said. "This boy has a tether curse. I need to get him back to Stull or he'll die. Dr. Critchlore will be very angry if this boy does not return safely."

She smiled. "Do you think I care how Dr. Critchlore feels?"

"You should," Professor Murphy replied. "He could be a powerful ally for you. And a worse enemy, if anything should happen to this boy."

This was strange. Professor Murphy was talking like he actually cared about me.

Irma tilted her head and looked at me. "I remember you," she said, waving an index finger in the air. "Oh, yes, I spoke with you in the capital. You get around, don't you?"

I shrugged.

"Let me see that curse."

I lifted my shirt, and she studied me carefully for a moment. "Fascinating. I haven't seen a curse like that in . . . years. Someone wants you dead. Whatever have you been up to?"

I shrugged again. "I've lived at Dr. Critchlore's school as long as I can remember."

"Well, you're going to die here, I'm afraid," she said. "Nobody is getting out until the storm passes. And if I'm not mistaken, it looks like you've got less than twenty-four hours. Tough luck, kid."

She turned to one of her men. "Where's the coffee? Why wasn't it here already? I will not tolerate subordinates who fail to antici-pate my needs."

"Yes, Your Amazingness." The seal-man left in a hurry.

Two other seal-men dragged Reythor into the office.

"This one's in charge," one of them said. "And we found this on their dragon." He dropped the three bags of sudithium on the table.

Irma smiled. "I knew it," she said. "I knew these villagers were hiding it. And I knew if I started letting search teams in, sooner or later someone would find it—or the locals here would just give it to me to keep people out again."

She was quite pleased with herself.

Back in the hangar we huddled in groups, the Pravus team near the baggage claim area, and us at the opposite end.

The seal-men stood guard around us.

Darthin, Frankie, and Meztli sat next to me, not knowing what to say.

I felt shock but also anger. It wasn't fair. I'd known I was cursed to die for months now, but I guess I never believed it.

Until now.

"I have twenty-four hours," I said, again. "Twenty-four hours. Twenty-four hours."

Living requires hope. I'd had hope before. Hope that the tether had been defeated and I could live a long and happy life in some remote corner of the continent, maybe in the Forgotten Realm. At the very least, I thought I'd have more time to find the curser.

"There's no hope left," I mumbled.

"You don't know that," Darthin said. "Why, right this minute Mistress Moira might be finding the witch. Right this minute, the witch might be removing the curse."

I shook my head because my chest was telling me otherwise. I couldn't take a deep breath—I could feel my lungs aching for a giant inhale of oxygen, but all I could manage were short, quick breaths.

Darthin looked to Alasie. "Is there any other way out of here?"

She thought about this, then looked at Meztli and Frankie. "Come with me."

They left. I felt dizzy. "I need to do something," I said. "Darthin, can I borrow your notebook? A pen?"

He opened his bag and handed it to me. I wrote a quick note of thanks to Cook, telling her that I loved her, that she was a fantastic mother. I wrote notes to my friends, telling them how much I appreciated their support and how I knew they were all going to do great things. Finally, I wrote a note to Tootles, telling him not to give up on Syke.

"How can you say that?" Darthin said, reading over my shoulder. "She would have let you die."

"No, she was going to save me," I said. "She propped open the luggage hatch so I could sneak on. She pretty much told me so when she mentioned I liked to sneak into places. I hate sneaking into places, and she knows that."

"So why did she say she wasn't sure about your curse, then?"

"Because she's smart. Think about it. If she's trying to prove she's trustworthy to them, being unsure is the only answer that is one hundred percent believable. If she'd said, 'Yes, he's cursed,' then Reythor might think she was trying to save me. If she'd said, 'No,' then Reythor might think she was trying too hard to prove she was with them. The only honest answer was the one she gave—'I don't know.'"

Darthin shrugged, not really buying it.

And then I wrote my last note, to Dr. Critchlore. I thanked him for taking me in when I'd been left at the gate. And then I told him that I was sorry for failing him, for failing to bring back the sudithium.

But I realized that there *was* something I could do to help him. What did I have to lose? If Irma had allowed us to come here in order to see the Pravus team go up against us, I was going to put her straight. I owed it to Dr. Critchlore.

I hurried over to her office. I could see through the glass wall that she was examining the sudithium rocks.

"I'd like to talk to Her Wonderfulness," I told the guard.

The guard turned to Irma Trackno.

She shrugged, so I went in.

"Lucky for you, I'm a bit bored right now. Something on your mind?"

"I just want you to know that if you think Dr. Pravus is a better trainer of minions than Dr. Critchlore, you're wrong."

She smiled. "It seems that I have evidence to the contrary." She motioned to the bags on her desk. "You were both after this resource, and yet they were the ones in possession of it."

"But they wouldn't have gotten it without us," I said. "They needed us. We didn't need them. *I* found the sudithium."

She was silent. Her stare made me really nervous.

"If you're looking for minions," I said, "you'd be a fool to pick Pravus over Critchlore. It would be like picking someone who cheated on a test instead of the person he cheated off of. Once a cheater is on his own, he's useless."

"That's very loyal of you," she said. "I have to admit, your plea does throw a wrench in my plans. Everything I've heard about Critchlore leads me to believe that that loyalty doesn't flow both ways."

"He may act tough and aloof," I said. "But I know it's an act."

"No, it's not," she said, shaking her head. "The man has abandonment issues. Keeping people at arm's length is how he keeps himself from being hurt."

"What?" I asked. "Who abandoned him?"

"I did. I'm his mother."

257

CHAPTER 39

"Irma Trackno will do anything, sacrifice everything and everyone around her, to achieve her goal of reuniting Upper and Lower Worb with herself as ruler."
—FROM *THE UNAUTHORIZED BIOGRAPHY OF IRMA TRACKNO*

I laughed, but quickly realized that this was the wrong response when I felt the full power of the scowl that Irma Trackno leveled in my direction.

"I'm sorry, it's just that—" I didn't know what to say. I was shocked. The Great and Powerful Irma Trackno was *Dr. Critchlore's mother?*

Impossible.

She smiled at me. "I know, I don't look old enough to be his mother. But it's true." She stood up and gazed out a small window. "I married young, before I realized my true ambitions. My husband was much older and settled in his ways. Soon it became apparent that we had different interests. He enjoyed the quiet life of an estate owner; I was more interested in world domination. I divorced him and married Wedgemont Trackno, Titan of the North."

"You left your son?" That made me so sad.

"Not entirely. I came back to visit a few times. He was doing quite well with his stable of nannies and his doting father."

"But now you want to reconcile with him, don't you?" She didn't answer, but I could tell it was true. "That's why you asked me about him in the capital."

"I need to reconcile with him, yes," she said.

"I could help you," I said. "Listen, I know you burned down the forest that killed Karya."

She turned on me, furious. Fear slammed through me until I told myself that I was going to die anyway. She seemed to realize this, too, because she sighed.

I remembered all the times Dr. Critchlore had said that he would never send a minion to Upper Worb. He never allowed us to use Upper Worb as a float during the Minion Games. It made sense now. He hated his mother—she'd killed the woman he loved.

"It wasn't my fault," she said. "It was around the time he came back from university that I realized he had the same drive as me. The desire to be the best, to rule whatever enterprise he took over. He was making a huge mistake falling in love with a tree nymph.

"The tree nymph had had a daughter with another man. I tried to convince my son to do the honorable thing and let them go. Don't break up a family. Unfortunately, the man in question was a scoundrel, and he tricked me. He'd lost the love of the nymph, and he knew it."

"She loved Dr. Critchlore."

"Who wouldn't? He has so much charisma. He gets that from me. At any rate, this nobody of a man promised me that they'd leave, and then he convinced me to destroy the forest so she couldn't return to my son. I believed him. It was only later that I learned that he'd left Karya behind, to perish."

"That's awful. You know that Dr. Critchlore has raised Karya's daughter. She's his ward."

"Really?"

"Yes, but she just ran away. She thinks that Dr. Critchlore burned down the forest to make a boulderball field."

"He didn't tell her?"

"No. He told me that he wants to protect her. That he would rather have her hate him than learn the truth about her father."

"That's remarkably noble of him," she said with a sour face. "Eww."

"He said that no kid should grow up knowing that her parent is a terrible person." At Irma's shocked expression I quickly added, "He probably didn't mean you."

She didn't look so sure.

"If you want to reconcile with your son, you could tell Karya's daughter, Syke, the truth—that *you* burned down the forest. Then she won't hate Dr. Critchlore anymore."

"Derek needs to listen to me," she said, still gazing out the window. "He has no idea what Dr. Pravus is planning."

"Syke is right out there," I continued, pointing. "With the Pravus team. Don't tell her about her father. Just tell her that Dr. Critchlore was protecting you. If she forgives him, she'll come back to Critchlore's, and he'll be so happy. He loves her like a daughter, I know he does. He hasn't been the same since she left."

It was possible I was projecting my own feelings there.

Irma returned to her chair and sat down, her face blank. I couldn't tell if she was going to laugh in my face or agree with me.

"Interesting idea." She pondered. "I didn't do anything wrong, you know. That tree nymph would have driven him to distraction. He wouldn't be half the titan of industry that he is if I hadn't done it. Should I have checked the trees before burning them down? Yes, I should have. I was too trusting. I learned an important lesson. I never wanted her to die, but my motivation was to protect my son. I knew he'd be better off without her."

She was trying really, really hard to justify what she had done.

"It was that scoundrel husband of hers who's to blame. But he got his, all right. Derek had his harpies swoop down on the man. I'm pretty sure they dropped him in the middle of Skelterdam."

She became quiet then, staring off into space.

"Thank you for telling me about Syke," she said. "I'm going to do something for you in return. I'm going to give you a chance to live. It won't be easy, but if it were me, I'd want to fight to the end."

"What is it?"

"It's probably going to cost me my best snow ox, but bundle up, kiddo. You're going to have a chilly ride."

I waited in the hangar as Irma talked to Syke in her glass-walled office. Syke kept shaking her head. I felt so bad. I hoped I hadn't just unleashed on her everything that Dr. Critchlore had been trying to protect her from.

As I rebundled to go outside, one of the giant hangar doors lifted up, and a cold wind swept ice and snow inside before a giant beast came through, blocking the opening. The snow ox was a strange looking creature. It had a huge head that hung lower than its body, with curvy horns and thick white fur.

Apparently Alasie had had the same idea as Irma, because she,

Meztli, and Frankie had snuck out to steal Irma's snow ox for me. Eight seal-men had their weapons pointed at my friends as they followed the snow ox inside.

"Aww, that's so sweet of you guys," I told them.

Irma came out when she noticed her royal steed in the hangar.

I pointed to my friends. "They were just anticipating your orders," I said. "They go free, right?"

She scowled but then nodded. The seal-men lowered their weapons.

An attendant brought a ladder for me to climb onto the beast's back. A flat riding saddle rested just behind his hump-like shoulders. It could seat a few people, it was so large.

"I'll go with you," Alasie said. "I know the way to the next town. You could get lost in this storm."

"Thank you, Alasie."

Professor Murphy strode over. "Good luck, Runt," he said. "Listen, just in case . . . I want you to know why I've been extra hard on you—"

"It's okay, Professor Murphy," I said. "I'll see you back at school."

Alasie climbed up the ladder perched next to the beast's side and took her place at the front, reins in hand. I climbed up behind her. A guard guided the ox forward. The beast smelled really bad, I have to say. I almost welcomed the blast of wind that met us at the door.

We walked out slowly, the ox moving reluctantly. The guard ran back inside as soon as we were completely out. As Alasie urged the beast to the right, heading for the road, I felt something grab me from behind. I turned around and saw someone in red clinging to my leg as she tried to pull herself up next to me.

"Syke?" I said. I could just make out her eyes through her goggles. The rest of her was covered under thick layers.

"Yeah!" she answered. "Couldn't let you get away."

"Syke, you're crazy," I said. "Get back to the hangar, where it's warm!"

"I'm coming with you," she said. "I don't want to go to jail with the rest of my team. Can't this thing go any faster?"

The snow ox was strong and solid in the wind but not very fast. Alasie yelled something at it while snapping the reins, and it picked up speed. Sort of.

The going was slow, and we were too cold to talk. I felt strength seep out of me bit by bit until I could barely hang on any longer. Syke held me in place from behind. Alasie kept the beast on track, and somehow we made it past the crater and through the mountains. I had to take little shallow breaths while trying not to panic because panicking made me need a whole lot more air.

I felt so weak.

I drifted in and out of consciousness. I vaguely heard Syke yelling at Alasie to go faster. I think I fell off once, because I felt a sharp pain on my side. Then I felt a rope tied around my waist. Screams zipped past my ear. The wind whipped around us like a tornado. I'm not sure, but I think we were shot at by locals in the next town.

I heard ravens screeching. Or maybe that was my imagination and it was just the wind.

"Have to keep going!" I heard someone yell. Alasie and Syke switched places, with me in the middle. I noticed Alasie had her bow and arrow out. Syke's arm was red with blood. I passed out.

I woke up inside a compartment, lying across a bench seat with my jacket under my head. We were moving.

"Train?" I asked. I still could barely breathe.

Syke leaned over the back of the seat in front of me. "Van," she said. "Alasie traded Irma's ox for it so we could go faster on the roads here, but she doesn't know how to drive."

As if to prove her point, Alasie swerved violently to the right, before overcorrecting to the left.

"We're heading south . . . mostly. Hang in there."

Syke was still pale, her eyes bloodshot, her hair tangled. She looked as tired as I felt.

Judging by her expression, I must have looked worse.

"You left . . . the hatch . . . open for me, didn't you?" I asked, unsure if I had just been hoping it was true. "On the dragon?"

She nodded. "I was worried you wouldn't take the hint."

"Did Irma tell you everything?"

"Yeah, she did," Syke said. She rested her chin on the seat and gazed out the window behind me. "I can't believe she's Critchlore's mother."

"I know," I said, smiling at her. "It's crazy."

"She gave me the sudithium," Syke said. "She told me she knows it doesn't make up for what she did, and that she was just trying to do the right thing. It was my father who . . ."

"I'm sorry, Syke," I said. "Everyone was trying to protect you from knowing about your father. And now I've ruined everything."

"You didn't," she said. "I already knew."

"What? How?"

"Sylveria, a hamadryad in the forest by the Great Library, told me. Those hamadryads know everything. They've got this network of roots and fungus that stretches across the continent and . . . Well, it doesn't matter. The only thing that matters is that I found out the truth after you visited that one time. I felt so bad about every-thing I'd done at Critchlore's, and I wanted to make it right. I decided to go undercover at the Pravus Academy and steal that book back."

"You're a spy . . . ," I said. "I should have known—you were so mad when I told you I thought Janet was a spy, because you thought being a spy was cool, and you hate her."

"That's true. I have new respect for her, though. Being a spy isn't easy. I had to pass all these ridiculous tests, and then I had to pretend to like Victus . . . *ew*. And, Runt, you really are in dan-ger. Pravus suspects that you turned his girl explorers against him. He's remembering stuff. That's why I tried to hide you during our hoopsmash game."

"You should have told me," I said.

"C'mon, Runt. You and I both know you can't keep a secret."

"But you took my sudithium—"

"They would've taken it from you as soon as we landed, and I needed you to look hurt and defeated. Then they'd know I was on their side. They trust me now."

"But why did you send the Pravus team after me and Alasie?"

"I didn't trust her." She turned forward. "Sorry, Alasie."

"It's okay," Alasie said, waving the apology away. The car swerved, but she corrected before we hit a tree.

"I thought Alasie was going to let that squid monster kill you," Syke said. "I knew she wouldn't dare if there were witnesses."

"You told Victus I thought I was a werewolf."

"I had to, Runt. I had to convince Pravus that you were a nobody. Think about it. The only person who could turn the girl explorers against him was someone from the royal family of Andirat. If Pravus put that together, he'd know you're the missing prince. So I told him you were the campus joke."

"But what about—"

"Just rest now," she said. "We'll get you home. Everything's going to be okay."

The van lurched again, but not as violently as before. "Sorry!" Alasie shouted.

"I'm sorry you had to learn the truth about your father," I said as I closed my eyes.

"So my dad was a dirtbag. So what?"

"Exactly," I agreed. "Lots of people have sucky parents."

"Look, I know who I am," she said. "I don't believe we inherit goodness or rottenness from our parents, like hair color . . . or musical talent or . . . a hatred of cilantro. I just don't. I get to decide who I want to be."

"Exactly," I agreed again. "I'll never know my parents, because they're dead, but they could have been terrible."

"If you're Prince Auberon, you came from good people—you know that," she said.

I knew she didn't think that the prince in the picture I'd shown her was me. "If?"

"I'm not convinced," she said. "But if you are, then you're part of a family that includes some of the most admired people in history."

It was true, and ever since I'd found out who I was, I'd felt proud. But if Syke shouldn't feel shame about her evil dad, then why should I feel pride about my famous family? *I* didn't have anything to do with what had made them great.

"Don't worry, Syke," I said, closing my eyes. "I won't make you kneel in my presence. A simple curtsy will do." I think she slugged me before I passed out again.

CHAPTER 40

A whiteout blizzard, a journey through the treacherous cliffs of Iqapaki, an attack by locals who mistook them for Irma Trackno, and Runt falling off the snow ox . . . twice.

—THINGS THAT HAPPENED WHILE RUNT WAS UNCONSCIOUS

I woke up to Syke and Alasie running around, screaming at people. "Get him to the missile train!" "Someone get a witch!" "Mistress Moira, what are you doing here?"

Clearly, I must have been hallucinating that last one.

The next thing I knew, I was lying across another bench seat, this one in a private compartment on the missile train, which had just entered Stull and was heading for the capital, Stull City.

"I can breathe again," I said. I inhaled deeply and opened my eyes.

I rolled over onto a very bruised hip, and quickly rolled back. "Ouch," I said. "What happened to me?"

Syke, lying on the seat across from me, laughed. "You rode a snow ox through a blizzard and nearly died. Runt, you idiot—how does someone not change their shirt for a week! You could have found the tether and gotten out of there days ago. You—"

I zoned out with a smile on my face. I was okay. And Syke was coming home.

Cook had sent my foster brother, Pierre, to pick us up at the station. I'd lost my backpack somewhere during the journey, so I didn't have any luggage. I sat next to Pierre in the front while I replenished my strength with the food Cook had sent along with him.

Thank you, Cook!

"We might get back in time for the float parade," he said.

"I should warn you, Syke." I turned in my seat to talk to her. "A few things have changed around school. It's a lot more dangerous than it used to be. The monsters have definitely gotten scarier."

"No, it's back to normal," Pierre said. "Critchlore got rid of Vodum's recruits and fired him. Again." He laughed. "I saw it happen! Critchlore told Vodum he was an incompetent fool who couldn't tell the difference between random monstrosities and trainable minions. It was hilarious. Oh, and the rest of the teams are back."

"Not Professor Murphy?" I asked.

"Yeah, him too. Apparently the dragons got out shortly after you did, and they beat you to the trains, too."

"Figures," I said.

We reached the gate, and I shook Syke, who'd collapsed from exhaustion. "Look, we have one of Pravus's giant gorillas." I pointed at Kumi.

"Of course you do. I sent him here." She grabbed her backpack and jumped out of the van. When Kumi saw her, he pounded his chest and whooped.

Wait . . . he'd been looking for *Syke*?

Pierre turned to me. "Come on, Runt," he said. "It's float time."

"Go ahead," I said. "Syke and I will catch up."

I walked over to Kumi just as he lifted Syke up in his giant hand.

"How did you send a giant gorilla here?" I shouted.

"I figured out what Pravus was planning to do. That he was going to . . ." She shook her head. "I wasn't able to save the others, but I got Kumi away from the enclosure before the whole thing went down. I told him to come here and wait for me."

"Wait for you here? When were you planning to come back?"

"As soon as I could steal back *The Top Secret Book of Minions*," she said. "I need to return it to Critchlore, to make up for my sabotage. Kumi, put me down, please." Back on the ground she turned serious. "Runt, what I've discovered is crazy. Pravus is planning something huge. I don't know the details just yet, but I was able to sneak into his office and grab this." She opened her backpack and took out a map of the Porvian Continent. "Give it to Critchlore—he'll know what it means."

"Why don't you give it to him?"

"I'm going back to Pravus's," she said.

"Syke, you can't!"

"I have to," she said. "I have to get that book back. I've heard his scientists talking about other secrets it contains. Even if Pravus already knows how to make a UM, we have to keep him from learning anything else. Don't worry—they'll trust me even more now because they know I was going to let you die. And I'll tell them I had to follow you, in case you were up to something."

"Syke. It's too dangerous there."

"I'm taking Kumi with me. I'll tell them that you guys stole him,

270

and I stole him back. They won't hurt him now. It would look too suspicious."

"Syke, *please* stay here. Critchlore can get his book back."

"I'm the best person for the job, Runt. Pravus loves me. Just don't tell anyone." She grabbed me and looked me in the eye with a hard glare. "You can tell Critchlore when you give him the map, but nobody else. And I promise that I'll send another raven if I need help."

"Another . . . raven?" I felt my jaw drop. "*You* sent the sudithium to Dr. Critchlore?"

"Um . . . yeah. Who did you think sent it?"

"Mistress Moira," I said. "It was her raven."

"True. I think Mistress Moira sent him to find me." She looked at Kumi. "Let's go," she said.

She turned to me. "I got you a clean shirt in Nostopako," she said, handing me her backpack. "I know you don't think you need to change your shirt, but for everyone else's sake, try to do it at least once a day from now on."

She climbed up to Kumi's shoulder and they left.

I opened Syke's backpack and found a clean shirt—ha ha ha—and the map she'd shown me and all of the sudithium that Irma had given her.

I looked back at her. She'd turned around and was waving good-bye, smiling wide. I smiled back, so happy I felt like I could fly. She didn't hate me. She'd been working undercover all along. A giant weight fell off me, taking all the hurt and anger with it. I'd been so scared that I'd lost her friendship, but it had been an act. A very good act. Wow, she was a great spy.

I put the backpack on and walked through the gates of my home.

I couldn't help but feel on edge. Over the past few weeks school hadn't been as safe as it usually was, what with all of Vodum's monsters roaming around—the leech-men, the matango, and those freaky skeletons. Even though I knew they were gone, I walked down the tree-lined drive feeling like something was hiding in the shadows.

And something was.

Rufus.

He sauntered toward me from the dorm road. Behind him was a large group of minions. The whole blue team, including my toddler trees, I was happy to see. They were heading from the dorms to the boulderball field for the presentation of the floats.

"You made it back," Rufus said. "I had money on you croaking."

"I guess you lose this time," I said, turning my back on him and continuing up the road.

He grabbed me and spun me around, stripping the backpack off my back. "I really, really hate you, Runt. Don't mess with me. I will shred you like cheese." He looked confused for a second. "Why is your bag so heavy?" I slumped. He was going to steal the sudithium. Again.

He opened the bag. "How did you—" he began. Then he laughed. "Doesn't matter. It's mine now."

I shook my head.

He snapped his jaw at me. "You're such a loser. You're not even going to try and get it back, are you?"

"I don't have to." I looked him in the eye, and then I walked away, heading toward the castle. After a few steps, I turned my head and shouted, "Trees! Rufus is a cheater!"

"Cheater! Nooooooo!" they said, surrounding him and grabbing the backpack. They wrapped their branches around his arms and legs so tightly that he couldn't move. He thrashed and screamed.

"Mummies!" he yelled. "Where are my mummies! I want my mummies!"

I laughed, the trees laughed, the other onlookers laughed.

"You know what I mean," Rufus said. "SHUT UP!"

The mummies didn't move. Rufus screamed at them. "Get these trees off me!"

The mummies watched Rufus struggle, but didn't come any closer. One mummy tapped another on the shoulder, then tilted his head toward the boulderball field. They walked away, ignoring Rufus.

"Mummies! I will unwrap you! Get back here!"

I followed them, listening to the sweet sound of Rufus being ignored. Googa caught up and handed me the backpack.

Most of the kids were in the float parade, but I was too tired to take another step, so I headed to the stands. I waved to Professor Zaida, sitting next to a very happy Uncle Ludwig, who gave me a thumbs-up. Cook sat with Tootles and Riga, and I hugged each one on my way up to see Professor Murphy.

I sat down next to him, and he smiled and patted me on the back. I was surprised to see Janet on the other side of him.

"I'm glad you're okay, Runt," she said, leaning forward. She stood up and came to sit on my other side.

Music blared from the loudspeakers. The stands were filled with kids and teachers and castle workers. I smiled at Janet but then noticed the freaky skeletons heading toward us.

Janet turned around to see what had caused my obvious panic. She stood up, raising both hands. "Guys, I've got this now."

The short one made some motions with his hands.

"Fine, you can watch the parade, but then you have to return to . . . you know."

What was going on? The skeletons sat down next to Janet.

"Janet, you know these guys?" I whispered.

She sat down and nodded. "My . . . associate sent the skeletons to keep you safe while I was gone on a secret . . . visit to my family."

"Keep me *safe*? They kept coming after me!"

The skeletons used sign language to tell her something.

"Yes. They were protecting you." She looked at the smallest one, who signed something more. Janet translated for me. "They stopped Rufus from attacking you." She looked back at him again. "And they saved you from a stampede of giants." She turned back to the skeletons. "And they scared off the Night Prowl that had been mocking you."

"Janet . . . who are you?"

She smiled. "A friend. Never forget that, Runt." She looked over at the teams congregating by the road with the floats. I followed her gaze to Rufus, who looked very disheveled and angry. "I need to go break up with someone. See you around, Runt." And she left.

This was turning into a really bad day for Rufus.

Professor Murphy tapped me on the shoulder. "I'm glad you made it back safely, Runt."

"Thanks, Professor Murphy," I said.

"You are quite resilient, I must say," he continued. "I've spent most of this term telling you that you are unfit for my program, but you didn't let that stop you. That's an important trait for a leader."

"It is?"

"Yes. A leader has to face constant questioning of his or her abilities—both from others and from himself or herself. I'm glad you passed that test."

"That was a test? Your hating me was an act?"

"I never hated you, Runt. I did resent that you were placed in my class. But I could see after the business with Miss Merrybench that you might have something. It was Professor Zaida's idea to test your resilience, and I'm glad it worked. I was starting to feel a little bad about how I was treating you."

"I was too."

"In Upper Worb, I knew it was a long shot, but I thought if anyone could win the support of the locals, it would be you with your guileless vulnerability." He laughed. "You have a knack for befriending monsters, Runt."

"Thanks." I wasn't sure what he meant by "guileless vulnerability," but I decided to take it as a compliment.

We watched Janet argue with Rufus on the far side of the field.

"You know what else makes a great leader?" he went on. "Someone who brings out the best in his or her followers. Rufus hasn't learned this lesson, but you have. Your friend Darthin was a completely different kid on our second trip to Upper Worb. When I asked him about the change, he told me that you kept getting monsters to ask him for help. And you somehow convinced Frankie to join a search team. And Meztli defeated his apathy, thanks to your example. That's leadership, Runt."

"I don't think I taught Meztli anything," I said. "It was the other way around, really. If it wasn't for him, I wouldn't have thought about breaking a rule."

"Another excellent trait in a leader," Professor Murphy went on, "is knowing you have much to learn from others. All in all, I think it's been a successful term for you."

"Thanks," I said. "You know, of all my grades, I'm going to be proudest of the A that I'm getting in your class."

He frowned. "Runt," he said. "The promise of an A was for—"

I handed him the backpack. "—whoever brought you the sudithium."

He opened the backpack. His jaw dropped as he looked from me to the bag and back again.

I smiled and spread my arms wide for that congratulatory hug, but Dr. Critchlore was approaching, and Professor Murphy stood up to show him the backpack.

"Dr. Frankenhammer is in his lab," Dr. Critchlore said.

Professor Murphy left before giving me my hug. Foiled again!

"Be sure to tell him what Frankie did!" I yelled after him. "He took out the entire Pravus team and got the sudithium back from them. He was amazing."

"Everyone knows what he did to the Pravus team," Professor Murphy replied, pointing to the field. I turned and saw Frankie atop the green team's float, lifting heavy objects and throwing them. The crowd cheered his name. The purple team's float followed, and I stood up to see who was playing Dark Victor. Oh, it was Frieda!

Dr. Critchlore took Professor Murphy's seat next to me. He was dressed a little casually, for him. Gone was the military-style suit, and in its place he wore a white open-collar shirt under a camel-colored blazer with a blue gryphon crest on the pocket.

"Well done," he said.

I sat down and smiled at him. "It was Syke. I told Irma who she was, and Irma told her everything. She gave Syke the sudithium as a way to say sorry."

"So . . . Syke knows about her father?"

I nodded. "She already knew. From the hamadryads in the forest. I'm so sorry, I know you wanted to keep that from her."

"Yes, I did."

"You won't believe what she's been up to," I said. "She was the one who sent the sudithium by raven, not Mistress Moira. She sent Kumi here, when Pravus destroyed the gorilla enclosure. She rode a dragon! And parachuted into some mountains. Oh, and she told me to give you this."

I handed him the map that Syke had put in my backpack. There were marks and numbers and scribbles all over it. Dr. Critchlore studied it for a few minutes. Then he looked off into the distance, lost in thought.

"Where did she get this?" he asked.

"She stole it from Dr. Pravus's office. What does it mean?"

"At first glance, it appears to be a map of Lower Worb. I wonder if these marks in red, GG—124, RT—115, are tallies of the minions he's placed with Wexmir Smarvy. And the other colors? Those might represent minions from other minion schools. I placed seventeen flying monkeys with him just last year, which matches this mark here."

He looked up again, thinking.

"Now, why would Dr. Pravus keep that kind of information?"

"I think your mother knows," I said. Dr. Critchlore scowled. "She told me that she wants to reconcile with you."

Before he could say anything, another voice interrupted us.

"Any chance I can squeeze in with you two?"

We looked up and saw Mistress Moira heading up the aisle holding two bags of popcorn. A huge smile burst out on Dr. Critchlore's face as he stood. She smiled back at him.

I jumped up, edged past Dr. Critchlore, and hugged her. "Welcome back," I said. "We missed you."

"You could have died, Runt," she said, taking a seat next to me. I sat down between the two of them. "You wore your underwear during the chant, didn't you? That's why it didn't work."

"Um . . . yes."

I avoided her disappointed look by turning my attention to the parade. My blue team's float looked great, with Jud taking Rufus's place as Fraze Coldheart. The red team's float followed—a seventh-year human dressed as Wexmir Smarvy was pushing minions off the float in a fit of rage. The crowd cheered.

"Have you found out who cursed me?" I asked her.

"I believe so. She's hiding in Skelterdam. Nobody knows exactly where, and nobody can find out because—"

"Because no human can survive in Skelterdam," I finished for her.

"Which is why I brought back an old friend." She nodded to the top of the stands, where a familiar-looking zombie with a hair bun and a flowery shirt swayed on hesitant feet. She was standing next to Barry Merrybench.

"Is that—?"

"Yes, it is," she answered. "Karen Merrybench. Recently undead and ready to make up for her past transgressions against you. It's part of her Twelve-Step After-Life Redemption Program."

"*She's* going to find the witch who cursed me?"

Mistress Moira smiled and nodded. "Yes, she is."

The yellow team's float was last. Bianca looked fierce, dressed as the powerful Maya Tupo. Darthin sat regally on the throne next to hers on a float covered with monsters. All the floats circled the field now in a terrifying display of Evil Overlord power.

"You know, none of those overlords are as scary as Dr. Pravus," I said. "We have to get Syke away from him."

Dr. Critchlore nodded. His gaze met Mistress Moira's, and she nodded and stood up, her robe swishing in a wind that hadn't been there a second ago. Her face was dark with concentration as she turned toward the west and raised her arms. She chanted something I couldn't hear, and then a dozen ravens flew over my head in the direction of the Pravus Academy.

"We'll get her back," she said.

"And we'll stop Dr. Pravus," Dr. Critchlore added.

I smiled, relieved that everything was now in capable hands. I could relax and get back to being a normal student, taking my normal classes.

Dr. Critchlore patted me on the shoulder. "And you, Prince Auberon, can return to your home country and lead it out of disaster."